Mystery
of the
Lazy
Loggerhead

Mystery
of the
Lazy
Loggerhead

BY LISA TRAVIS

ILLUSTRATIONS BY ADAM TURNER

Published by WorldTrek Publishing

Copyright © 2016 by Pack-n-Go Girls

Printed in the USA

Visit our website at www.packngogirls.com.

This is a work of fiction. Names, characters, places, and incidents either are the product of the author's imagination or are used fictitiously. The city of Praia do Forte, Brazil, is real, and it's a wonderful place to visit. Any other resemblance to actual events, locales, organizations, or persons, living or dead, is entirely coincidental and beyond the intent of either the author or the publisher.

Illustrations by Adam Turner

ISBN 978-1-936376-27-8

Cataloging-in-Publication Data available from the Library of Congress.

To Will & Sarah, who inspire me to make a difference every day.

Mystery of the Lazy Loggerhead is the second book in the Pack-n-Go Girls Brazil adventures. The first book, *Mystery of the Troubled Toucan*, tells how Sofia and Júlia first met. Here's a bit about the book:

Nine-year-old Sofia Diaz's world is coming apart. So is the rickety old boat that carries her far up the Rio Negro river in Brazil. Crocodiles swim in the dark waters. Spiders scurry up the twisted tree trunks. And a crazy toucan yelps a warning. It chases Sofia and Júlia, her new friend, deep into the steamy rainforest.

There they stumble upon a shocking discovery.

Contents

Meet the Characters

Sofia Diaz
loves a good mystery. She didn't know she would need to use what she learned in Florida to help solve a mystery in Brazil.

Júlia Santos
is excited to visit Brazil's beaches. She wants to become a ranger and protect the animals of Brazil.

Mr. Diaz

is Sofia's dad. He works for a motorcycle factory that has offices in Brazil.

Senhor Santos

is Júlia's dad. He works with Mr. Diaz. He's excited to show Mr. Diaz and Sofia the beaches of Brazil.

The Lazy Loggerhead

should not be this lazy.

What's going on?

And now, the mystery begins . . .

Mystery of the Lazy Loggerhead

Chapter 1

Sunrise

"What's that?" Sofia Diaz asked.

"Onde?" Her Brazilian friend, Júlia Santos, scanned the edge of the beach. She squinted from the early morning rays of the sun. A few seagulls floated by on their morning beach patrol. They squawked at the girls. "Where? I don't see anything?"

"It's moving." Sofia kicked her new Havaianas off her tan feet. She made sure to pick them up. They were only the most famous flip flops in the world. She did NOT want to lose them. Sandals safely in hand, she dashed down the beach. The familiar smell of the salt air filled her lungs. The sand kicked up behind her speedy feet.

"Wait—" Júlia sprinted to keep up with her.

"Yuck!" Gobs of dark green seaweed squished between Sofia's toes. She looked ahead to find the spots with the least seaweed. Then she hopscotched her way through. "I hate seaweed." She scowled.

"I did not know gym girls could . . . run so fast," Júlia panted. She bent over to catch her breath. Long strands of dark brown hair fell out of the clip holding it back. "I thought you just did flips and cartwheels."

"Yeah, but I'm a bear too, remember?" Sofia put her arms up and growled softly. "Bears can run fast!" Her mom had told her she'd cried so loud when she was born she'd scared all the nurses. They started calling her "the bear." Sofie-Bear. She still liked that nickname. It gave her speed when she wanted it. And courage when she needed it.

Sofia stopped a few yards away and pointed. "It's a sea turtle. See her giant head and big jaws? And the reddish-brown and yellow color of her shell? I think she's a loggerhead."

Júlia's dark brown eyes opened wide. *"Uma tartaruga marinha?"* A sea turtle? She lived on the edge of the Amazon rainforest in Manaus. So she'd seen lots of animals. Sloths, pink dolphins, monkeys, snakes, poison dart frogs. You name it. She'd seen it. She'd sworn she'd even seen a jaguar run through the bushes beside her once. But she'd never come face-to-face with a sea turtle. She wondered how similar they were to the river turtles she'd seen.

The sea turtle pulled herself slowly along the edge of the water with her flippers. It looked like she dragged a heavy checkered stone on her back.

How hard must that be with only flippers?

"Yeah, a sea turtle. And definitely a loggerhead." Sofia shadowed the turtle.

"How do you know she is, how do you say, logger—head?" Júlia asked.

"I know a little about sea turtles. My grandparents in Florida live near a sea turtle rescue place. I go there every time we visit. I've seen loads of loggerheads there. And she looks the same. I didn't know they had loggerheads in Brazil though." She kept trailing the turtle. "She seems slow," Sofia observed.

"Turtles are *all* slow, no?" Júlia giggled. Her brown eyes sparkled. Her light brown skin glowed in the sun.

Sofia spun around and smiled. "Yesssss. But she seems really, really slow. They are usually all gone by morning. I hope she's not sick." She shook her head. "Strange," she murmured.

Júlia shrugged her shoulders. "*Preguiçoso?* Maybe she is lazy?"

"We should follow her and see what she does," Sofia said.

"*Sim.* Yes. But we should stay far away from her. So we don't scare her. That is the right thing to do." Júlia had her sights set on being an Amazon ranger when she grew up. She knew leaving animals alone was always best.

The girls followed the lazy loggerhead.

They walked farther away from the white lighthouse that overlooked the beach. Palm trees lined the shore as far as their eyes could see. The palm fronds swayed in the light wind. A lone fishing boat bobbed in the surf. They could hear a seagull's cry above the sound of the waves hitting the sand. Each wave that rolled in covered their feet with cool water. A hint of orange lingered from the morning sunrise.

"I love the sunrise," Júlia said. "*Lindo maravilhoso!* So beautiful. Is the prettiest time of day."

"Really? I'm more of a sunset girl myself," Sofia replied. "I like all the colors in the sunset. The reds, oranges, purples, blues . . . it's like a different painting every evening."

"But the sunrise is a new day. A new beginning. And each new day can be a great day." Júlia sighed dreamily.

Sofia nodded. She stared at the sea turtle ahead. "I like that thought—about new days being great." She looked over at Júlia and smiled.

"Yes, like today. A new day. And a great one because you are here." Júlia gave Sofia a quick hug. "*Que saudade!* I missed you so much! I jumped up and down when I heard our dads had a meeting near Salvador. I hoped we would have another Amazon adventure. But I am happy to see you anywhere."

"Yeah. I hoped we'd see our bird buddy, the troubled toucan, again. NOT." Sofia snorted and gave her friend a wry smile.

"*Não se preocupe.* Don't worry. He is not troubled anymore!" Júlia smiled brightly. "And now we both get to see more of Brazil."

Sofia agreed. They'd have a different kind of adventure in Praia do Forte. And any adventure with a beach would be a good one.

"How are things with your parents?" Júlia asked.

"It's been hard with them apart." Sofia looked away. Her brown eyes started to tear up. "But we're still trying to be a family. My brothers and I split our time with them. One week with my mom. And one week with my dad." She breathed in, stood a little taller, and tightened the pony tail in her dark brown hair.

"I'm sorry," Júlia replied. She put her hand on Sofia's shoulder.

"Well, there is a bright side. I've gotten really good at packing my bags to go places. Maybe someday I'll be a world traveler."

"You already are." Júlia patted Sofia's back.

Sofia froze and pointed at the sand next to them. "Look at this!"

Júlia stared at the strange markings in the sand. "They look like small tire tracks."

Sofia kneeled down to inspect the tracks. "They *are* tracks. But not from tires. From a loggerhead turtle."

"Do you think the lazy loggerhead made them?" Júlia scratched her head.

"Maybe." Sofia looked up and scanned the beach. The lazy loggerhead still crawled slowly along the water's edge. More tracks made zig-zag patterns on the beach ahead.

Júlia knelt down and brushed her hand over the tracks. "Or do you think she led us here?"

"Well, normally, I would say no. But after the troubled toucan . . ." Sofia tilted her head to one side. "Never say never."

Chapter 2

Tartarugas Marinhas

"Welcome to Centarmar. Are you here for a tour?"

A young woman smiled brightly. Her white teeth stood out against her dark brown skin. Turtle earrings dangled against her shoulder-length, kinky brown hair. Sofia admired the turtle necklace that lay against her turtle t-shirt. She certainly liked turtles Sofia thought to herself.

Júlia and the woman spoke back and forth in Portuguese.

"This is Camila," Júlia said. "I told her we are here to meet my dad's friend, Rodrigo Montes."

"*Vamos.* Let's go. I will show you," Camila said. They walked under a handmade wooden sign with a sea turtle carved into it. A sandy path twisted around tall palm trees. The lighthouse towered above them. It looked much bigger close up.

Camila talked as they walked. "The name, Centarmar, is from **Centro de Tartarugas Marinhas.** It means Sea Turtle Center in Portuguese."

When they rounded the corner, they saw several large pools. Visitors peered over the sides. So Sofia did too. A smaller brown turtle covered in barnacles glided by in the first pool. A staff member tended to a few tiny green turtles in the second pool.

They walked by a third pool. Three loggerheads floated toward them. "That one is Daniela. They rescued her two weeks ago." Camila pointed to the one in the middle. "The thing on the back of the boat? How do you say . . ." She spun her hands around in a circular motion.

"The propeller?"

"*Sim.* Yes. It hit her and cut her flipper." The turtle paddled slowly with its one healthy flipper. "We rescue turtles and help them get better here. We also protect the nests sea turtles make on the beach."

Sofia tapped Júlia on the shoulder.

"This is just like the sea turtle

12

rescue place in Florida I told you about."

Sofia wondered if she should tell Camila about the lazy loggerhead. In Florida, she probably would. But she was in Brazil. And it was probably nothing. She didn't want to look silly. But then again, her dad always told her that some people *talk* about making a difference. Other people *make* a difference.

She could talk to Júlia about the lazy loggerhead for the next few days. Or she could make a difference. She'd need to find someone who could help them though. Even if she did look silly.

"Camila, we saw something strange on the beach this morning." Sofia paused. "A loggerhead turtle. She seemed very slow. I mean, I know turtles are slow and all . . ."

"She was *lazy*," Júlia said with a sly smile.

"Hmmm. That *is* strange. Not a slow turtle," Camila chuckled. "A turtle still on the beach in the morning."

"That's what I thought." Sofia frowned and rubbed her chin. "Should we do something?" Maybe Camila would have some sort of plan.

"Where did you see the turtle?"

"The beach on the other side of the lighthouse. Over there." Júlia pointed past the lighthouse to the sandy beach on the other side. "But farther down."

"I will ask our *tartaruguiero*, the turtle experts," Camila said. "Ah, here is Rodrigo." She led the girls over to two men deep in conversation.

The men stood just outside a small gray building with a white tent-like roof. A skinny man looked out from under a straw hat. His tangled hair, frayed shorts, and old sandals gave him a bit of a wild look. Twinkling eyes shone against his weathered face and wrinkled skin.

He turned to the girls and opened his arms wide. *"Boa tarde. Boa tarde. Bem-vindo ao Centarmar."* Good Afternoon. Centarmar welcomes you.

"Boa tarde, Senhor Montes. Meu nome é Sofia. Prazer em conhencé-lo." Sofia introduced herself, practicing her Portuguese.

"Igualmente. Nice to meet you too. Call me Rodrigo, yes?" He grasped Sofia's shoulders and kissed her lightly on the cheek. Then he kissed her on the other cheek. "And this is Júlia, yes?" A smile peeked through the gray hair of his scraggly beard. "Your dad shares many stories about you." He kissed her lightly on both cheeks too.

Júlia smiled. *"Olá. Prazer em conhencé-lo, Rodrigo.* Thank you for showing us around while our dads are working."

"Com certeza! Of course. Of course. I hope Camila spoke well of Centarmar, yes? That is her job, after all." He winked at

Camila. "And please meet Senhor Costa. He plans to donate money to help the turtles." He patted Senhor Costa on the back. "Very generous, he is."

Senhor Costa stood straight and tall. He tipped his head and looked at them through tired eyes. Under his blue suit jacket, a white button-down shirt looked wrinkled from the heat. The sun reflected off his shiny black shoes. He seemed out of place on the sandy path.

"Rodrigo, you need not tell people that. It's quite embarrassing." He looked down and fidgeted with his hands.

"He is humble, yes?" Rodrigo reached up and grabbed his shoulder. "*Me perdoe.* Forgive me. But it is good to spread the word about those who help the turtles, no? Then others, they decide to help too."

"*Obrigado.* Thank you for the tour." Senhor Costa tilted his head forward. "Now I must go." He signaled toward the exit. *"Adeus."* Goodbye.

He spun on his heel and left.

"Tchau. Tchau." Bye. Bye. Rodrigo shrugged his shoulders and turned to the girls. "Are you ready for us to show you the rest of Centarmar?"

The girls nodded.

"Come, come then. *Vamos.*" The girls followed Rodrigo and Camila down the sandy path.

"Can we go up in the lighthouse?" Sofia pointed to the white lighthouse that towered above them.

"Today? No." Rodrigo shook his head. "Sorry. It is locked up. No key today. But I can show you the turtle nests."

They walked down a narrow footpath. Rodrigo opened a small wooden gate. Inside sat rows and rows of turtle nests protected by circles of wire netting.

"We find the nests. If they are not in a safe place, we move them here," Rodrigo said.

They knelt in the sand by one of the nests. Sofia

peppered Camila with questions. "So what do you think is wrong with the turtle on the beach? Have you seen that before? Why do you think she is so lazy?"

"*Não sei.* I don't know. But our team will find out."

"How? How will they find out?" Sofia wanted answers.

Camila looked over at Júlia and shrugged her shoulders.

"*Não se preocupe.* Don't worry. Is okay, Sofia," Júlia put her hand on Sofia's arm. "They will handle it. They are experts."

"I hope so. Or else."

"Or else what?" Júlia looked alarmed.

"Or else we will be rescuing turtles instead of *botos.*"

Júlia remembered the pink dolphins from their last adventure and laughed quietly. "Now *you* want to be the ranger?"

Chapter 3

Pirate Fishermen

Sofia yawned and half-opened one eye. The early morning light peeked through the curtains of their tiny hotel room. Sunrise. Júlia would say another great day had begun. But Sofia thought the day could wait a few minutes. Even if it would be great. She turned over to go back to sleep.

Then she remembered. The lazy loggerhead. She did *not* feel like getting up, but she *did* want to help the turtle. She wanted to make a difference.

Maybe Centarmar was looking for the lazy loggerhead this morning. If so, they might need her help. And if they weren't looking, well, she would need to craft her own plan. Decision made.

She rolled out of bed and grabbed her Havaianas. She was happy she'd slept in her shorts and t-shirt. Now she could make a quick getaway. She wrote a short note to her dad and tip-toed out the door.

Her mind still in a fog, Sofia rounded the corner of the hotel building.

SMASH!

"*Ai!* Ouch!" Júlia collapsed to her knees. "You stepped on my toe."

"You stepped on mine." Sofia croaked. "What are you doing up anyway?"

Júlia rubbed her toe. "I could ask you the same question." She looked up and flashed Sofia a half smile. "Let me guess. You have a plan to save the lazy loggerhead?"

Sofia shrugged her shoulders. "Maybe. And you? I suppose you're headed out on ranger duty to check on the lazy loggerhead yourself?"

Júlia nodded and burst out laughing. "Okay then. *Vamos!* Let's go!"

Sofia reached down and pulled her friend up. The girls hobbled down the path to the beach.

The morning rays of the sun glowed off the dark blue water. Two fishing boats drifted by in the distance. The waves splashed on the sand. Peaceful, Sofia thought.

It was too early for grandparents who walked the beach in the mornings. And it was too early for children who played in the pools of water formed by the coral reefs just off shore. And it was too early for teenagers who sunbathed on Saturdays. But it should be too late for a sea turtle. Yet there she was. She slowly dragged herself along the edge of the surf.

The girls followed the lazy loggerhead down

the beach. One slow step at a time. They picked their way through clumps of seaweed. They passed an old hotel. They heard the hammering of construction workers adding new rooms to the hotel.

The girls explored the hotel's old tiki huts, pretending to be marooned by pirates on a desert island. And they skipped through the waves to catch back up to the lazy loggerhead again (not that she ever got that far ahead).

"Júlia! Look! More tracks in the sand. Do you think they are the same ones?"

"Não. Não." Júlia knelt down to take a closer look. "Lots of people go to the beach during the day. There would be footprints all over the tracks from yesterday. These are new. Maybe the lazy loggerhead *is* making the tracks."

Sofia tilted her head and shrugged her shoulders. "Maybe she's trying to tell us something."

Júlia stood up and took five giant steps backwards. She looked up and down the beach. "Just tracks." She sighed. "I see no pattern. No message."

"Or she could be leading us to the tracks." Sofia followed the tracks away from the water. She bent down to look closer. "There are no nests here." Her eyebrows wrinkled together in deep thought. "In Florida, you can follow turtle tracks to a nest. The sea turtle rescue place marks the nests so people don't disturb them. But I don't see any nests."

Júlia bent down and took a look. "Remember, sometimes Centarmar moves the eggs. They bring them to the nesting area we saw to protect them. Do you think they did that?"

"Maybe—"

"Bom dia!" a voice behind them boomed.

Sofia's heart skipped a beat.

Júlia stumbled backwards. She squinted into the sun. "Senhor Costa? Is that you?"

"You remember." He tipped his head.

"Oi! Hi! You scared us."

"What are you two young girls doing on the beach so early?" The edges of his mouth crept open into a forced smile. "I thought little girls needed their rest?" He leaned over and winked one of his drooping eyelids.

"We were just checking on the lazy loggerhead," Sofia answered.

"Como?" Say again?

"The slow sea turtle over there," Júlia pointed up the beach. "We are worried about her."

"*Fique tranquilo.* I'm quite certain there's nothing to worry your little head about," Senhor Costa patted Júlia on the head. Sofia could tell Júlia didn't really like that. But she just smiled and nodded.

"And these tracks," Sofia added. "They look like sea turtles came up to lay their nests, but there are no nests."

He looked closer and frowned. "I'm afraid

it appears that these nests have been raided. You see those fishing boats out there?" He pointed to the two boats they saw earlier. "Sometimes the fishermen come on shore early in the morning and take the eggs."

Júlia's mouth dropped open.

"Raided?" Sofia mouthed to Júlia.

"You must be careful coming out here so early in the morning. You might run into one of them. Their boats look friendly in the water. In person, however, it's like meeting a *pirate*." Senhor Costa emphasized the last word. "And pirates aren't nice to little girls." He swished his arm like a sword. "Maybe you should run along home now before you meet one of them. You don't want to walk the plank." He snickered.

"Adios!" he yelled after them as they ran. And ran. And ran. They ran as hard and as fast as they could. Sofia almost lost her Havaianas. Almost.

Chapter 4

A Fisherman's Tale

Sofia really needed to know what was going on.

They found Camila talking to some tourists underneath a thatched umbrella.

"Hey Camila," Sofia interrupted. "Did your turtle experts find the lazy loggerhead this morning?"

Camila put a finger to her mouth to shush Sofia. Then she turned her back to the girls and continued talking. "We untangled the nets from Davi. The doctors gave him fluids and antibiotics.

He will go back into the ocean next month." The tourists nodded their heads and moved around the pool to get a closer look.

"So? Have they found her yet?" Sofia asked again.

"They looked this morning. They did not see her."

"That's odd. We went down there this morning too. We saw the lazy loggerhead. But we didn't see anyone from Centarmar."

"*Fique tranquilo.* No worries. They will find her," Camila replied.

Sofia was getting tired of people telling her not to worry. Compared to her cousins in Florida, she seemed relaxed. But in Brazil, clearly she was not.

"And there were no nests. There were tracks. But no nests." Sofia stood in front of Camila with her hands on her hips.

"We did not move any nests this morning," Camila said. She shrugged her shoulders.

Sofia looked over at Júlia. Her lips pressed together in a thin line. She could tell Júlia was thinking the same thing. If Centarmar didn't move the nests, then Senhor Costa must be right. The pirate fishermen raided them.

"Bom dia." Rodrigo rounded the bend of the turtle pool and opened his arms wide. "Happy to be back, yes? I am happy you are here. I have the key." He held up an old black key. "The key to show you the lighthouse today, yes?"

Sofia's face lit up. She grabbed Júlia's hand and squeezed it.

"Come. Come. *Vamos.*" Rodrigo signaled with his hands. The girls paraded off behind him toward the lighthouse.

"They built this lighthouse to warn sailors of the coral reefs." Rodrigo pointed just off shore. "An old tale, there is. Of a captain," he said as they entered the lighthouse. Sofia shivered in the cool air.

She ran her fingers over the old stone walls. "His ship crashed into the reef one night when the light went out. Now he haunts the lighthouse in search of the keeper who did not fix the light. They have not been able to fix the light to this day." Rodrigo turned around and grinned wide. His yellowish teeth and wild eyes made him look just a little crazy. "They say if you see him, no one ever sees *you* again."

Sofia's hands shook as she climbed the winding staircase. The waves crashing against the shore outside hissed in her ears over and over. At least she hoped it was the waves. Below them, the door blew open and banged against the stone wall. Wind swirled up the tower steps. Goosebumps covered Sofia's arms. Was it the cool air? Or the captain's ghost?

"But I have not seen him yet," Rodrigo chuckled. He continued up, up, up the stairs. At the top, he offered his hand to Sofia to help her up the last step.

"Glad to hear that," Sofia panted. Her legs felt weak. Was she scared or just tired? She honestly wasn't sure.

The sun burst through the windows that lined the round walls of the lighthouse. Whatever breath Sofia had, the view took it away. "What did you say about the sunrise, Júlia? *Lindo . . .?*"

"*Lindo maravilhoso?*"

"Yeah, that. The view. You can see everything. It's amazing."

Júlia nodded. Then she poked Sofia in the ribs and pointed. "Look. A few of the turtle tracks still in the sand."

"Rodrigo, you must know a lot about the sea turtles since you work here," Sofia said. She circled around to each of the windows looking for more turtle tracks.

"*Sim*. Yes, the turtles have always been a way of life here in Praia do Forte, in one way or another."

Sofia gave Júlia a confused look. "What does that mean?" she mouthed. Júlia shrugged.

"Well, we saw turtle tracks in the sand this morning," Sofia said.

"Oh, you did, did you?" Rodrigo walked over to the girls and pointed out the window. "Those?"

"Yup, but we didn't see any nests."

"No nests, say you?" Rodrigo looked off into the distance. "A lot of nests there usually. But this season, not so many. No good reason why though."

"We saw Senhor Costa walking the beach this morning. He told us pirates raided the nests," Sofia said.

"Not pirates. Fishermen." Júlia corrected her. "He said the fishermen are mean like pirates."

Rodrigo turned and raised his eyebrows. "He said that, did he?"

"What do *you* think?" Sofia crossed her arms and leaned against the side of the lighthouse.

"What do *I* think? I think no. It is not fishermen." Rodrigo's brows furrowed together. His eyes grew darker. "Before Centarmar came, it is true, many fishermen did take eggs from the nests. That is how we lived back then. When Centarmar began, they asked many of us to work for them."

"Wait, *you* were a fisherman?" Júlia snuck a worried glance at Sofia.

"*Sim*. Yes, yes. I was. We knew the turtles. How to spot them when they came ashore. How to read their tracks. How to find their nests. Find and protect the eggs, they said. And we will give you food and money. So we did." Rodrigo waved a hand in the air. "Why would Senhor Costa say such a thing?"

34

"I'm . . . I'm not sure," Sofia stammered. "Who else could it be? I mean. We checked with Centarmar. They didn't move any nests . . ."

Rodrigo scratched his chin through his scraggly beard. He leaned in closer to Sofia. "Sometimes the construction workers are crooked. They steal the eggs to sell them." He gave the girls a quick nod of the head. "You know, yes?"

Sofia *didn't* know. What was she supposed to believe? Her heart pounded in her chest. Were they stuck up in a lighthouse with a pirate fisherman? Or could it be the construction workers?

Rodrigo reached out toward Sofia's shoulder. "You okay?"

Sofia dodged his hand and stepped toward the stairs. Was he trying to kidnap her? Maybe he was the pirate fisherman afterall.

Sofia wanted to run all the way down the winding stairs as fast as she could. She stood on her tip-toes and peeked over to inspect her escape route. Yikes! She got dizzy just looking down. It definitely wouldn't be a quick escape. She needed to channel her inner bear. She needed courage.

Júlia put her best fake smile on and nodded back to Rodrigo. "You are probably right. The construction workers." She looked at Sofia and signaled toward the stairs with her eyes. "*Obrigada.* Thank you for the tour and the turtle information, Rodrigo."

Sofia took a deep breath. "Yeah, *obrigada.* We should go now. I'm sure our dads are waiting."

Júlia darted down the winding stairs. Sofia stumbled down behind her.

"*Esperem!* Wait! I can walk you down." Rodrigo's voice echoed down the narrow stairway. From the bottom, Sofia could've sworn it sounded like the wail of a ghost.

Chapter 5

Turtle Rescue

BANG! BANG! BANG! BANG! BANG!

The loud noise woke Sofia from a deep sleep.

BANG! BANG! BANG!

"All right already. I'm coming." She rolled out of bed and looked through the peep hole of her hotel room door. Júlia paced in front of the door.

"*Bom dia,* Júlia," Sofia grunted as she opened the door.

"Is a new day, Sofia!" Júlia's bright smile just

made Sofia more tired. "Time to check on the lazy loggerhead. *Vamos!*"

"Seriously?" Sofia yawned. "Already?"

Júlia nodded.

"Fine." Sofia sighed. "Let me get my shoes." She picked up her Havaianas and told her dad where they were headed.

Júlia waited against the wall outside the door. When Sofia came out, she reached into her pocket. She held up two pieces of bright ribbon. "My dad brought back *fitas* for us from their meeting in Salvador. He got them from *Igreja de Nosso Senhor do Bonfim.* That means the Church of Our Lord of the Good End. The church is known for its miracles."

"The church cures things?"

"Many people believe that. So they go there to pray for a miracle. That is probably where the *fita* tradition of wishes came from. Anyway, these are right from the church's gates." She turned to Sofia.

"For each knot I tie, make a wish. But don't tell me your wishes."

Sofia scrunched her eyes tightly shut and made three wishes. She looked at the lime green *fita* on her wrist. "And I keep it on until it falls off, right?"

Júlia nodded. "Now you do mine." She stuck her wrist out. Sofia tied a light blue *fita* on with three knots just like Júlia had done. After Sofia tied the *fita* on, Júlia used her fingers to make

39

a locking motion in front of her mouth. "We cannot tell anyone our wishes. Even each other." Sofia nodded.

Sofia twisted the *fita* around and around on her wrist as they walked. She remembered the *fita* Júlia gave her during the last trip. She wore that wish bracelet until it fell off. She supposed some of her wishes had come true. She was still best friends with Júlia after all. She had also wished for her family to stay together. That didn't quite happen as she had imagined. But they *were* still a family. Just a little different than before.

So maybe these did work. She didn't know for sure, but she planned to keep her mouth shut. She might really need a miracle for her wishes to come true this time.

"Look! The lazy loggerhead." Júlia pointed down the beach. Sofia sprinted ahead to catch up to the turtle.

The lazy loggerhead pulled herself slowly along the edge of the surf. Only this time four turtle experts from Centarmar surrounded her. They carried a large tarp with four straps on it. It looked like a giant sling.

"*Oi meninas!* Hi girls, can you help us load her?" Camila stepped out from behind the four men.

"*Com certeza!*" Of course! Júlia got on her hands and knees. She pulled the tarp into the lazy loggerhead's path. The waves splashed around her legs. The water soaked her, but she didn't care.

Sofia knelt down on the other side and pulled it tight. Her knees squished into the seaweed scattered along the edge of the water. Ugh. Kneeling in seaweed? Only to rescue a sea turtle, she thought.

They watched as the lazy loggerhead moved slowly along. She didn't seem to want to crawl onto the tarp. Sofia didn't blame her. The turtle didn't know they were trying to help her.

Júlia coaxed her along using her best ranger skills. "Is okay," she said softly.

The men all spoke in Portuguese. Sofia had a hard time understanding their turtle rescue plan. But she figured it out when they each grabbed a part of the turtle's shell. The turtle was huge and awkward. Sofia hadn't thought about the logistics of rescuing a sea turtle. It clearly wasn't easy, though.

"*Ai!*" A flailing flipper clawed one of the men. His arm buckled and her shell rocked as he let go.

"*Cuidado!* Careful!" Júlia gulped. The girls scrambled over to grab the turtle's shell before it hit the ground. They slowly lowered her onto the tarp.

The men carefully wrapped the sling around her. Then they picked her up with the straps. Sweat dripped down the sides of their faces as they loaded her into the pickup truck.

"Would you like to ride back in the truck with us?" Camila asked.

"Com certeza!" Sofia replied practicing her Portuguese. Definitely!

Back at Centarmar, the men unloaded the turtle. They hauled her inside to the veterinarian's office. Sofia and Júlia walked on each side ready to jump in and help.

The doctor greeted the girls at the door. "She's lucky that you girls told us about her," she said. "It's always a miracle when we're able to rescue one of these grand sea turtles. And you girls really made the difference." She gave each of the girls a hug.

"But what's wrong with her?" Sofia peeked over the doctor's shoulder into the room behind her. "Why is she so slow? Will she be okay?"

The doctor put a hand on Sofia's shoulder. "I don't know girls. I'll find out what's wrong though." She gave them a worried smile. "And I'll do my best to save her." She walked back into the room and shut the door behind her.

Sofia didn't feel reassured. Her eyes started to tear up. She turned to Júlia. "Do you think she'll be okay?"

Júlia shook her head sadly. "*Não sei*. I don't know. Maybe we did not rescue her in time."

Then Sofia's eyes lit up. They glistened with leftover tears. "Or maybe she's just fine. Maybe she didn't make the tracks. Maybe she *is* like the troubled toucan." Sofia willed herself to believe it was true. "She just crawled slowly so we would follow her to the tracks."

Júlia nodded slowly. "That must be it." She also wanted to believe. "She wanted to tell us about the pirate fishermen. Or the crooked construction workers."

"She wants us to stop the raiders," Sofia said gravely.

Chapter 6

The Stake Out

"I don't know, Sofia. Maybe we should just let Centarmar figure it out," Júlia said with her arms crossed.

Sofia gritted her teeth and dug her feet deep into the warm sand. "That doesn't sound like the ranger Júlia I know. The one who wanted to stake out the Amazon in the middle of the night."

"Stake out? I wanted to eat steak in the Amazon? Maybe for dinner, but not in the middle of the night." Júlia blocked Sofia from walking farther down the beach. "*Fala sério*. You are kidding, right?"

"No. I'm not kidding. A 'stake out' is where you wait and spy on the bad guys. The lazy loggerhead wants us to find the raiders. How else are we going to do it?" Sofia sighed and put her hand on Júlia's shoulder. "You still want to be a ranger, right?"

"*Sim*. Yes, but what if the pirate fishermen see us? Or the crooked construction workers?"

"We're fast runners, right?" Sofia smirked. "Well, I'm faster than you. So maybe you *should* worry." She winked at Júlia. Júlia didn't laugh at her joke. "Seriously, though, we don't even have to go alone."

"*Como?*" What?

"We can do a turtle walk," Sofia replied. "Back in Florida, they do evening turtle walks so people

47

can see the turtles come in to nest. You think they do that here?"

Júlia cracked a tiny smile. "I'll go ask."

Sofia leaned against one of the turtle pools while she waited. A group of tourists from Australia (not Austria!) moved in next to her. They pointed and talked in their cool Australian accents. Sofia spun around to see what they chattered about.

The lazy loggerhead's deep black eyes stared back at her. Sofia hoped upon hope that she felt okay. They locked eyes. She gave the lazy loggerhead a quick nod. "I'm working on it," she said. "I'm going to find those raiders." And she could've sworn the lazy loggerhead nodded back.

"I found Camila," Júlia puffed as she joined Sofia by the side of the turtle pool. "She can take us this evening with our dads."

"Legal!" Cool! Sofia tried out another

Portuguese phrase she remembered. She high-fived Júlia. *"Vamos!"* Sofia pointed her finger down the path. "To find our dads." She skipped off.

Breathless, the girls raced up to their dads. They sat under a thatched umbrella in front of their hotel. Mr. Diaz flipped through an overstuffed notebook. Senhor Santos tapped furiously on his laptop.

"Can we go on a turtle walk tonight?" Sofia wheezed.

"Nós podemos? Can we?" Júlia pleaded. She clasped her hands in front of her heart.

"Sure, we're just finishing up for the day. Maybe we should get something to eat first though," Mr. Diaz replied.

"I've got an idea." Senhor Santos shut his laptop and hopped up. "Let's get some *acarajé* over there." He pointed to a small wooden stand a few hundred yards down the beach.

A woman in a long white dress greeted them with a broad smile. A red and white patterned scarf wrapped her hair up on top of her head. A black beaded necklace hung around her neck. Large gold hoop earrings dangled as she moved. She handed Senhor Santos an overflowing paper wrapper. Inside yellowish filling oozed out of a large fried ball. A few shrimp popped out of the sides.

"So good," Senhor Santos said as he munched. "It's deep-fried black-eyed peas. They cook the stuffing inside with things like shrimp, cashews, peanuts, coconut milk, onion and palm oil." He handed each of the girls their own overflowing paper wrappers. Júlia opened her mouth wide and began eating.

Sofia looked down at it and then up at her dad. He gave her the "be polite" nod. So she took a little nibble. Hmmmm. She didn't think this would top her list of best Brazilian foods. She took another nibble from the other end.

"What is wrong?" Júlia wrinkled her eyebrows. "Do you not like it?"

"No, I like it." Sofia nodded her head and shot Júlia a small smile. She took another small bite. "I'm just not that hungry right now."

Júlia shrugged her shoulders.

"Ice cream!" Sofia pointed to a stand tucked behind a cluster of palm trees.

"I thought you are not hungry?" Júlia winked.

"I'm always hungry for ice cream," Sofia said.

"You see, I have two stomachs." Sofia pointed to her left side. "This one's for breakfast, lunch, and dinner." Sofia pointed to her right side. "And this one's for ice cream." She giggled and grabbed her dad's hand. *"Vamos!"*

Sofia piled her bowl with all kinds of ice cream. They were made from Brazilian fruits she had never even heard of. She tried flavors such as *taperebá* and *cajarana*. The *soursop* ice cream tasted like strawberries, pineapple, coconut, and banana all swirled together. She reached over to add another scoop of passion fruit to her bowl. A familiar hand pulled her arm back.

"That's enough, Sofie-Bear," her dad said gently but firmly.

"But we've got a long walk tonight," Sofia grumbled.

"Yes, so you'd better eat up what you have." Her dad steered her away from the ice cream. If she'd had her way, Sofia would've eaten ice cream for the next few hours. But instead, they waited (and waited and waited) to meet Camila by the lighthouse. Finally, she arrived.

"*Vamos!* It is a perfect night to watch nesting turtles," Camila said. The glow of the moon gave off just enough light to see the way. "Maybe we will have some luck and see some. But the *tartaruguiero* have not found many nests on this beach yet."

"Why is that?" Senhor Santos asked.

Camila shrugged her shoulders.

"We heard that it could be pirate fishermen or crooked construction workers," Júlia piped in.

Senhor Santos chuckled. "Always my little ranger, JuJu." He poked her in the side and smiled wide.

"Dad, no. Is true!"

"What's that?" Sofia pointed up ahead. Shadows danced against the sand.

Júlia squinted. "*Não sei.* I don't know. Let's go see."

They tiptoed slowly down the beach. The shadows moved eerily this way and that. Their bare feet made no noise in the soft sand. The closer they got, the bigger the shadows became. Sofia's spine tingled.

The shadows looked like a crowd of giant scary spiders dancing on the sand. Sofia squeezed

her eyes shut for a moment. She knew they must be playing tricks on her. Still, her heart pounded in her chest. She pulled her dad close beside her. She didn't like spiders. Even if they were just shadows. And if they weren't spiders . . . what if pirate fishermen or crooked construction workers were in the middle of raiding nests? She shuddered at the thought. She squeezed her dad's hand as they tip-toed closer.

"Sofie-Bear, where's that inner bear of yours?" Mr. Diaz elbowed Sofia in the ribs. "You're not afraid of the pirates, are you?" He winked.

"Not funny, Dad," she growled.

"Actually, I don't think you need the bear right now," Mr. Diaz replied. "The shadows are just palm trees blowing in the wind."

Sofia sighed in relief.

"Ai!" A loud shriek echoed behind them.

"A pirate fisherman!" Júlia gasped.

Sofia whirled around. She expected to see an old fisherman with an eye patch threatening them with a sword. Instead she saw Senhor Costa flat on the ground.

"Sorry, Júlia. No pirate here," he said with a small laugh. He leaned on his right hand and struggled to get up.

"What are *you* doing here?" Júlia asked.

"Rodrigo told me you were going on a turtle walk tonight. He said I should try to see the nesting turtles. So I ran to catch up with you. And then this." He pointed at the coral reef behind him.

"Seems you tripped," Mr. Diaz said. "Your pant leg is ripped." He pulled at the edges of the rip. "Looks like the coral cut your leg pretty badly. We'll have to go back. Girls, come here and assist Senhor Costa." He bent down to give Senhor Costa a hand up.

"I'm so very sorry for scaring you," Senhor Costa grunted. He hobbled between the girls as they walked back. Sofia turned her head to steal one more glance. The palm trees swayed in the wind while the spiders danced. The dark ocean water splashed near the shore. She didn't see any turtles. Or raiders. They had missed their chance.

Chapter 7

Turtle Tracking

The morning waves rolled onto the beach. The sound soothed Sofia's soul as they walked. She didn't need to be nervous she told herself. She looked out into the ocean waters. Two fishing boats floated toward them. Surely, those were just plain fishermen. Not pirates. Down the way some construction workers pulled out their hammers and nails. Surely, those were just plain construction workers. Not crooked turtle nest raiders.

"You are too quiet," Júlia said.

"I wish we'd found the raiders last night," Sofia said.

"I hope those are not the raiders." Júlia pointed to the fishing boats that drifted close to shore.

"That's why I wish we'd found them." Sofia wanted to shake her *fita* off and make her wish come true. But then, of course, the wish wouldn't come true. Why did Júlia tie it so tight? She gritted her teeth. Grrrr. She let out her inner bear with a mumbled roar.

"Look!" Júlia pointed up ahead. "More turtle tracks."

Sofia nodded. "Since the lazy loggerhead is at Centarmar, she must not be making the tracks!"

"Is like you said before at the doctor's office," Júlia said. "She was leading us to the empty nests. So we would try to find the raiders."

Sofia veered right following a set of tracks. She

inspected the empty nest. "But this is strange . . . I don't think the turtles nested here to begin with."

"*Como?* What?"

I think these are false crawls," Sofia said.

"False crawls?" Júlia looked puzzled. *"Tem macaquinhos em sua cabeça?"*

Sofia giggled. "No. No monkeys in my head." She knew Júlia just used a Brazilian saying that meant you had strange ideas in your head.

"A false crawl is when a turtle goes up on the

beach to lay a nest but then doesn't." Sofia stood up and put her hands on her hips. She pointed to the tracks. "Do you see how the tracks go up into the sand and then come right back down? There's no nest at all. It's a false crawl."

Júlia followed the tracks with her eyes.

"And this one over here." Sofia jogged to the next set of tracks. "Here the tracks go up. Then there's just a little pushed sand." Sofia pointed to the small mound in the sand no wider than the tracks. "Then the tracks keep going up the beach. That never happens if the turtle made her nest. She would go back into the ocean."

"So a turtle never nested here?"

"I don't think so."

"So there are no pirate fishermen? Or crooked construction workers?"

Sofia shrugged her shoulders. "Depends on who you believe. But maybe not."

"How do you know all this?"

"From the sea turtle rescue place in Florida." Sofia blushed. "I ask a lot of questions."

"You? Ask questions? Noooo," Júlia teased. "So, no nests. No raiders. No mystery, right?"

"Wrong."

"*Como?* Come again?" Júlia looked puzzled again.

"Something fishy—no, 'turtle-y'—is going on." Sofia laughed at her own joke. Júlia just looked confused.

Sofia explained. "Why would the turtles crawl up the beach night after night to make a nest but never make one?"

Júlia raised one eyebrow. "Good question."

Chapter 8

Night in the Light

Sofia sat cross-legged on the reclining chair with her head in her hands. A thatched umbrella shielded her from the afternoon sun. She kept trying to move the puzzle pieces around in her head. A lazy loggerhead. Pirate fishermen. Crooked construction workers. False crawls. No nests. It didn't make sense.

"I just don't get it. What was the lazy loggerhead leading us to? Or trying to tell us? If those were really false crawls, why? How are we ever going to figure this out?" Sofia sighed. She played with the *fita* on her wrist, twisting it around and around. She wished she could put the pieces of this way too strange puzzle together.

"*Não se preocupe. Vamos descascar o abacaxi.*" Júlia got up and sat together with Sofia in her chair.

"What? Peel the pineapple? What are you talking about?" Sofia scrunched her eyebrows together. "Now, *you* are the one with monkeys in your head."

Júlia laughed. "Is another Brazilian saying. It means we will solve the problem." She put her arm around her best friend. "We will think of a plan. We always do."

"What's up girls?" Mr. Diaz plopped down next to the girls.

"Nothing," Sofia said dully.

"Well, I've got a cool surprise for you. Rodrigo asked if we wanted to camp out in the lighthouse tonight." Mr. Diaz's face lit up with excitement.

"He said they let boy scouts and girl scouts stay overnight, so why not us?"

Sofia shot Júlia a frightened glance. Júlia squeezed Sofia's hand. "Well, um, Dad, I'm not so sure. I'm kinda tired."

"What?" Mr. Diaz leaned forward in his chair and put his hands on his knees. "Are you kidding me? This is a once in a lifetime chance to build a memory."

Sofia rolled her eyes at Júlia. But Júlia leaned over and whispered, "Maybe *this* can be our plan." Then she stood up and reached for Sofia's hand. "*Sim.* Yes, Mr. Diaz. You are right. *Vamos*, Sofia. Let's get ready to go."

Sofia couldn't believe that Júlia had just agreed to stay the night in the lighthouse. Did she forget that Rodrigo could be a pirate? Or worse, that a ghost haunted the lighthouse?

Sofia spent the next few hours trying to

change everyone's minds. But no luck. Now they all climbed up, up, up the stone steps behind Rodrigo.

"Have you seen any pirate fishermen?" Rodrigo asked. He laughed.

Was it a scary laugh? Sofia wasn't sure. It could've just been an ordinary laugh. Or a tired laugh. Or a coughing laugh.

He turned around and offered his hand to Sofia to help her up the last step. "No worries. There are not too many of us left around." He winked.

Did he just say "us?" Sofia checked her ears. Was he the pirate and he planned to lock them all up here to find out what they knew? She had to warn her dad. But he still huffed and puffed his way up the steps carrying their gear.

"No," Júlia replied. She stepped into the lantern room. "We did not find any pirate fishermen. I think you are right. No pirate fishermen." Júlia nodded her head slightly. Her lips parted into a tiny fake smile.

"*Sim.* Yes, we fishermen are honest men. And many of us are now working for Centarmar. We spend our time protecting turtles, not harming them."

"Well, then, maybe you can help us," Sofia said in a tiny voice. She reached deep down inside herself hoping to find the inner bear she needed to make a difference. "We found false crawls on the beach. Lots and lots of false crawls. Why would the turtles keep coming up on the beach and then not make their nests?"

Rodrigo's bushy eyebrows raised up into the straw hat he wore. "False crawls, you say?"

Sofia nodded.

"Now that is strange, it is."

"Sofia thought so too," Júlia added.

"And quite the turtle detectives, you girls are." He paced around the room looking out each of the windows.

The girls followed him with their eyes. Had she

made a mistake saying something? Sofia peeked down the stairs to check on her dad and Senhor Santos. They were coming. Just waaaay too slowly. She sucked in a deep breath and looked at Rodrigo who still paced around the lantern room.

"Something is scaring them," he said finally. The girls glanced at each other. "What?" Júlia mouthed. Sofia shrugged.

"Here you go, Sofia." A rolled up sleeping bag

bounced off her head. Mr. Diaz poked his head up the last step.

Sofia sighed in relief. Finally!

"A hand," Rodrigo offered his hand to help Mr. Diaz and Senhor Santos with the last of their overnight gear.

"*Obrigado,*" Senhor Santos panted.

"*De nada.* You are welcome." Rodrigo nodded his head and helped Senhor Santos up the last step. "I will see you all in the morning. Have a good night. *Boa noite.*" He turned and stepped down the tower stairs. "Watch out for the ghoooost . . ." he yelled from half-way down. His voice echoed off the stone walls and his footsteps faded. Together they sounded just like someone, or something, creeping up the tower stairs.

Mr. Diaz and Senhor Santos looked at each other. Mr. Diaz raised an eyebrow. That certainly didn't make Sofia feel any better. She unrolled her sleeping bag and snuggled in. If she could've zipped it up over her head, she would've. But then she wouldn't be able to watch for the ghost.

"Where's your inner bear, Sofie-Bear?" Mr. Diaz grinned.

"The bear left," Sofia grumbled.

"It's okay, Sofia. There are no ghosts here," Mr. Diaz replied. He rubbed her back through the sleeping bag.

"Plus, we're here to keep you safe," Senhor Santos added. He zipped up Júlia's sleeping bag and patted her on the back.

Sofia still wasn't sure. The moonlight's eerie glow seeped through the windows of the lighthouse. The waves hissed over and over as they crashed against the shore. A shiver went up and down her spine. She gritted her teeth and rolled over to face Júlia. "I won't go to sleep," she whispered.

"Me neither." They made a pact. And a secret handshake to go along with it. And a secret hug. Then they whispered and whispered. About the wild animals of the Amazon. About gymnastics. About school. About friends. Anything to keep their minds off the ghost. Or the pirate fishermen. Or the crooked construction workers. They whispered until their dads fell asleep.

"I guess they're not going to protect us after all," Sofia muttered.

"Then we will have to keep watch." Júlia took a deep breath and stood up. She tip-toed around the lantern room. "No ghost," she sighed in relief. She turned around to check out the window and sucked in her breath again.

"Look!" Júlia grabbed Sofia's hand to help her up. A dark heart-shaped shadow crept across the sand.

"Is it a turtle?" Sofia put her hand up on the

glass as if to trace its path. "Is it turning around again?" Sofia cried softly. "Why? Why?" She buried her head in her hands.

"There is another shadow. Behind it. Do you see?"

"Where?" Sofia looked up from her hands.

The shadow lurched with each step. "Is some kind of limping monster," Júlia gasped. "With a laser beam!" Her face filled with horror. A bright beam lit up a turtle's head.

Sofia squinted to see. Her heart pounded. She was *not* going to look away until she solved this mystery. False crawls. No turtle nests. A limping monster. A laser beam. She moved each of the puzzle pieces around in her head. And then it hit her.

Night in the Light

Chapter 9

For the Love of Turtles

The sun had risen on another brand new day. A great day. The morning rays warmed Sofia's skin as she and Júlia bolted out of the lighthouse.

Her dad was right. She really had built memories last night. She remembered the scary talk with Rodrigo. She remembered the limping monster on the beach. And she remembered the moment she knew the truth.

She had told Júlia right away, of course. And

they had wanted to tell their dads, of course. But waking her dad up from a sound sleep was kind of like waking up a bear from hibernation. She knew where she had gotten her bear-like qualities.

Instead they talked until dawn. Then they watched a stunning sunrise from the top of the lighthouse.

At the break of dawn, their dads hopped on an early morning conference call with some people in London. So they still hadn't gotten a chance to tell them. And now here they were, bursting at the seams to tell someone.

"Bom dia." Good morning. Rodrigo greeted them right outside of the lighthouse. "A good night, yes? Up early to greet the day, yes?"

"Bom dia," Júlia replied. "We did not sleep much, but the stars sparkled all night long. And we watched the sunrise start a new day. A great day." They walked under the palm trees.

"We think Senhor Costa is scaring the turtles," Sofia blurted out.

Rodrigo stopped in his tracks right by the loggerhead pool. "Senhor Costa, say you?" He wrinkled his nose and crossed his arms. "No, I do not think so. He loves the turtles. He plans to give us money to save turtles."

"Sofia is right. Is Senhor Costa," Júlia agreed. She put her arm around Sofia. "We saw a limping monster chasing the turtles with a laser beam."

Rodrigo looked confused.

"The *shadow* of a limping person—with a *flashlight*," Sofia explained. "He may love the turtles, but scaring them is a weird way to show it."

"Anyone." Rodrigo flicked his hand in the air. "Anyone could be chasing the turtles with a flashlight," he argued.

"Yes, but not anyone would be limping," Sofia said. "Senhor Costa cut his leg on coral during our turtle walk the other night. So he would be limping. But we still don't know *why* he would scare the turtles."

"Silly girls. What tales are you telling?" Senhor Costa limped up the winding path toward them.

Sofia gulped. Júlia stumbled backwards against the turtle pool wall. She almost took a swim with the lazy loggerhead.

"Senhor Costa, tell me this is not true?" The

wrinkles around Rodrigo's eyes got bigger as he scrunched them with worry. "These girls here say they saw a limping man chasing the turtles. And you are limping, no?"

"I came to bring you the money for my donation to Centarmar, Rodrigo. I didn't hurt the turtles. I love them as you do." He scowled at the girls.

Sofia grabbed Júlia's hand. What would happen if Rodrigo didn't believe them? Would Senhor Costa throw them in the pool? Bury them in the sand? Tie them up in a palm tree? She looked around. Her mind raced to find an escape plan.

Rodrigo looked up from under his straw hat. "You do, do you?"

Senhor Costa nodded curtly. "*Eu faço*. I do. Yes. The turtles bring tourists. And tourists stay in my hotels. I wouldn't hurt the turtles. I just urged them to nest somewhere else." He tilted his head and looked into Rodrigo's eyes. "No harm was done."

"It is true then?" Rodrigo choked. He bowed his head and clenched his fists.

Senhor Costa straightened his jacket and held his head high. "I just bought the hotel on the beach. We're repairing it and adding on some rooms. But there are problems with the lighting. Centarmar won't allow us to use the lights we bought. They're too bright."

"Too bright, are they?" Rodrigo knit his bushy eyebrows together under the brim of his straw hat.

"The project is costing more money than we thought. There's no more money to buy new lights." Senhor Costa put his hands out with the palms up. "I thought if I scared the turtles a little, they wouldn't nest there. I thought if there were no new nests in front of the hotel this season, Centarmar would let us use the lights we have."

"You thought that, did you?" Rodrigo tilted

his head. His eyes grew dark. "You know the rules. Always low lights by the beach. The turtles will not nest if they are disturbed by the lights. And the baby turtles, they will crawl to the light instead of the ocean. Low lights. Always low lights." He shook his head.

Senhor Costa's eyes narrowed. He pressed his hands together in front of his mouth and looked down for a moment. He took a deep breath and then clasped his hands in front of him. "I'm trying to save money. Money that I can give to help the turtles," he pleaded. "If not for these girls . . . if they had just believed the story about the pirate fishermen, we'd have more money for the turtles . . ."

Rodrigo abruptly raised his hand to stop him from talking further. "More money for you and your hotel, you mean." He took a slow breath in through his nose and let it out slowly through his tight lips.

Rodrigo turned toward the girls. He put one arm on Júlia's left shoulder and the other arm on Sofia's right shoulder. *"Obrigada meninas."* Thank you girls. "I can see you love the turtles. You made the right decision."

Senhor Costa glared at him. Rodrigo stood tall and returned the gaze. "Scaring the turtles is not love, I do not think. You made the wrong decision. We do not need your money." He grabbed Senhor Costa by the elbow and dragged the limping man back down the winding path.

Chapter 10

Sunset

By the end of the day, the girls were the talk
of Centarmar. They had become "the turtle
detectives." People turned and whispered to one
another when they walked by. Little girls and boys
waved and pointed.

The girls rounded the last corner of the
winding path. They saw the Centarmar staff.
Everyone cheered and clapped. Camila stepped out
of the crowd.

"Obrigada de Centarmar," Camila said with a broad smile. "Thank you. You are now honorary staff of Centarmar." She reached up and hung a turtle necklace around each of their necks. Then she tucked turtle earrings just like hers in each of their hands. "And, more good news. The lazy loggerhead is fine. You do not need to worry."

"There's nothing really wrong with her, right?" Sofia gave Júlia a knowing glance. "She's not lazy after all."

Júlia leaned over. "She just inched along the beach slowly to show us the false crawls," she whispered. "So we could solve the mystery."

Camila looked surprised by Sofia's comment. "No. We are glad you told us. She was *more* than lazy. She was sick. The doctor found a plastic bag inside her."

Júlia looked puzzled. "A plastic bag? How would that make her slow?"

Sofia thought a moment. "She probably thought the bag was a jellyfish. So she ate it. The plastic bag got trapped inside, right?"

Camila nodded.

"It rots and causes gas," Sofia continued. "Then she floats. She can't swim. She can't dive down to eat. She would've starved." Sofia shook her head sadly. "That's probably why she crawled so slowly by the edge of the water. She couldn't swim. The waves kept washing her ashore."

Júlia looked alarmed. Sofia pressed her lips together in a thin line. She'd seen this too many times before in Florida.

"You two are great turtle detectives *and* turtle rescuers," Rodrigo said. "But, Sofia, you are from Miami, no? How do you know so much about sea turtles in Brazil?" A twinkle in his eye stood out like a giant question mark.

"We have a sea turtle rescue place near my grandparent's house in Florida." Sofia looked around at the staff as she talked. "Just like Brazil, we have loggerheads too. I've been there a ton of times. And I ask a lot of questions." She blushed. Júlia gave a hearty nod. Actually, she kept nodding until Sofia elbowed her in the ribs.

Then Sofia had another idea. It might be silly, but it could make a difference. "Maybe I can introduce you to the sea turtle people in Florida? We can work together—in Brazil and the United

States to save the sea turtles." She held her breath and waited for their reaction.

"*Com certeza!* Of course!" Rodrigo's wide smile burst out of his beard. "We will learn much from one another, I am sure. *Obrigado.* For all you have done at Centarmar, we thank you." He gave both of the girls a kiss on each cheek.

Senhor Santos stepped out from the parting crowd and gave Júlia a big hug. "Another day. Another ranger adventure. *Bravo*, JuJu," he whispered in her ear.

Mr. Diaz came over and grasped Sofia's shoulders. "Aww, my Sofie-Bear. I'm so proud of you. You really made a difference this week." He gave her a great big bear hug.

"Thanks, Dad." Sofia hugged him back.

"That was nice of them to give us this necklace and the earrings." She played with the turtle around her neck. "They'll go well with my *fita*."

Sofia looked down at her wrist. "My *fita*. It fell off!" Tears started to well up in her eyes. She had lost it not even *one* week from the day she got it.

"Fique tranquilo," Júlia said. "Don't worry. Is supposed to fall off when the time is right."

Sofia's eyes lit up. Her wishes! Yes, that's it. She had wished that she stayed best friends with Júlia. And, of course, she still was. She had wished that the lazy loggerhead would be rescued. And she was. And she had wished that they would solve the mystery. And they did. "My wishes! They came true! It *is* a miracle!"

"Maybe," Mr. Diaz said. "But I think it's more about you than the *fita*. You and Júlia didn't just talk about things. You stood up for what you believed in. You took action. Your actions saved the lazy loggerhead. And your actions protected the turtles. Now we can watch them safely nest on our last night in Brazil."

Sofia looked up at her dad. Her brown eyes sparkled.

"Really? We can go on another turtle walk?"

"Well, the last one wasn't the best, was it?" Mr. Diaz titled his head and smiled.

Sofia grabbed Júlia's hand and squeezed it tight. "We get to watch the turtles tonight. Did you hear that?"

Júlia nodded. She gazed out toward the horizon. "But first, we watch the sunset." She strolled down to the beach and sat down on the cool sand. "I see why you like it. *Lindo maravilhoso!* The colors *are* amazing."

Sofia took off her Havaianas and flopped down beside Júlia. She scanned the horizon. Oranges, blues, purples, and pinks all mixed together. Their reflection rippled in the water. The fishing boats still bobbed up and down. They didn't look scary anymore though. "Yes. It *is* amazing."

Sunset

"Look, a turtle."

"Where?" Sofia looked up and down the beach.

"No. A painting. Like you said. In the sunset."
Júlia pointed to the clouds. "A lazy loggerhead.
Saying thank you to us."

"You're welcome," Sofia whispered under her
breath.

Mystery of the Min Min Lights

Chapter One

Wendy Lee watched the men carrying boxes into the tidy yellow house. She stood on a dry patch of grass and chewed her thumbnail. She knew she shouldn't bite her nails but couldn't help it. This was just one of those days.

"Hey! *G'day, mate!*"

A squeaky voice from somewhere in the sky yelled at Wendy.

She twisted her head and looked up.

"Ow yar goin?" The voice squeaked again. Wendy had no idea what the voice said. None.

Wendy shaded her eyes against the sun. Holy smokes was it ever sunny. And hot. And dusty. The dry wind blew her straight black hair in tangles around her face. A fine layer of grit covered her teeth. She squinted at the bright, cloudless sky and looked for where the voice came from.

A giant tree towered over the neighbor's yard. It looked, really, like a dozen trees all twisted together.

"You! Mate!" The tree seemed to be calling to her. "Whatcha' doin'?"

Finally. English. Sort of.

Wendy cocked her head and studied the branches. The noise seemed to come from two skinny legs wrapped around a thick tree branch. Wendy caught a glimpse of blond curls and a red sports jersey in between the broad emerald leaves.

Beyond the tree, a screen door slammed. "Jacko?" A girl about Wendy's age stepped out onto the wide wooden porch. She had lots of curly blond hair pulled back into a thick ponytail. Her tan arms and long legs matched the color of Wendy's skin, except the other girl got her color from being in the sun. The girl put her hands on her hips and huffed loudly. "Are you in the tree again, Jacko? Mum's gonna' be *cross as a frog in a sock*. I'm *dobbing on you* as soon as she gets home from the police."

"Police?" Wendy shifted her eyes nervously.

The girl sighed. "We've a bit of a problem with sheep rustlers."

"Rustlers? You mean people are stealing sheep?" Wendy asked.

"Yeh. But it's not people who are doing it." She scanned the sky and then leaned close to Wendy. Her voice dropped to a whisper. "It's UFOs."

Find out what happens to Wendy and Chloe in the Pack-n-Go Girls book, Mystery of the Min Min Lights.

Meet More Pack-n-Go Girls!

Discover Australia with Wendy and Chloe!

Mystery of the Min Min Lights

It's hot. It's windy. It's dusty. It's the Australian outback. Wendy Lee arrives from California. She's lucky to meet Chloe Taylor, who invites Wendy to their sheep station. It sounds like fun except that someone is stealing the sheep. And the thief just might be something as crazy as a UFO.

Discover Austria with Brooke and Eva!

Mystery of the Ballerina Ghost

Nine-year-old Brooke Mason is headed to Austria. She'll stay in Schloss Mueller, an ancient Austrian castle. Eva, the girl who lives in Schloss Mueller, is thrilled to meet Brooke. Unfortunately, the castle's ghost isn't quite so happy. Don't miss the second and third Austria books: *Mystery of the Secret Room* and *Mystery at the Christmas Market.*

Meet More Pack-n-Go Girls!

Discover Mexico with Izzy and Patti!
Mystery of the Thief in the Night
Izzy's family sails into a quiet lagoon in Mexico and drops their anchor. Izzy can't wait to explore the pretty little village, eat yummy tacos, and practice her Spanish. When she meets nine-year-old Patti, Izzy's thrilled. Now she can do all that and have a new friend to play with too. Life is perfect. At least it's perfect until they realize there's a midnight thief on the loose! Don't miss the second Mexico book, *Mystery of the Disappearing Dolphin.*

Discover Thailand with Jess and Nong May!
Mystery of the Golden Temple
Nong May and her family have had a lot of bad luck lately. When nine-year-old Jess arrives in Thailand and accidentally breaks a special family treasure, it seems to only get worse. It turns out the treasure holds a secret that could change things forever!

What to Know Before You Go!

Where is Brazil?

Brazil is the largest country in South America. North of Brazil is Venezuela and the small countries of Guyana, Suriname, and French Guiana. West of Brazil you can find Bolivia, Peru, and Colombia. South of Brazil are Paraguay, Uruguay, and Argentina. The Atlantic Ocean borders the east side of Brazil. The shoreline is a whopping 4,655 miles long!

How Big is Brazil

Brazil and the United States are close in size. Brazil is slightly smaller, though. It's 8,511,965 square miles. Brazil is the fifth largest country in the world. It's the largest country in South America. Brazil is also the fifth largest country in terms of population with 208 million people.

Brazilian Money

Did you know that every country has its own money? In the United States, we use dollars and cents for our money system. Brazilians use the real. We use this symbol to mean dollar: $. This is the symbol for the real: R$. The real is made up of 100 centavos. Their coins have the Southern Cross constellation printed on them. This is the symbolic constellation of the southern hemisphere.

In Brazil, the use of periods and commas in writing amounts is exactly the opposite of what is used in the United States. For example, one thousand dollars and fifty cents in the United States is written as $1,000.50. In Brazil, it would be written as R$1.000,50. If Sofia buys ice cream in Miami, the price looks like this: $2.75. When Sofia and Júlia buy ice cream in Praia do Forte, the price looks like this: R$2,75.

Brazilian Sayings

Just like in the United States, Brazilians have many sayings. Brazilians are very affectionate. So, they will often end a conversation or an email with a friend by saying, "*um beijo*" (a kiss) or "*um abraço*" (a hug). Brazilians also value being positive, even when there's a problem. If the problem can't be solved or someone is stressed, they will say, "*fique tranquilo*" (don't worry). For example, if you lose your bracelet, "*fique tranquilo.*" You can surely get another one. And we can go shopping together!

Turtle Rescue Centers

Praia do Forte is home to Projeto Tamar. Their mission is to protect endangered sea turtles in Brazil. They have 23 bases in 9 Brazilian states. They protect 1,100 kilometers of coastline and islands. Projeto Tamar conducts research, monitors turtle nests, and provides environmental education. If you cannot visit Brazil, visit the Loggerhead Marinelife Center in Juno Beach, Florida. They are leaders in sea turtle protection, education, research, and nursing sea turtles back to health. There are many other sea turtle rescue centers around the world. Find one on your next trip to the ocean.

Brazilian Ice Cream

People love ice cream in Brazil. At the *sorveteria*, or ice cream store, there are hundreds of different flavors. You can try *jabuticaba* ice cream, made of a fruit that looks and tastes like grapes but with a citrus twist and hint of spicy wasabi. Don't miss out on the *umbu* ice cream. It's made from Brazilian plums. Many people say that *pitanga* ice cream is their favorite. It's made from Brazilian cherries. Júlia's favorite is *nata goiaba*, or sweet guava and cream.

Recipe for Pão de Queijo

Try this amazing recipe for yummy Brazilian cheese bread.

Ingredients *(If you make this recipe, be sure to get an adult to help you.)*

1 egg (room temperature)	1/2 cup cheese (packed)
1/3 cup olive oil	1 teaspoon salt
2/3 cup milk	
1 1/2 cups tapioca flour	

1. Preheat oven to 400°F.
2. Grease insides of a mini muffin tin (use olive oil).
3. Blend all ingredients until smooth (in a blender).
4. Pour batter into the mini muffin tin - not quite to the top.
5. Bake in oven for 15-20 minutes, until puffy and lightly browned.

Say It in Portuguese!

English	Portuguese	Portuguese Pronunciation
Hello	Ola	Oh-LAH
Good morning/day	Bom dia	Bhon DEE-ah
Good afternoon	Boa tarde	BOH-ah TAHR-deh
Good night	Boa noite	BOH-ah NOY-teh
Hi	Oi!	OH-ee
Goodbye	Adeus	Ah-DEH-oosh
Bye	Tchau	Chow
Please	Por favor	Poor fah-VOHR
Thank you	Obrigado/Obrigada	Oh-bree-GAH-doh/dah
Nothing	Nada	NAH-da
Yes/No	Sim/Não	Seen/Now
I don't know	Não sei	Now say
My name is . . .	Meu nome é . . .	MEH-ooh NOH-meh eh
Nice to meet you	Prazer em conhecé-la/lo	Pra-ZAIR eh con-YO-seh-la/lo
Mrs.	Senhora	SENN-yoh-dah
Mr.	Senhor	SEEN-yoh
Let's go!	Vamos!	VA-mos
Cool	Legal	Lay-gah-oo
You're kidding!	Fala sério!	FAH-lah SEH-dee-oh

English	Portuguese	Portuguese Pronunciation
Careful	Cuidado	Kwi-DAH-doh
I missed you so much!	Que saudade!	Kay sah-ooh-DAH-jee
Don't worry	Não se preocupe	Now seh Pray-o-COO-pe
Beautiful! Marvelous!	Lindo maravilhoso!	LEEN-doh MAH-dah-veel-yoh-zoo
Great!	Bravo!	BRA-voh
Good	Bem	Behn
Of course!	Com certeza!	Com ser-TEH-zah
0	Zero	ZEH-roo
1	Um/Uma	Oon/Ooma
2	Dois/Duas	Doysh/Doo-ahsh
3	Três	Trehyesh
4	Quatro	KWAH-troo
5	Cinco	SEEN-koo
6	Seis	Saysh
7	Sete	SEH-chee
8	Oito	OY-too
9	Nove	NOH-vee
10	Dez	Daysh

My Brazilian Trip Planner

Where to go: _____

_____

_____

_____

_____

_____

_____

_____

_____

_____

_____

_____

_____

_____

_____

_____

_____

What to do: _____

_____

My Brazilian Trip Planner

_____

_____

_____

_____

_____

_____

_____

_____

_____

_____

_____

_____

_____

_____

_____

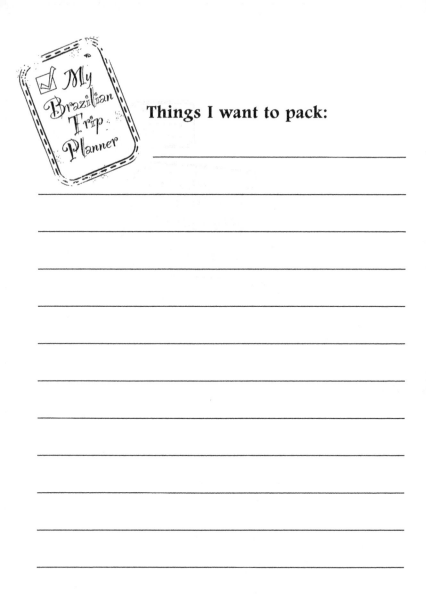

My Brazilian Trip Planner

Things I want to pack:

_____

_____

_____

_____

_____

_____

_____

_____

_____

_____

_____

_____

_____

_____

_____

Friends to send postcards to:

My Brazilian Trip Planner

_____

_____

_____

_____

_____

_____

_____

_____

_____

_____

_____

_____

_____

_____

_____

Thank you to the following Pack-n-Go Girls and Pack-n-Go Boys:

Maia Caprice	Jack Falender
Keira Clotfelter	Lisa Muehlfellner
Elizabeth De Pry	Abby Rice
Audrey Duncan	Faith Sheeks
Madeline Duncan	Sarah Travis
Kate Falender	Caroline Yoder

Thank you also to Marjorie Ehrhardt and John Ehrhardt.

And a special thanks to my Pack-n-Go Girls co-founder, Janelle Diller, and our husbands, Steve Diller and Rich Travis, who have been along with us on this adventure.

Lisa Travis has always dreamed of faraway places. Her childhood days of exploring old National Geographic magazines in her attic led her to the world beyond. She studied in Germany, traveled the USA in a Volkswagen camper, and lived and worked in South Korea. She currently finds ways to pack and go by designing global leadership programs. Her experiences around the world inspired her to write Pack-n-Go Girls stories that deliver positive messages around independence, adventure, and global awareness. Lisa lives, bikes, and skis in Colorado with her husband, two kids, and two dogs.

Adam Turner has been working as a freelance illustrator since 1987. He has illustrated coloring books, puzzle books, magazine articles, game packaging, and children's books. He's loved to draw ever since he picked up his first pencil as a toddler. Instead of doing the usual two-year-old thing of chewing on it or poking his eye out

with it, he actually put it on paper and thus began the journey. Adam also loves to travel and has had some crazy adventures. He's swum with crocodiles in the Zambezi, jumped out of a perfectly good airplane, and even fished for piranha in the Amazon. It's a good thing drawing relaxes his nerves! Adam lives in Arizona with his wife and their daughter.

Pack-n-Go Girls Online

Dying to know when the next Pack-n-Go Girls book will be out? Want to learn more Portuguese? Trying to figure out what to pack for your next trip? Looking for cool family travel tips? Interested in some fun learning activities about Brazil to use at home or at school while you are reading *Mystery of the Lazy Loggerhead?*

- Check out our website:
  www.packngogirls.com
- Follow us on Twitter:
  @packngogirls
- Like us on Facebook:
  facebook.com/packngogirls
- Follow us on Instagram:
  packngogirlsadventures
- Discover great ideas on Pinterest:
  Pack-n-Go Girls

SILVER

MOON

A RILEY HUNTER NOVEL

AMANDA LYNN

∞ ∞ ∞

Cover designed by Coverinked Book Cover Design
http://coverinked.com/

This book is a work of fiction. Names, characters, places, and incidents either are products of the author's imagination or are used fictitiously. Any resemblance to actual persons, living or dead, events, or locales is entirely coincidental.

Amanda Lynn
Visit my website at https://amandalynnauthor.com/

Printed in the United States of America

First Printing: November 2018
Amanda Lynn

ISBN-9781728793344

CONTENTS

FOR MY FAMILY, THANK YOU FOR
THE ENCOURAGEMENT TO CHASE
MY DREAMS.

*"Never give up on a dream just because of the time it will take to
accomplish it. The time will pass anyway."*

CHAPTER I

Mrs. Greenwell was a typical elderly woman of about eighty. She had snow-white hair wrapped in a tight bun, outdated glasses–purchased at least twenty years ago–a matching tweed blazer and skirt, and a black handbag that never left her hands. Her reason for seeking me, however, was anything but typical.

Her granddaughter had recently disappeared under mysterious circumstances, yet the local police department weren't going to file a report or search for her. She was desperate to find her granddaughter and decided to hire me, a private investigator, to track her down. The only lead she had to offer me were her granddaughter's last known whereabouts—a local club called *Silver Moon*.

"I'll go tonight," I offered with a warm smile. "I'll take the photograph you gave me and ask around. I'll also see if I can get a meeting with the owner or the head of security while I'm there."

"I can't thank you enough," she said with a sigh of relief. "I just can't understand why they won't take this seriously. My Jessica would never just leave. I don't care what she said on the phone, I *know* she wouldn't.

Her granddaughter, Jessica, had called her the night she disappeared and left a voicemail stating her intentions of running away. But since Jessica didn't go home first to pack anything, Mrs. Greenwell was convinced Jessica didn't leave willingly.

"I tried to tell the officer that someone forced her to make that call, but he wouldn't listen."

I was still on the fence about what had happened. I would have agreed with the officer's reasoning, if it hadn't been for her not packing anything first. When people ran away, they usually had a plan, or at the very least, they would take items with them. Jessica didn't have any money or a car, and she'd only had the clothes on her back when she took off. Things just didn't add up for me.

"Hopefully, I can find something out tonight. And I'll call her friend you mentioned and set something up with her as well."

Thank you again, Riley." She stood up. "And please call me to let me know how it went. I'd rather know if you can't make any progress than be left in the dark."

"Absolutely. I'll make sure to let you know every lead I get and how it turns out," I reassured her as I stood to walk her out.

Several hours and clients later, I had to practically push my last customer out the door, so I could get to the nightclub with time to spare before my meeting with the owner. He'd agreed to meet with me at nine that night, but I wanted to have plenty of time to show Jessica's photograph to as many of the club workers as I could.

When I got there, I explained the situation to the outside bouncer, and after he told me he didn't recognize her, he let me in, so I could show the picture to other employees. For the next two hours, I weaved through the crowd and asked every worker I could find; they all had the same response—they'd never seen her before.

Deflated, I found an empty seat at the end of the bar. I knew it had been almost a week since she'd gone missing, and the employees saw hundreds of people daily, but I still thought at least one of them would have recognized her.

"Excuse me," a woman's voice sounded behind me. I turned to see a petite brunette dressed in the all-black uniform of the employees at *Silver Moon*.

"Yes?"

"Are you Lucian's nine o' clock?"

I sat there for a moment, confused, until I remembered Lucian was the name of the owner of the club.

"Oh, yeah, that's me." I glanced at my phone. It was only about five minutes till nine. I didn't realize it was already that late.

She gave me a half smile; one that clearly said she had better things to do besides fetch me. "Follow me, he'll see you now."

"Okay." I grabbed my phone and wristlet wallet from the bar and followed her through the crowd until we reached a door right off the dancefloor. She scanned a badge to let us in, and we walked down a long hallway, not stopping until we reached a closed door near the end.

"Wait right here. He'll be out in a minute," she said.

7

"Before you go," I opened my wallet and pulled Jessica's picture out, then I showed it to her, "do you recognize this girl? She was in here last week."

She glanced quickly at the picture and shook her head. "No, never seen her before." She gave me another fake smile before turning and walking back down the hallway.

I rolled my eyes, put the picture back, and leaned against the wall. Girls like her, the ones that pretended to be nice but would stab you in the back the moment you weren't looking, were a dime a dozen and were one of the reasons I didn't go out to places like this. Well, that and the too-handsy drunks who thought they'd get lucky if they grabbed your ass.

The door opened, sending a wave of chills pouring over my skin. I shivered, straightened from the wall to face the door, and almost had to pick my jaw up off the floor. Standing there was the most gorgeous man I'd ever seen. He had wavy sandy-brown hair that just covered his ears and laid perfectly out of his eyes, a sun-kissed complexion only a few shades lighter than my own, defined cheekbones, and a jawline that had a day's worth of stubble.

He even had the perfect muscular build—for me anyway. He wore a black button-down shirt that was tight enough to hug and showcase his well-built physique. His muscles were clearly well-defined, but he didn't have that excessively bulky body-builder frame some men thought all women preferred.

The most startling feature of this man, though, were his penetrating emerald eyes. I'd never really described a man as gorgeous before; I'd always said they were handsome, cute, or good-looking, but this guy was in a league all on his own.

"Are you okay?" he asked.

I pulled out of my trance and realized that wasn't the first time he'd said something to me. I blushed and tried to shake it off. "Yeah, I'm fine. It's just been a long day."

He grinned, clearly knowing the effect he had on women. "Are you Ms. Hunter?"

I hated it when people called me that. "Please, call me Riley." I offered a warm smile.

He held out his hand. "I'm Lucian. It's a pleasure to make your acquaintance, Riley."

I shook his hand, and the moment our skin touched, a jolt of something, electricity maybe, shot through my arm. Startled, I jerked my hand back.

"Sorry," he said. "Must be static." He stared at me intently and absently rubbed the hand that had shocked mine up and down his thigh.

Starting to squirm under his fixed gaze, I cleared my throat and said, "Thank you so much for meeting with me. I'm sure you're busy, so I appreciate you taking the time."

He blinked, seeming to come out of his own trance. "It's no problem." He gestured toward the open doorway. "Please, go in and have a seat."

As I walked past him, I glanced up and saw his nostrils flare as he leaned slightly down toward me. Did he just sniff me? I continued toward the desk in the corner of the room and tried to remember if I had put on perfume that morning; was it too strong? Maybe I smelled bad? I'd taken a shower and put on deodorant before work, so I knew that couldn't be it. I inwardly groaned as I realized I must've picked up a weird smell over the last couple of hours as I'd pushed through the crowd and rubbed against people.

9

Wasn't that just my luck? I met the hottest guy I'd ever seen, and I probably smelled like sweat and alcohol. Oh well, it's not like I really dated anyway, and I was pretty sure I didn't have a chance with this guy, even if I wanted to. I brushed it off and sat down in one of the chairs in front of the desk and waited for Lucian to take his seat behind it.

"So, you're a private investigator?" he asked once he was seated.

"Yes. I was hired to track down a missing person since the police department won't file a report." I paused, but he nodded for me to continue. "The missing person is a twenty-one-year old girl named Jessica Smith. She has brown hair, she's about five-two, and lives with her grandmother. She works at a game store part-time, and last Tuesday, she told a co-worker she had plans to come here after work that night. She clocked out, and that was the last time anyone's seen her."

"So," he leaned back in his chair, carefully touching his fingertips together, "she's been missing for one week?"

I nodded my head in agreement. He let his eyes trail off, staring at nothing in particular on the wall. His intense concentration gave me a moment to shamelessly admire him some more. His lips, even though currently set in a firm line, looked soft, and I found myself wondering what they would feel like pressed to mine.

Startled by that thought even crossing my mind, I shifted in my seat and tried to stay focused on my reason for being there. I'd managed to make it through college and the last two years without being distracted by men, and I planned on keeping it that way.

It's not like I hadn't dated, because I had; I just always found an excuse to pass on a second date. And the first one was usually because of an obligation to a friend to go on a blind date with someone they knew, but that first date was where my obligation ended. I couldn't even remember the last time I'd went out with a guy because I'd wanted to and not because of a guilt trip.

"You said that was the last time anyone saw her." His eyes flashed back to me. "I assume someone has heard from her then? That would explain why the police won't file a report."

"You're right." I smiled, despite a feeble attempt not to. "That night before she disappeared, she called her grandmother while she was here. It was late, and her grandmother was already in bed, so Jessica left a message saying she'd met a man at the club and was going to run off with him. The next morning when her grandmother heard the message, she went straight to Jessica's room to see if she was there. She wasn't, but all of her stuff still was.

"At first, she thought Jessica was drunk and rambling when she'd called her, but when Jessica didn't return home that day or show up for work later that night, she got worried and called the police. The officer said that since Jessica had stated her intentions of leaving, they wouldn't file a missing person report."

Lucian finished for me, "And since she didn't go home to get her personal belongings before she left, her grandmother suspected foul play." He mischievously smirked. "The police refused to help, so she hired you, hoping you could find Jessica."

"Exactly. It doesn't take you long to catch on, does it?" It was more of a statement than a question. One hazard of my occupation was the realization that common sense, wasn't really that common. I was usually forced to frustratingly spell everything out for people, regardless of how obvious something seemed to be.

He answered regardless. "No, it doesn't. Over the years, I've learned how to read between the lines."

I wondered what else he'd perfected over the years and realized almost instantly, I shouldn't have. I could feel my cheeks beginning to burn again. I averted my eyes, in an attempt to calm my blush.

"They should have thought of this," Lucian mumbled.

My eyes shot back to him. Confused, I asked, "What are you talking about? Who should have thought of what?"

His eyes bore into mine, just as intently, if not more so, than they had in the hallway. He was searching for something, but I had no idea what he was searching for. After what felt like hours, Lucian sighed and broke eye contact.

"I've already received a phone call from the police department about your missing person."

That was news to me. Mrs. Greenwell had made it sound like the officer had flat-out refused to do anything regarding Jessica's disappearance. "So, they are investigating this?" I asked.

"No."

I was starting to get irritated. "Okay, so why did they call you, if they aren't investigating?"

"Because that's what they're supposed to do when a call comes in regarding this club." His gaze returned to me.

Taken aback, I sat there for a moment, contemplating how I should handle this. If the police notified him anytime they received a call involving *Silver Moon,* it could mean one of two things—either he had friends, and they were just giving him a heads-up, or he had officers in his pocket, and they turned a blind eye when it came to this club. If the latter, I knew I needed to be careful.

Up until that moment, I hadn't gotten any of those, *'mob boss I do what I want in this club'* type of vibes, but every employee I'd spoken to had barely glanced at the photograph before giving me an automatic no. Did they just tell me that, even though they'd recognized her?

"So," I started, "is everyone on the police force instructed to call you first?"

He snorted. "No, it's not what you're thinking." He leaned back in his chair. "It's just a handful of officers and detectives that handle calls involving this club. I can assure you, there's not many incidents that happen here, but if anything does, they personally handle it." Lucian paused, "Well, they call me, so I can personally handle it."

I didn't know what to say. Lucian had admitted the police ignored calls about the club. I knew I should tread carefully, but that really pissed me off. "Not what I'm thinking, huh?" Fuck it. "So, you don't have those officers in your pocket?"

Lucian smirked. "No, I don't." I raised an eyebrow and gave him a look that clearly expressed how much I didn't believe him. "I've never paid anyone to look the other way and let me handle the calls they receive," he insisted. "Those officers just know exactly what goes on here and agree it would be best that I handle it."

"What goes on here?" I asked out loud before I could stop myself. I'd never heard of any illegal activity happening at *Silver Moon*, but since I didn't frequent the club, I couldn't say for sure nothing like that happened there.

Lucian was studying me again. "There are areas of this club that are reserved for a selective clientele," he carefully began. "And if the wrong people found out, or it became public knowledge, there would be repercussions for all those involved."

Selective clientele? I didn't want to know what he was referring to; the less I knew, the better off I'd be. Unless, he had sex slaves or something equally disturbing, and that's what happened to Jessica. I hated to ask, but if it was related to my case, then I had to, "Does Jessica's disappearance have anything to do with your selective clientele?"

"Honestly, I'm not sure."

"What do you mean, you're not sure? Was she secretly working in one of your rooms? What if one of your client's took her home, so they could have their way with her anytime they wanted?" I blurted out. I knew my questions were pushing it, but if that's what had happened to Jessica I needed to know.

Confusion laced his face, and he shook his head, "Riley, I think you've got this wrong."

"Oh, really?" I knew I would regret my next words, but, "Why don't you enlighten me, then?"

For the third time tonight—well, fourth if you counted the hallway—Lucian's emerald eyes searched mine like he was trying to read my soul. "Fine," he said, "this club has rooms in an area the human partygoers aren't allowed in. They're reserved for vampire patrons and the human donors that work for me."

I laughed. And when I saw his expression was stone-cold-serious, I got pissed. Why was he treating this as a joke? There was a missing person, and since the police looked the other way when it came to this club, he was my only hope in trying to find her, but he wasn't taking the situation seriously. Why were the hot ones always assholes?

"Okay," I decided to placate him for a moment. Maybe this was his way of not saying, out-loud, what those rooms were really for. Vampire could be code for *'client who pays for sex'* and human donor could be *'sex slave'*. "So, let's pretend what you're saying is the truth. Did Jessica work in those rooms?"

"No. I don't have anyone working here by that name, and none of my employees are missing."

"Why did you say you weren't sure if one of your clients had something to do with her disappearance, then?"

"Because even though I know she didn't work here, if she was last seen here, a vampire could have taken her home. While that's highly unlikely, I can't guarantee it couldn't have happened."

I snorted. I couldn't keep playing along; it was too ridiculous. "Look, I don't want to know what goes on here, especially if it's something the police turn a blind-eye to, but can we cut the vampire bullshit and focus on why I came here?"

Lucian leaned forward. "I'm not joking, Riley. Vampires are real, and those rooms are for allowing them to feed from the vein of willing humans in a controlled environment."

I rolled my eyes and grabbed my cellphone and wallet. If he wasn't going to help and was adamant about continuing to play this game then I was done. I would try to get access to surveillance footage from nearby businesses. Hopefully, I'd be able to see who she left with on one of them. I stood up. "Thanks for your time, Lucian."

Before I could take one step, Lucian moved faster than my eyes could track to block the closed door. "I told you I wasn't joking," he said and grinned, revealing long, pointed canines.

Unable to remain standing, I dropped back down into my seat. As Lucian made his way, in human speed, back to the desk, I followed his every movement. He smiled again and I watched, spellbound, as the two elongated teeth slid back up to a normal length.

All thoughts of my missing person's case had vanished from my mind as I desperately struggled to grasp reality. I averted my eyes from Lucian, and looked anywhere but at him. I needed to think, and he was a distraction.

He wasn't trying to play a prank on me and wasn't using code words when he'd said vampire and human donor. And as much as I wanted to believe what he'd just done was an illusion, I knew there wasn't any way he could've pulled that off. No, what I witnessed was real.

Vampires existed.

What did that mean for me? There couldn't be many people who knew that truth, so was I in danger now? Or was it normal for a vampire to tell a human? There were too many variables and what-ifs for me to be comfortable with.

At least he'd said they fed from willing humans in a controlled environment. Surprisingly, that made me feel a little easier about the situation I found myself in. Another unsettling thought came up, though—was the reason for my unusual attraction to him because of a vampire power which made him desirable to humans?

"Are you going to be okay? You look ill."

I looked up at him, and took a deep breath. "Yeah, I'll be fine. I just needed a minute to collect my thoughts." And my sanity. "Finding out a world you thought only existed in movies and books is real is a lot to take in." Lucian was casually leaning against the front of his desk, gazing down at me with curiosity.

"You're accepting this really well."

As much as I hated to admit it to myself, finding out he was a predator, didn't make him any less attractive. What was wrong with me? It had to be a vampire ability. I'd seen those movies; the ones where the human girl was helpless when it came to falling in love with the vampire boy. "Really. How do you figure that?"

He gave me a wistful smile, making me want nothing more than to melt in my seat. Stupid vampire powers.

"Most people usually scream, faint, or run away." He gently pushed away from the desk and began slowly pacing around the room, occasionally stealing glances at me. "You, on the other hand, have calmly remained seated in my office and are accepting, what you had believed to be tales for horror movies and Halloween, to actually be very true and very real."

"Well," I shifted in my seat, positioning myself for a better view of him. I liked to look at who I was talking to. "I don't see the point in overreacting. You're obviously not planning on hurting me or taking my blood," I paused, "or whatever it is that vampires do."

He stopped walking and turned to face me, "And what makes you think I won't harm you, Riley?"

I opened my mouth to tell him, but then closed it. What did make me think that? Beside the fact that they drank from people who were willing, and I didn't think he would expose himself

17

and then want to talk about it, he'd also been genuinely nice to me—even when trying to convince me vampires were real. "If you wanted to hurt me, then I'm pretty sure you would've already done so. You wouldn't have taken the time to talk to me first and tell me what you are."

He seemed satisfied with my answer. "Good point." Then a more serious expression came over Lucian's face. "I would never harm you." He made his way back toward me. "For one, it's against our rules. And two, I like you."

That made me blush. I tried to turn my head before he could see my reddened face, but I wasn't quick enough.

"Riley, please don't be embarrassed." I could tell he was close, possibly even right next to me. "Let's change the subject, shall we? What else can you tell me about the missing girl, besides she was last seen here at my club?"

A surge of guilt echoed through me when he mentioned my reason for being there. Between the revelation that vampires existed and the strange magnetism I had toward Lucian, I kept allowing myself to get distracted. A missing person was serious, and I needed to stay focused. Besides, even though I was attracted to him, and now knew he wasn't an asshole with a mob-boss mentality, I didn't know how I felt about dating a vampire.

Did he date humans? If so, and he was interested in me, would I want to? Or was he dangerous? He said it was against their rules to harm me, and for reasons I couldn't understand, I had a gut-feeling that I would be safer with him than I'd be with most human men. And other than that glimpse of his true self he gave me to prove he wasn't lying, I never would've thought he wasn't human. Since I normally didn't willingly date, sitting there, contemplating those things was messing with my head, and was another reason I leaned toward the idea he had vampire voodoo where my attraction was concerned.

I cleared my train of thought and turned around. He was sitting behind his desk again. "No," I looked up to meet those mesmerizing eyes once again. I cleared my throat. "At this point, that's all I really know. I decided coming here would be the best starting point, since this was her last known location. And I was hoping one of your employees would recognize her from the picture I brought, but no one did." I gave him a pointed look.

He smiled impishly, "I'd say if you ask again after this meeting, some of them may have a different answer." I nodded, it was just as I'd thought. They didn't want to tell me anything since it could've been vampire-related. "Can I see her picture?"

"Absolutely." I opened my wallet and pulled out the picture Mrs. Greenwell had given me. I'd intended to pass it directly to him, but when I glimpsed Jessica's face, I helplessly studied it, searching for a hidden clue I'd somehow overlooked. "Tomorrow I'm going to the game store to talk to her friend. Hopefully, she'll be able to give me some insight into what kind of person Jessica is."

"Her grandmother didn't tell you?"

I shifted my focus from the photograph back to him, "Friends usually know more of the intimate details in a person's life than family."

I placed the picture face down on the desktop and slid it across, pausing midway where Lucian's outstretched hand awaited. He lifted the photograph from the desk and turned it over. It seemed like there was a hint of recognition in his face, but it was for such a brief moment I wasn't sure if I'd imagined it. "Do you recognize her?"

There was a long silence before he reluctantly answered, "I believe so."

I could feel myself suddenly teetering on the edge of my seat with excitement at the prospect of an early lead. "Did you see her last week? Did you see who she was with?" What was meant to be two simple questions spilled out more like a drunken ramble.

"I was out of town last week, but I think she's been in here before." His eyes darted from the picture back to me. "Can I keep this?" He rose from his chair and walked in my direction. "I'll show it to everyone that works here. They'll be more likely to give me details about Jessica, and I'll let you know if anyone can recall seeing her."

I tried to hide the disappointment in my voice as I spoke, "Sure, I have more copies at my office." I slouched back in my chair with all the former enthusiasm drained from my body. "Could I also get a copy of the surveillance videos from that night?"

"I'll give the photograph to my security team. They'll go through the footage to see if she shows up on any of them. If they find her, I'll make sure you get copies." He paused a few steps in front of me, placing the picture in his shirt pocket. His expectant stance suggested he was ready to end our meeting. I sighed and rose from my seat to face him.

He closed the gap between us and took one of my hands in his. I wasn't sure what he was doing until Lucian lifted my hand to his lips and gently placed a kiss on the back of it. "I give you my word, I'll do everything in my power to assist you."

Somehow, I managed not to blush. "Thank you, Lucian. You have no idea how much of a help this will be to me."

He lowered my hand, "Don't mention it. It'll be my pleasure. And I'm sure I don't have to say this, but . . . what I told you is not something that many humans know, and I'd prefer you not mention it to anyone. The world isn't ready to find out vampires exist."

Was he serious? Even if I did tell someone, I knew they wouldn't believe me. "Don't worry, I won't say anything." There was something else that was bothering me, though. "Why did you tell me, and show me, what you are?"

His eyes pierced mine once again, "I wasn't going to. I was going to give you the run-around and send you on your way until I could look into it further and make sure a vampire wasn't involved. But, each time I gazed into your eyes, I couldn't make myself lie to you."

His brow wrinkled with soft lines of concentration as he glanced toward the door. "Unfortunately, my job calls to me." Lucian focused on me again, "I hate to be rude and end this meeting, but . . ."

Had he felt the same magnetic attraction for me that I'd been experiencing toward him? As much as I wanted to find out, I also didn't want to know the answer to that question. "It's okay, I understand."

Lucian smiled and led the way to the door. He opened it and motioned for me to go first. As I exited his office, an enormous man wearing all black, from his skin-tight t-shirt and jeans to his boots, caught my attention. He was sprinting down the hallway right toward us.

"Lucian." His voice was deep. Just the kind you would expect bellowing from that monstrous body. As he drew nearer, it became clear that enormous didn't even begin to describe this guy. His body was a canvas of rippling muscles dancing underneath his skin with every movement he made.

"Yes, Avery?"

I turned to find Lucian beside me.

"Sir, there's been an incident." He halted just mere inches in front of us, his six-foot-three stature towering over Lucian's five-foot-nine. He wasn't even out of breath. Either he hadn't ran far to get there, or he was on some amazing steroids.

"I know. What happened?"

Avery anxiously glanced my way, then back to Lucian. He was bald and not particularly handsome. There was something about his face that suggested it wasn't quite symmetrical—maybe a broken nose one too many times?

"It's okay," Lucian's tone contained a hint of displeasure. "What did he do this time?"

Avery glanced my way again, deciding whether to trust Lucian's judgment. He must be security; that would explain the black outfit.

He relaxed a little, giving Lucian his full attention. "There was a fight between two guys by the bar. Danny was the first one there. He broke it up, but one of them hit him, and he got angry and started to lose control. Aiden and Jimmy got there just in time to grab Danny and throw him in the tank."

Worry was written on Lucian's face. "Did anyone see him?"

"No. He was in the tank by the time he completely lost control."

It was Lucian's turn to relax; he let out a quiet sigh of relief. "Good. Go down and wait by the tank door." He turned to me and smiled, "I'll escort Riley out then I'll join you."

Avery gave him a slight nod of his head, turned, and trampled back down the corridor. I watched his hypnotic canter until he disappeared behind the door. With the sheer massiveness that was Avery, I was astonished at the gracefulness his body emitted.

"Shall we?" Lucian brought me out of my stupor as he raised his arm like an old-fashioned gentleman, waiting for me to wrap mine around it. I smiled and graciously accepted the awaiting gesture.

We made the journey to the entrance of the dance floor in a comfortable silence. It wasn't until we approached the door that he spoke. "I really do hate having to end this so soon."

"It's okay." I released his arm. "Thanks again, Lucian." I retrieved a business card from my back pocket. "Here. If you find out anything, please call me. My cell phone is always on."

He took the card, letting his eyes quickly sweep over it, before placing it in his shirt pocket alongside the photograph of Jessica. "You know," he began as he focused back on me, "you have a very unusual eye color."

I knew few people shared my grayish hue growing up, but I didn't think it was that uncommon. And like most people, my eyes varied in color depending on my mood. Sometimes they were a striking blue, and later in the day they'd transform back to their normal gray. "Um," I began.

"That's not a bad thing." Lucian quickly added. "I've just only seen your particular color a handful of times. And only in the same family."

23

"That's odd." I didn't know what to say about that revelation. "Well, maybe I'm related? My Dad had the same color. I've never met anyone in his family, but I assume he got them from somewhere."

He regarded me in silence for a moment, before cryptically replying, "Maybe." He then asked, "You said *had*. Does that mean your father is no longer living?"

I swallowed hard. "No, he's not. Both of my parents passed away when I was little."

"I apologize. I shouldn't have said anything."

"No, it's okay." And it was. I'd gotten used to telling people I was an orphan over the years, but it always made conversations awkward.

Before this conversation could go that route, and to be honest I didn't really know where to take it from there, I reached out to open the door. Before I was even halfway there Lucian already had it open and waiting for me. I looked up to behold a handsome, grinning face.

"You escort women, kiss their hands, and you open doors for them?" I felt myself grinning again. It'd been a long time since I'd done it, but I think I was flirting with Lucian. "You're just too good to be true."

"Ah, but there is a downside."

"What?" I gave him a skeptical expression.

"I'm a vampire, or had you forgotten?"

Oh yeah, I had. For a moment there, I was just an out-of-practice girl flirting with a cute guy. "Minor complication, nothing too serious."

His face showed both amazement and bewilderment. "It really doesn't bother you, does it?"

"No." It was automatic; I didn't even have to think about it. I guess I knew how I felt about dating a vampire. Now, I just had to decide if I wanted to date someone at all.

His smile widened even more. "I have a feeling you're going to be an enigma, Miss Riley Hunter."

I chuckled. Yep, definitely flirting. "Good." I gave him one last flirtatious grin before stepping through the doorway and into the deafening roar of the club.

The sudden burst of music blasting me from all sides was enough to temporarily daze me. Once I regained myself, I scanned the dance floor looming before me. It didn't look like a fight had just been settled. It was over halfway filled with intoxicated dancers—not bad for a Monday night.

I turned to get one last glimpse of Lucian before leaving, but he was nowhere in sight. He must have already left for the tank, whatever that was. I couldn't see him anywhere; it was almost like he'd vanished. I sighed and headed for the door.

I made my way through the twists and turns of the inebriated crowd, finally reaching the exit. I pushed through the doors and stepped out into the cool night air. The five-degree temperature drop since I'd been inside made me shiver. I crossed my bare arms and let my hair fall over them in an attempt to stay warm. I usually pulled my long, dirty-blonde hair back into a ponytail, but I'd kept it down tonight. A decision I was grateful for now.

The glowing blue neon lights above the entrance shone down on me, casting an unusual hue on everything in its wake. I glanced up at the sign that read *Silver Moon*. An uncanny feeling emerged, filling me with a certainty that this sign would become very familiar to me over the next few weeks.

I had only been to *Silver Moon* on one other occasion before that night, and it wasn't willingly. About a year ago I was forced to accompany Hattie, my best friend since elementary school, to her sister's bachelorette party. At first, not being an avid drinker or an eager participant in social events, I was steadfast in my resolve not to attend. But after weeks of Hattie pleading and insisting she needed me to help her survive an entire night of her sister and her sorority friends, I finally caved and agreed.

We both volunteered to be designated drivers for the night, allowing everyone else to drink themselves into a stupor and humiliate themselves. Despite having to endure the snobbish antics of her sister and friends, I was surprised I actually enjoyed myself. But I think that was because of the endless wreckage available for my viewing pleasure. Needless to say, Hattie took plenty of incriminating photos for future blackmail use.

But even though I had a good time, my one and only club excursion only solidified my reasoning for neglecting the nightlife. When I was in high school, I had actively attended and even enjoyed the parties, but once I graduated, my focus switched from football games and pulling all-nighters to studying for my degree in Criminology and beginning my career. After so many years of immersing myself in work and disregarding all social events, I actually preferred to be alone now.

My preference, however, was not good enough for most of my leftover friends from high school and college. Most of them were already married, or had been with their boyfriends or fiancés so long that you might as well put them all in the same category. They didn't understand my unwillingness to settle down at the ripe old age of twenty-four and constantly tried to fill my weekends with dates of friends-of-friends.

I looked at my watch; it was after ten. I hadn't realized I'd been in there that long. I gave the entrance one last glance before reluctantly turning and beginning my two-block journey to the parking lot.

CHAPTER 2

eep. Beep. Beep.

The miserable sound I loathed woke me from my dreamless sleep. I slowly raised my head from the comfort of the pillow to peek at the clock on the nightstand.

Seven.

A long yawn escaped my lips as I leaned forward to silence the dreaded noise. As I fought the urge to fall back asleep, my thoughts drifted back to my encounter with Lucian the night before. I'd always enjoyed movies about vampires, but I never thought they actually existed. I went to bed as soon as I'd gotten home, so I hadn't had time to process it yet; it still seemed surreal.

Actually, surreal didn't even begin to cover how I was feeling about it all, especially the strange and unexpected attraction to Lucian. I hoped either someone at *Silver Moon* remembered seeing Jessica, or even better, they had security footage of her leaving the club. If so, and I had to see Lucian again, I'd have to keep reminding myself to be cautious and not act like a fan-girl. Even though Lucian seemed to feel something strange between us as well, I didn't know if the pull *I* was feeling toward him was legit, or the product of a vampire effect. And until I knew the answer to that, I was going to be careful.

The observation Lucian had regarding my eyes was something else that bothered me. While most people didn't comment on them, it certainly wasn't the first time someone had. But when he mentioned knowing only one particular family that had the same shade, it was unsettling. He either had to be mistaken, or mine only appeared to be the same color. Even though I've never met anyone in my dad's family, that seemed like too much of a coincidence. And as far as I was aware, his closest relatives had all passed away, just like him.

Both of my parents died when I was eight years old. They went to the Tennessee Mountains for a romantic anniversary weekend, while I stayed behind with my mother's parents. One morning they went on a hiking excursion in the mountains and were never seen again. Search teams scoured every inch of reachable mountainside daily for several weeks to no avail. The searches became less frequent until the day finally came when they stopped altogether. They'd found no sign of my parents, or what might have happened to them.

The devastating pain of losing them was still there, buried deep within. Now and then, it forcefully emerged, slicing with emotions so raw I felt like I was still that eight-year-old child, realizing I would never see my mom and dad again. It was difficult, but I tried not to think of them often—because even though it'd been sixteen years, the pleasant memories eventually led to the agonizing ones.

For fear of doing just that I switched my train of thought and reminisced about my teenage years living with my grandparents. They raised me after my parent's death, even though it wasn't always easy for them. It'd been a long time since they'd had to deal with the complications of raising a teenager.

A lazy smile crept on my face as I recalled the unintentional, but difficult, time I gave them every morning as they tried to wake me up for school. I could never get enough "five more minutes." Not much had changed since then. I still wasn't a morning person, but for the sake of work and a paycheck, I dutifully rose each day at a decent hour to begin my morning routine.

Realizing the time had come to do just that, I pushed all my adolescent memories aside, rubbed the sleep from my eyes, and sluggishly rolled out of bed. I slid on my fuzzy blue house slippers—a Christmas gift from my grandmother last year—and began the daunting task of making the bed.

Being a horrible procrastinator, if I didn't do that as soon as my feet hit the floor, it wouldn't get done. At five-five and with a king-size bed involved, it usually took me a few minutes and a moderate amount of stretching to get the bed made. Although, I wasn't sure why I even bothered since I rarely had visitors, and it was even rarer to get a visitor to my bedroom. I was the only one who ever saw if my sheets were clean or the comforter tidy, but it was one of those many habits my grandmother had drilled in my head when I was younger, and I hadn't been able to shake it.

With that finished, I needed to gather my clothes for the day and take a shower. My closet was an array of mostly jeans and t-shirts, so I never had to search long for an outfit. When I first started my business, I wore more traditional, business-appropriate attire, but I'd never felt comfortable in that style of clothing. Eventually, I got tired of my feet screaming in pain after being held hostage in heels all day, and I decided to dress in my normal garb. So far, I hadn't had any complaints from my clients and until I did, t-shirt and jeans it was.

By the time I'd finished blow drying my hair and applied my minimal amount of makeup, it was around eight. That gave me about an hour before I needed to head down to the office. When I say down, I meant literally. My apartment was directly above my office. It made commuting to work so much easier.

Seriously though, it was one of the perks that led to me leasing this building instead of a few others I'd been interested in. That and a private fenced-in parking lot behind the building. It was reserved for myself and a few other building owners that surrounded me. With a security guard posted at the entrance, I didn't have to worry about being mugged getting in or out of my car.

There were two entrances to my upstairs apartment—one from the office downstairs and the other from the back of the building. Stairs next to the back entrance of the first level office led up to a small deck and the entry to my apartment.

At first, without having saved enough money for the down payment, I didn't think I'd be able to lease the building. I've had a part-time job since high school, but all that money went to vehicles, insurance, and whatever else I needed. By the time I graduated college, I had a little bit of money saved up, but I was afraid to spend it. I qualified for a nice amount of financial aid during college, but it didn't cover everything, and I knew those payments would start before I could bring in enough money to stay afloat. I was counting on that savings to cover my college payments until I was financially comfortable.

That's when my grandparents surprised me with the inheritance from my parents. They'd sold my childhood home after it was clear my parents weren't coming back and placed the amount that was left, after paying the mortgage off, into a savings account. They never touched it or told me about it. I wasn't instantly rich, but it ended up being enough money to pay off my college debt, pay the down payment for the lease, and furnish the office and my apartment.

I got a bowl of cereal ready, placed it on the bar, and hopped onto one of the bar stools nestled underneath. Before digging in, I picked up the remote and turned on the television in the living room.

Most people would assume that living in Kentucky, there wouldn't be much news to report on. That may be the case in some parts, but not in Louisville. There was an almost constant stream of violence being reported about on the news each day, and I liked to stay informed of the happenings where I lived. Knowledge was power in my book, and you could never have enough.

After I finished my breakfast and placed the dishes in the sink, I became distracted by a weeping middle-aged woman on the television. I slipped into the living room to get a better view.

The woman sputtered through endless, gasping sobs that her daughter, Candace, had disappeared two nights ago after going club hopping with some friends after work. According to one of them, she met a twenty-something man halfway through the evening and left with him. Her friends pleaded with her not to go, but she assured them she would be fine and would see them in the morning. No one had seen her since.

I quickly ran back to the bar to grab a pen and some paper. The circumstances of this disappearance sounded a little too familiar to my case to be a coincidence. I scribbled down the important details about her vanishing and stuffed the paper in my pocket. Time to go to work.

Trudging down to the office to face, what I already knew would be a prolonged and boring day of the usual cheating spouses and faulty insurance claims, I mentally prepared myself. With the absolute abundance of the unfaithful I was forced to witness regularly, I often wondered if anyone actually honored their nuptials these days.

Several hours and walk-ins later I found myself face-to-face with an upset twenty-something woman, confessing her fear that her husband was having a little too much fun on his "late nights". I'm not heartless, but after you heard the same story, just change a few variables, at least three times a day, you became desensitized to the emotional meltdowns those people experienced in front of you.

I stifled a yawn as I dutifully wrote the when and where I should look for her husband. I realized, as my stomach grumbled with protest, that I'd been forced to skip lunch due to the abundant surge of walk-ins that day. I'd only barely kept my gnawing hunger at bay by snacking on miscellaneous items I had stashed in my drawer for emergencies. Not that I was complaining, but lately that had become a trend, and my food choices were dwindling. Today, I had to settle for a small bag of pretzels, half of a granola bar, and a handful of skittles.

As I finally bid my goodbyes to her—thankfully my last customer of the day, I anxiously glanced at my watch. It was five till eight, and Lucian was supposed to arrive any minute. A wave of nauseating butterflies soared into the pit of my stomach, and I felt myself grinning with the thought of him. I'd been like that all day, and not being able to explain why he had that effect on me was really making me uneasy. Just one thought of Lucian, and my body betrayed me, acting like I was in high school again with a crush on the cute boy in my class.

Lucian had called about an hour ago inquiring about my trip to the game store that night. After some small chat, he asked if he could go with me. When I questioned why, he hinted that he may have a lead on Jessica's disappearance, but would only discuss it with me after he heard what her friend had to say. He didn't want to give me any false information, and depending on what Amy had to offer, it may or may not have been. Lucian assured me he would know after speaking with her.

If he could help me figure this case out, then he could follow me everywhere I went. Being a vampire, he may have been able to pick up on things I couldn't. If the movies were accurate, then who knew what he was capable of, and I had a feeling this case was going to be a tricky one to solve.

Ding.

That must be him. A wave of tingling nervousness spread throughout my body as I jumped out of the chair in my office, almost sending it crashing to the floor, and hurried out into the hallway. From there I could see the entrance of the building in the waiting area. Since I hadn't been able to hire a dependable secretary, I had to follow that routine of up and down every time I was working at my desk. Recently, since business had been booming, I'd taken the habit of using the secretary's desk in the waiting area in between my appointments.

Lucian wasn't in my limited view of the front door, so I walked into the waiting area. He was there, seated in one of the empty chairs in front of the secretary desk, looking just as scrumptious as he did last night. He was dressed casually today, appearing to have stepped out of a GQ ad, wearing black jeans, brown boots, a dark-gray shirt, and leather jacket. Seeing him, though, sent my stomach into a frenzied panic.

"Hello, Riley." He rose from his chair, "Are you ready to leave?"

His soothing voice caressed and calmed my jittery body, "Almost. Give me just a second." I dashed back to my office to shut down the computer and grab the mini tape recorder that covertly fit in my purse or pocket. I never knew what a witness would reveal, so I recorded every conversation in case I needed to review it again later. I threw it in my purse and picked up my keys laying on the desk.

When I returned to the waiting area, blessedly free of those annoying butterflies, Lucian was standing beside the door. "Are you ready now?"

"Yeah," I quickly skimmed over the room, making sure I hadn't forgotten anything—an unfortunate habit of mine. "Are you?"

Lucian smirked, "I'm always ready. Do you want to take my car or yours?"

"I'll drive. I know exactly where we're going." I pointed to the door, "We can go out here; I'm parked out front."

Lucian opened the door and waited for me to pass through. I turned off the lights as I fumbled to find the correct key. He followed directly behind me, closing the door as we walked out. I locked up and engaged the security system with the handy remote I'd been given, since I always forgot to punch in the code before I walked out.

I unlocked my Jeep Cherokee, and we climbed in. Lucian immediately scanned the contents of the interior, finally settling his smoldering gaze on me, "I'm curious, why an SUV?"

I glanced over at him as I started the engine and put it in drive. "Why not?"

"I don't know. For some reason I just pictured you in something a little sportier."

I couldn't stop the smirk from forming, "It's the blonde hair, isn't it?"

He laughed, "You know, I think you're right. A blonde girl and a sports car, what guy would ask for more?"

I chuckled as I pulled out of the parking lot. "All joking aside, I do like sportier vehicles. But I wanted an SUV for the winter, just in case it snows."

"How far away do you live from the office?"

There were two things I was apparently unable to refrain from while around Lucian; one was smiling, the other was blushing—I did both. "I live upstairs."

He laughed again, "So, why do you need to go anywhere when it snows?"

Still blushing, "I never know when I'll get a call from a client and have to go out." The chances of that would be slim, though. I usually knew in advance when I needed to do a stakeout, and if the roads were bad, the person I was after more than likely wouldn't be out in the weather. My real reason was more out of pure stubbornness, than a necessity for work. I sighed as I admitted, "Mostly, though, I just like to know that if I do want to go somewhere, then I can." I stopped at a red light and gathered up enough courage to look over at him.

He was staring at me with amusement etched on that handsome face. "I'm sorry, I'm just teasing you. I also have a SUV for the same reason. You can never be too prepared for anything."

"Exactly. So let's change the subject, shall we?" The light turned green, and I focused my attention to the road again.

"What would you like to discuss?"

A million questions came sprinting through my mind. There were so many things I wanted to know about him, about vampires, even about why he chose to help me. After mulling it over a few moments, I finally settled on, "So, how old are you?"

"My last human birthday I turned twenty-five," Lucian hesitated, "but that was over a century and a half ago."

"Over?" I couldn't hide the shock in my voice.

He chuckled, which he seemed to do often around me. I wondered if all vampires were as friendly and good-natured as Lucian. It made me feel relaxed and comfortable around him— which I knew was going to make it difficult to keep my distance. "Yes, over. If you want to be precise, I was born in 1810 in London, England."

"So, that explains the accent." I thought I'd detected a hint of a foreign accent. If it wasn't for me listening to the distinct sound of southern drawls all day, I may not have noticed it.

"Yes. It's faint, though, since I've been in the U.S. for almost a hundred years."

"Why did you leave your home?"

"For the same reason thousands of other immigrants left theirs. America was supposed to be the land of opportunity, and I needed a change in scenery. You can only live in the same city for so long never aging and not have someone take notice."

"That makes sense." I contemplated what it would be like to live that long. Being a history buff, I would relish the chance to see what he's witnessed during his life. On the other hand, you'd have to withstand the agony of helplessly watching everyone important to you grow old and die, all the while you remained eternally youthful. I suddenly found myself not so much in awe of Lucian, but sorrowful for the anguish I was sure he's had to endure.

"You know I usually don't speak this openly about myself with anyone."

I quickly glanced at him again, "Then why are you so forthcoming with me?" I pulled into the game store and searched for a vacant spot.

There was a long silence as he collected his thoughts. Finally, he answered, "From the moment I first saw you, I've felt attracted and drawn to you. And I feel like I can share anything with you, even my most guarded secret."

I thought I was blushing a few moments ago, but that was nothing compared to now.

He continued, "Revealing my true nature to people isn't something I do often, but I felt like I needed to."

My thoughts drifted back to the night before. I thought it was odd how attracted I was to Lucian. When he showed me he was a vampire, shock took over, but it wasn't long before I was struggling again with the magnetism I felt toward him. Not once did fear cross my mind; of him or what he could do to me. I was more worried about dating someone in general and if what I was feeling was real or the product of a supernatural ability, than the fact that he was a vampire.

"Well, if we're being honest, then I should tell you that, strangely enough, I feel the same way about you." I parked, turned off the engine, and turned toward Lucian. His beaming smile said it all—he was pleased.

"Can I ask you something?"

I guess it was my turn to answer a few questions, "Sure."

"Why did you say, 'strangely enough'?"

"Well," I shifted in my seat. I always felt uncomfortable discussing my feelings. I had only been in one serious relationship, which lasted roughly two years. Most of our time together was during high school, but attending different colleges, and more importantly, his co-ed dorm, was too much for the endurance of our relationship.

Originally, I'd avoided jumping into another one by focusing on college and then my career, but it didn't take me long to realize I actually liked being single. And since it'd been several years since my last true relationship, I was rusty when it came to sharing my feelings. "I work a lot, and I don't date much. It's been a long time since I've been attracted to a guy, and I've never felt so drawn to anyone like I do you. It's only been a day since I met you, so it's strange to me."

"I understand completely. Honestly, I've never felt the pull I do toward you with anyone before," he gave me a pointed look, "and I've been around for a while." The irony in that comment brought out an amused snicker from both of us.

"Well, if I'm really being honest," I continued, "I'm not completely convinced that my feelings are real. I've been wondering if my reaction is due to some type of allure that vampires have."

He seemed confused. "Are you asking if you're attracted to me because of what I am?"

"Yes." I sheepishly admitted.

Lucian smirked. "Do you really think I have vampire mojo that draws unsuspecting women to me?"

Dammit, I was blushing again. "I don't know what vampires can and can't do."

"Good point," he admitted. "There are some things vampires can do that humans can't, but I promise that's not one of them."

I regarded him for a moment. I still wasn't completely convinced, and I wasn't sure if it was because I wasn't exactly getting any younger, or because of the overwhelming attraction I felt for Lucian, but there was a substantial part of me that wanted nothing more than to plunge headfirst into a relationship with him. Sitting there conversing so effortlessly with him, and undeniably sharing more intimate details than I had with anyone else for quite some time, I found myself almost hopeful of that possibility. So much for keeping my distance and being careful.

But I already had an obligation to speak with Amy that night, and I didn't need this distraction. Maybe later, but not then. "Okay. I believe you." *Sort of,* I added silently. Time would tell if this was real, or the product of something else that I didn't understand yet. I glanced over at the entrance to the game store, "I guess we should get this over with." I turned back to Lucian.

"As you wish." He smiled, filling me with a surging warmth I'd never felt before. It flowed throughout every inch of my body—some places more profoundly than others—and whispered assurances of Lucian, telling me that I should allow him to cross the barrier I'd unconsciously placed after my last failed attempt at a relationship. As I stared into those enchanting eyes, I wondered if I could. And I wondered if a relationship could even exist between the two of us. I slowly exhaled a silent sigh and opened the door.

CHAPTER 3

A s I sat across from Amy, I couldn't help but notice the uncanny resemblance she bore to Jessica. They both had similar upturned noses, high cheekbones, brown eyes, and thin lips. The only two immediately noticeable differences were several inches in height and hair color. Amy's hair was brown, where Jessica's was blonde. It was so uncanny, I even had to do a double take when we first entered the store, just to make sure I wasn't seeing Jessica with dyed hair.

I'd introduced myself and Lucian to her and explained why we were there. She appeared to be nervous, but agreed to answer any questions we had. After informing her manager she was going to take a break, Amy led us to their employee room for privacy.

"So, Amy," she absently stared at her fidgety hands while they rested on the table—which in my experience was usually a sign someone was hiding something, "has anyone ever told you that you and Jessica look alike?"

"Yeah, that's why we became friends in middle school. We thought it was fun pretending to be sisters when we were younger."

"You two have been friends for quite some time then."

"You could say that. We used to be closer, though."

I shifted in my chair and glanced at Lucian seated beside me. "What do you mean, you used to be?"

For the first time since we sat down, she met my gaze. Her sorrowful eyes confirmed my assumption, confessing there was something she desperately wanted to say, but was struggling with whether she should.

"Amy, it's alright." Lucian tried to soothe her fears. "If you have any information about Jessica, you can tell us. The more we know, the sooner we'll be able to locate her."

She shifted her focus from me to Lucian, then back again. "I haven't told anyone this." Her eyes yearned for more reassurance.

This time I answered their plea, "That's why it's important to tell us anything you can. Even the tiniest detail might be of some help."

Amy sighed, "Okay." She looked at Lucian once more before beginning. "It all started about six months ago. That's when she was assigned to write this stupid paper for our college psychology class about vampires and the cults that follow them."

When she mentioned vampires my body tensed. I anxiously peered at Lucian, wondering if he shared a similar reaction. His face was an indecipherable mask, careful not to illustrate whatever he was thinking. With no guidance from him, I directed my attention back to Amy, "Define vampires and the cults that follow them for me."

Confusion swept across her face, "Well, not like actual vampires." She casually rolled her eyes, "They obviously don't exist."

If she only knew.

Amy continued, "Jessica was supposed to research people that believed they were vampires and the cults that worshiped them. The purpose was to get into the minds of people that have these supernatural obsessions and get a glimpse of what makes them tick." Amy paused, inhaling a deep breath. "She went online for research and found an underground following right here in Louisville."

Lucian muttered underneath a gentle sigh, "Let me guess, she became involved with them."

Amy confirmed Lucian's theory with a slight nod of her head. Tears were on the verge of escaping.

"So, what happened after she became involved with them?" I needed to keep Amy focused on the story. I was afraid any distractions would leave me with a distraught witness and unanswered questions.

Blinking back the tears, she slowly began again, "At first, she was telling me how fucked up and crazy they were. But the longer she kept meeting with them, the more she believed their bullshit. Jessica even tried to convince *me* that vampires were real, and that she'd seen one."

Lucian interrupted, "Did she say what this vampire looked like?"

"No. I never asked, and she never offered any information about him." Amy paused again, "About a month and a half ago, after she realized I wouldn't convert to her new level of psycho, we stopped hanging out as much. That's when she started going to clubs with other members of the cult and skipping classes at school."

I leaned back in my chair, "Do you think one of the members is the guy she ran off with last week?"

"It wouldn't surprise me. She always talked about one guy in particular named Ben. He told her he was the vampire's right-hand man and could arrange a private meeting with him."

"When did she say that?" Lucian cautiously questioned.

Amy thought for a moment, "I guess it was about two weeks ago."

"Did she ever say where the meetings were held?"

Amy sat in silence again as she searched her memories for information, "No. But I don't think they were actually in Louisville."

That was an odd assumption, "Why not?" I asked.

"She told me once that it took almost an hour to get there. I know with traffic that's possible, but once when it had been raining, she came back with mud on her car, like she'd been driving down a dirt road or something. And there aren't any dirt roads that I know of in Louisville." Amy hesitated, "Look, I can't explain why, I just always had this feeling they were somewhere else; somewhere outside the city."

We all sat in silence for a moment, digesting her last comment. Lucian was the first to speak, "Thank you for your help, Amy." He turned to me, "That's all the information I need for the moment." He rose from his chair, "Ladies, if you would excuse me, I need to make a phone call."

As Lucian hurried out of the room, I reached into my purse and turned off the tape recorder. Amy gave us some important clues I needed to follow up on, but I didn't think she had any more vital information to give us.

With no further questions myself, I rose from my seat. Amy followed my lead, and we walked back to the main room of the game store together. As we approached the counter, I turned to her, "Amy, if you can think of anything else, please call me." I handed her a business card, "And thank you again for answering our questions."

"No problem," she paused. "I hope you can find her. I know we've drifted apart recently, but she's still my friend. I don't want anything bad to happen to her."

"I know." I gave her a reassuring smile and ended the conversation with that.

I somberly journeyed outside, breathing in the faint scent of a nearby restaurant as I scanned the almost vacant parking lot for Lucian. He wasn't there. With hunger pains rumbling deep down in my stomach, I made a mental note to call in a pizza order when I got home and began walking to the Jeep. I hoped Lucian's disappearing act wasn't a habit of his; this was the second time in two nights.

As I strolled to the Jeep, my thoughts wildly wandered, entangling themselves into a disheveled mess. Amy had answered our questions, but paved the way for several more. Could Jessica have become involved with vampires? Two days ago, my answer would have been no, there's another logical explanation. But two days ago, I didn't know Lucian, and I didn't know vampires actually existed.

With my mind submerged in endless thought, I didn't realize I'd reached my destination until an odd sensation filled my body and trickled over my skin. My eyes immediately emerged from their haze to focus on my surroundings, discovering the Jeep directly in front of me.

With the overwhelming feeling someone was watching me, I glanced around the parking lot. The moon was just days shy of being full, casting down enough light to see a parking lot vacant of life. I decided my sudden episode of paranoia was unwarranted; probably the result of my lack of sleep and unlocked the doors.

Suddenly, the sensation burned through me once again, this time with a potent urgency that couldn't be ignored and pushed aside. Realizing it couldn't be a hallucination, I quickly turned and surveyed the area again, searching for the hidden source of my uneasiness, but it was just as empty as before.

I was reluctantly about to give up on my search again, when a faint glow caught my attention. I turned to find a man standing across the street from the game store. He had shimmering elbow-length white-blond hair that flowed over a black tattered trench coat.

The iridescent glow was coming from his eyes; an illusion created from a nearby street lamp reflecting off of them—no doubt the effect from some hot-off-the-market contact lens I hadn't heard of yet. It was amazing what you could buy these days.

There was no question, his fiery gaze was focused on me. I strained my vision with no avail to distinguish any facial features. He was just too far away.

With his radiant eyes burning into mine, he was giving me the uncanny impression he had ill intentions. Not wanting to take my eyes off of him, I blindly dug in my purse for the pocket knife I always carried with me. It only took a moment to realize it wasn't there. I silently cursed myself after remembering I'd removed it the night before to open a package and hadn't put it back. I switched to finding my pepper spray. If he was coming after me, I wanted to be prepared. Obviously pepper spray wouldn't take a man out, but it might buy me a few seconds of surprise.

"Riley," Lucian's silky voice drifted from behind, startling me.

A small yelp tore from my throat as I jerked around to face him, "You scared the shit out of me."

"Sorry, I didn't mean to." His smile playfully expressed otherwise. "What are you doing just standing here?"

"I'm watching that weird guy over there." I motioned toward where the stranger was standing.

Lucian's gaze drifted beyond me, "What man?"

I swung around to discover an empty sidewalk. I took a few steps toward the street and scanned the area. No one was there. "That's odd."

"What?" Lucian came up to stand beside me. He also surveyed the area, trying to understand what had happened.

"He was just right there." I again pointed to the empty sidewalk. "It's like he just disappeared." With him nowhere in sight, I pushed it to the back of my mind for now_there were more important things to be concerned about at the moment besides a man standing on the side of a street. "Speaking of disappearing, where did you go?"

Lucian gestured toward the Jeep, "Do you want to get in first? I'll tell you about it on the way back."

"Sure." We climbed in and exited the parking lot. I drove out slowly, though, scanning the area again for the mysterious stranger, hoping to get a better glimpse of his face.

Lucian broke my concentration by beginning, "What I'm about to tell you is in strict confidence. Most donors don't even know as much about our way of life as you're about to."

We'd discussed it the night before, and I was fairly confident I knew what a donor was, but I still wanted confirmation from Lucian. "When you say donors, is that in the literal sense? You're talking about humans who actually let vampires drink their blood, right?"

"Yes. There've been donors almost as long as there have been vampires. Of course, it's a much more popular thing now, since the High Council made it a punishable crime to kill a human about two hundred years ago."

That was good to know. "So, what's the High Council exactly? Do they decide what is—and isn't—a crime?"

"Yes, and no." He sighed. "Vampire politics are very complicated. There's a High Council and several Low Councils. The High Council were our lawmakers and our judges. Once they decided a punishment, they sent their trained team of assassins, called the BloodGuard, to carry out justice. However, the responsibility became too much—or so we're told—for the High Council, and they relinquished their control over the people to the Low Councils. They're made up of mostly House

Heads. They're the ones that actually govern our world now and even control the BloodGuard."

"House Heads?" I asked.

"Many of the older vampires, and almost all of the Born ones belong to Houses. They have their own feudal system, their own rules—usually at the top of that list is not to associate with unHoused vampires—and are led by the most powerful vampire in the House."

"They sound kind of stuck up," I observed.

"You have no idea," Lucian agreed with a smirk.

"Only the most imperative issues are escalated to the High Council now, which has been ruled by the same three vampires ever since the Elders–who are the oldest of our kind–first decided we needed law and order. Before, vampires roamed freely doing as they pleased with no consequences." He paused in thought, "We basically govern ourselves much like humans do. We have laws, and when they're broken, there's punishments."

Thank goodness for the Elders, I couldn't imagine a world where vampires ran amuck, killing everything in their paths. "When did they set up the Council?"

"Several hundred years before my time."

Oh. It was a little unnerving to imagine vampires who, several hundred years ago, were old enough to be called Elders. It did make me curious to know just how old they actually were, but that was a conversation for another time. I had more important questions for now. "So, when you say *Born ones*, do you mean . . .?"

"Yes, exactly as it sounds. Some vampires are Born; others, such as myself, are Made."

That contradicted everything I thought I knew about vampires. Not to mention, opened the door to many more questions that we just didn't have time for at that moment. With the faint beginnings of a headache from lack of food, I switched the topic from Vampire Politics 101 to our present situation, "So, where did you go earlier?"

"I had to call Avery. He's the guard you met last night." Lucian hesitated, "He's the head of my security team and second in command of the local werewolf pack."

"Werewolf?" I jerked my head around to look at Lucian. Unfortunately when I did, I also took the Jeep with me. An explosion of car horns forced me to focus on the road once more while maneuvering the vehicle back in the correct lane.

Once all was calm, Lucian spoke, "I'm sorry. I didn't think you'd react that way. I assumed since you knew vampires existed, it wouldn't be a shock to discover werewolves do as well. I wouldn't have mentioned it until we were safely back to your office, had I known."

"It's okay. I just wasn't expecting it." I glanced over at Lucian, this time with my eyes only. "Is there anything else I should know about while I'm prepared to hear it?"

"I guess you should also know that werewolves from the local pack make up almost the entire security force at *Silver Moon*."

That definitely filled in a few missing pieces about last night. "Then I'm assuming the tank is for when a werewolf is about to shift."

He nodded in confirmation, "Yes. A full moon is only a few days away, which makes it hard to resist the urge to shift. Danny's usually good at suppressing it, but when you add a strong emotion, like anger, it makes it almost impossible. Luckily, he was able to refrain from completely shifting until Aiden and Jimmy could remove him from the crowd and put him in the tank."

I chuckled to myself with the thought of werewolf security. It made so much sense; you couldn't get much beefier than that. "Okay, so let's get back to the subject of Jessica and how a vampire cult could possibly be involved."

Lucian sighed, "You do realize this guy claiming to be a vampire could actually be one."

"Yeah," I briefly looked at him, "but how do we know for sure?"

"There are two things I know for certain. One, is that no vampire stepped foot in my club that night, other than the ones who were working. The security staff are quite sure of that." He paused, "The other is that I believe there's a new vampire in the area who hasn't made his presence known to me."

"Is he supposed to?" It felt like a stupid question, but I didn't know the answer.

"Yes. Every country is ruled by its own Low Council and is divided into territories, which are presided over by a Dominus. These territories are too large for any one vampire to watch over, so they appoint Consuls to look after smaller regions inside their territory. The Consul of each region is responsible for upholding the law in that area. Think of them as a sort of sheriff, and the Dominus as more of a governor. Consuls report to their designated Dominus, and they report directly to the Council."

So much for no more vampire politics. Keeping one hand on the steering wheel, I used the other to search the contents of my purse for a bottle of headache medicine.

Lucian continued, "In the United States, there are six territories, and those are further divided into varying regions, depending on vampire population."

"But you said Housed vampires had their own rules, so do they not fall under the Consul and Dominus?"

Another sigh came from Lucian. "Yes, and no. Technically, they're supposed to report to their assigned Dominus, but since several of the House Heads are council members, that rarely happens. And each House has its own sub-branch of the BloodGuard, called the HouseGuard assigned to them, so they tend to take care of their own rule-breakers. The rest of the BloodGuard are assigned in teams across the country where the vampire populations are the heaviest, so they can assist the Consuls with upholding vampire law."

There it was. I popped open the top, got two pills out and tossed them into my mouth. With nothing to wash them down with, it took several attempts before I managed to swallow them.

Lucian peered my way, "Am I giving you a headache? If you don't want me to explain all this, I don't have to."

"No, it's not you," I protested. "It's just an overload of information, and my brain is working on little sleep. But, it's information I need to hear. If Jessica's disappearance is connected to vampires, then I need to know as much about you guys as I possibly can." I pulled into the parking lot at my office.

There was one lone vehicle remaining, a Land Rover. Assuming it belonged to Lucian, I carefully parked beside it.

"The point in explaining all that was simply so you could understand how our system works. I'm a Consul, so it's my job to uphold vampire law in my region. And to do that, I have to know which vampires are here at all times. If a crime is committed, it gives me an idea of who to look for. When a vampire crosses into a new region, they're supposed to identify themselves with the local Consul and inform them of their intentions while in their area—whether it's just passing through, or setting up a permanent residency."

I unbuckled my seat belt and twisted around to face him, "How do you even know he's here?"

"I've picked up his scent in various places across the city."

"You can smell him?" I carefully suppressed an amused grin.

"We have several abilities humans don't."

My mind immediately began producing images of vampires flying through the air, hypnotizing people. I knew it was cliché, but after watching as many horror movies as I had, it was kind of hard to break out of the box.

Lucian continued, "For example, we can see, hear, and smell farther and clearer than any human being could possibly ever imagine. Especially in the dead of night; our ability to see in the dark rivals none other."

"So, let me get this straight—this new guy was supposed to check in with you when he came here, but he didn't. And now there's a cult claiming to serve a vampire, and people are disappearing."

"That's not all."

I raised a quizzical eyebrow, "Is this about the lead you mentioned earlier?"

Lucian nodded, "Unfortunately, Amy confirmed my suspicions with her knowledge of the cult. Over the last couple of months, we've had several humans come to the club who smelled like they'd been in close contact to a vampire, but none of them are donors who're employed at the club. Some vampires have personal donors, but the guards haven't recognized the scent of the vampire that's on them. While I was away last week, another group came in, and when I got back, Avery showed me the surveillance tapes to see if I recognized any of them. I didn't, but the girl you're looking for was with them."

"Did she leave with them?"

"Yes."

A rush of fury swelled up inside me with the thought Lucian had been withholding information from me, "Why didn't you tell me this last night?"

"Since I wasn't there that night, I wasn't sure it was the same girl. I wanted to be certain it was her first by showing the picture you gave me to a few of the guards who were actually there that night. I didn't want to give you false information."

The sudden surge of anger that had filled my body deflated as fast as it had come, and I sighed as I leaned forward and rested my head on the steering wheel.

Vampires.

What the fuck did I get myself into this time? If I had half a mind I would call Mrs. Greenwell, explain that all I came across were dead ends, say I was sorry I couldn't help her, and give her back her money.

I might've done just that if a scenario of my grandmother desperately searching for me hadn't crept into my head. Wouldn't I want someone to help her find me if I was the one missing, especially if I were taken by a vampire? Shit. Me and my stupid conscience; I had to find her, or at least try to.

I raised my head and looked at Lucian. We locked eyes and, without uttering a word, exchanged a series of silent understandings between the both of us. I assured him I was in for the ride, no matter how bumpy it got. Lucian simply gave me reassurance.

Knowing I'd have Lucian by my side through this was the only thing keeping me from running away screaming. What better way to head into a lion's den than with a lion?

Lucian broke our silence, "this isn't the first disappearance that I've heard of lately, and I'm almost positive he's connected with all of them. The first disappearance occurred the night after I first detected his scent."

I remembered the story on the news earlier that day about Candace. I'd suspected her similar disappearance wasn't a coincidence.

"I'm not sure, yet, what he's planning," Lucian carried on, "it has to be something or else he would've checked in with me. I assure you, however, that whatever it may be, it'll be big. A rogue vampire would have taken one person and moved on to avoid detection, but he's firmly decided to stay, and there has to be a reason. What the missing girls' role in all of this is, I don't know. I assume he's either planning to turn them into vampires, or he's feeding from them."

"I thought you said it was against your laws to kill humans."

Lucian shamefully turned away, "Our society, unfortunately, is just as flawed as yours. There are vampires that occasionally break our laws, just as you have humans that break yours. If everyone obeyed the law, then we wouldn't require Consuls, Domini, or even the Council."

"Do you think he'll kill someone?"

"Perhaps."

"Then if he has Jessica, time is running out; if it's not too late already."

Lucian sadly nodded.

An unnerving thought crept into my mind, "If he's trying to stay as far under the radar as possible and people are mysteriously disappearing, then we could potentially have a vampire serial killer on our hands."

Lucian finally met my worried gaze, "Exactly."

CHAPTER 4

There was someone in my room, I could feel it. The air was thick with an intruding presence that caused every hair on my body to prickle with anticipation and my heartbeat to race wildly out of control. Logic screamed at me to grab my cell phone and call the police. But skepticism whispered the simple truth that I could never reach it in time—it was on my nightstand. Even if I could get it and dial 911 before my trespasser could stop me, the police would never get there in time.

"Riley." An eerie male voice softly spoke my name. It was barely audible, but it floated throughout the room, wrapping around and surrounding my body like a comforting blanket.

Realizing there was no point in pretending to be asleep; obviously the intruder knew me and had a very direct reason for breaking into my apartment, I turned my head toward the unfamiliar voice. I expected to open my eyes and see a large, obtrusive man hovering over me, but no one was there.

Slowly, I raised myself up to a sitting position in the bed. I allowed my eyes a moment to adjust to the darkness before I scanned my bedroom in its entirety. There was still no sign of the burglar.

Having a guard posted at the back entrance of my building, in addition to an extensive security system, I'd always scoffed at my grandfather's suggestion to buy a pistol for protection. I wasn't in a crime-ridden area of Louisville, so I thought I was safe with those two defensive factors. If I survived this, I would take his advice and get one. But for now, I was left defenseless.

"Riley."

My head jerked toward the source of the mysterious voice— the open doorway that led to the living room. The distant glow of an outside street lamp was trickling through the curtains of the living room window, giving off just enough light to create ghostly dramatized shadows.

I squinted and strained my eyes, but I all could decipher was the outline of the sofa. I had perfect vision, but unfortunately it was only perfect human vision. I'd give almost anything at that moment to have the aid of Lucian and his immaculate vampire sight.

I glanced over at the phone, snuggly nestled between the lamp and alarm clock. A fleeting thought, or more like common sense, crept up and tried to convince me to contact the police. He was more than likely watching me that very instant, as I struggled with my debate, but at least I would've made a conscious effort to save myself.

"Riley."

I focused my attention to the doorway once again. The sultry voice urged me to get up and discover the source. If I wasn't so curious to find out who was in my apartment and how he knew who I was, I could've resisted the intoxicating pull. But as they say, curiosity killed the cat, and I hoped I had a few lives left at my disposal. Besides, there was a good chance that if I cooperated he'd leave with whatever valuables he came to collect and not harm me.

Yeah, right.

It was nice to have hope, though.

With my mind stubbornly, yet decidedly set, I threw back the comforter and silently slid out of the bed. As I cautiously tiptoed into the living room, my eyes swept over every visible inch of the apartment. I knew my hopeless attempt at discretion was pointless; more than likely he was camped out in a covert spot watching my every move and found my effort at being sneaky hilarious. But, it gave me a sense of empowerment in the situation I found myself in, and I'd take empowerment over scared shitless any day.

After walking the living room in its entirety and determining it to be free of intruders, I decided to make the kitchen, with an abundance of blunt objects and knives, my next target for inspection. I continued my tiptoe dance, while sending fleeting glances toward the two shadowy, vacant doorways that led to the spare bedroom and guest bathroom, until I reached the bar and quickly peeked around it—the last thing I needed was a hand emerging from nowhere to grab my legs.

Thankfully, it was void of burglars as well. The knife block was on the adjacent counter, which I swiftly reached with one lengthy stride. Without making a sound, I cautiously withdrew the butcher knife from the block.

Suddenly my skin, which had maintained its prickling uneasiness since I'd awakened, electrified with an unnerving sense of foreboding. My body involuntarily stiffened with alarm and expectation as a faint rustling sounded behind me. I inhaled a deep breath and slowly turned around to meet my illusive intruder.

I choked on a stunned gasp as I found myself face to face with the stranger from outside the game store. He was much taller and much more handsome than I would've expected. He had to be at least six-foot-four, and his face was slightly feminine with its delicate features, but handsome enough to never question its masculinity. His billowing white hair traveled downward past his elbows and flowed over the tattered trench coat he still wore. His hair, combined with the pale sunless complexion of his skin contrasted with the ebony coat to give an ethereal façade.

"Hello, Riley." His voice was low, but smooth and seductive, and his pale crystal-blue eyes smoldered down on me with a sapphire blaze.

I finally managed to exhale the breath I had been subconsciously holding, "Who are you and how do you know me?" I firmly tightened my already unyielding grip on the knife.

He grinned maliciously, revealing fangs, "My name is Malus, and I know a great deal about you." He took a step closer, "But what I'm more interested in, is what I don't know."

A long string of profanity stretched through my mind as I grasped the tremendous amount of danger I was in. A gut instinct told me this was the very vampire that Lucian and I were discussing just a few short hours ago; the vampire that we suspected of being a serial killer. Now he was in my apartment and for some reason, interested in me.

"What do you want to know?" I tried to remain calm, but my shaky voice cracked with fear.

"How are you able to sense my presence?"

I shook my head, perplexed, "I don't know what you're talking about."

His cobalt eyes glowed with cold rage, "Do not play games with me, human," Malus snarled. "You know what I am; what I'm capable of. Do not test my patience."

He jerked the knife from my unsuspecting hand with lightning speed, propelling it across the room with a mere flick of his wrist. Before I had time to even acknowledge the sudden confiscation of my only weapon, he was in my face, "I've been following that pitiful excuse for a Consul for some time, making sure he suspects nothing. And he didn't. At least until you showed up two nights ago, filling his head with your piteous woes of disappearing humans. Last night while you were alone in the parking lot, I was going to kidnap you and take you back to my followers, so you could feed them."

"What stopped you?" I managed in a hushed tone. My undeveloped plan was to keep him rambling long enough for me to think of a way out of this. Although, I was fairly sure that wasn't going to work. How were you supposed to escape the clutches of a sadistic vampire?

He leaned his head back slightly to let out a hearty laugh, exposing his pearly-white fangs once again. "You did."

At least I managed to do something right. I took the opportunity, while he was distracted, to try gradually backing away from him. I had a feeble hope that if I could get just a little bit of distance between us, I would have more options at an escape attempt. As soon as I took one miniscule step backward he quickly placed an impenetrable arm behind my back, forcing me closer until our bodies almost touched.

"You sensed my presence in the parking lot. I saw your body react to it, giving you a warning. Even now your body reacts to my very presence. Few vampires can sense when one of our kind is near like that, and I've never heard of a human that could do it." He lowered his face to mine and pulled me closer, forcing the front of our bodies to press together. A wave of nausea hit as I felt his arousal. "How are you able to accomplish this?" His voice had reverted to the calm, seductive lure as before.

Fighting back the urge to vomit as his hard length continued to press into my stomach, I was having trouble processing what he implied. I couldn't sense vampires—that was absolutely ridiculous. I started to open my mouth to tell him just that, but I quickly closed it. Hadn't I been warned in the parking lot? And when I woke up and was exploring the apartment, didn't I sense a presence other than mine?

That still didn't explain Lucian, though. Wouldn't I have felt something similar with him?

Dread slowly crept through my body, and my face went pale as I realized the truth. I had gotten, what I'd thought at the time, were cold chills when Lucian opened his office door. And when he came into the office the night before, I'd felt the same sensation, but I'd passed it off as being nervous.

Malus smirked as he saw the enlightenment flood across my face. He inclined his head until he was able to brush his lips against my cheek. Then he slowly traced the line of my jaw downward with faint kisses until he reached my neck. "If you're capable of such extraordinary things as a human," he breathed onto my skin, sending shivers down my spine, "just think of how remarkable you could be as a vampire. As one of my vampires."

An altogether different shiver swept through my body with the thought of spending eternity with this creature. I had no doubt in my mind he'd force me to carry out whatever monstrous scheme he had planned.

"And what would being one of your vampires consist of?" All I could muster was a faint whisper, barely audible to my own ears, but somehow I knew he'd heard me.

I felt his lips curl into a smile against my neck. "You'll find out soon enough," he breathed onto my neck, "I have a feeling you'll be a very powerful young vampire. Maybe even powerful enough to become my second in command. With you by my side, I'm confident we can achieve my world-shattering plan. And if nothing else, I can use you for ransom. I'm sure those eyes have something to do with your uniqueness, and I know of a few vampires who would be very interested to know you exist. But don't worry, that's only a last resort."

Abruptly, Malus became motionless. Even the heat of his breath ceased against my skin.

I knew it was time. He was done talking, but strangely enough, I wanted him to continue. That was the second time a vampire had commented about my eyes, and I needed to know what was so special about them. Lucian had mentioned seeing them in a particular family, and now Malus insinuated certain vampires would like to know I existed because of them.

Malus couldn't risk revealing any more information or details about his plan, though, until I was his vampire servant, so I closed my eyes, squeezing them shut tight. I braced for the impact of his fangs, but his firm grip relaxed, and his lips left my skin. I cautiously opened my eyes, to see his face directly in front of mine.

"It seems Lucian has come to save you." While his pursed lips visibly epitomized his aggravation at the interruption, I was ecstatic. "We shall continue this discussion at a later time. But remember Riley, you will be *mine*."

He released his hold on me completely, giving me one last fangy grin as he vanished right before my eyes. I stood there for a moment in shock; vampires couldn't just disappear . . . could they?

"Riley."

Hearing my name whispered, yet again, brought me back to my senses. It urgently resonated once more before I realized this time the source of the voice was Lucian. At the same instant of recognition, the kitchen gradually faded, and an ominous darkness took its place. Unable to stand any longer, I fell to my knees as my surroundings disappeared. I frantically searched with my evaporating vision for Lucian, but the darkness was much quicker. When the dusky gloom had devoured everything in its sight and threatened to swallow me along with it, I closed my eyes with defeat and embraced it.

CHAPTER 5

I sluggishly opened my eyes as I woke to Lucian's soft, comforting voice. His gentle hands were cupping my face as he leaned over me with a worried scowl. Seeing him allowed all the fear and panic I'd just experienced to vanish, becoming nothing more than distant memory.

I was left experiencing a dazed confusion, and wasn't able to remember why I had an underlying feeling of apprehension. Unable to concentrate on anything else, I seized the moment to admire the simple beauty of Lucian's face. His eyes held vague traces of laugh lines, and I felt myself getting lost in them. He smiled warmly, and it transformed his handsome features into something younger; perhaps how he might've looked before he became a vampire.

"I was worried about you," Lucian's smile slowly vanished, concern taking its place again.

I frowned, unable to understand why he'd be worried about me. The newfound doubt and uncertainty acted as an anchor, letting the events that had just occurred to slip through the hazy confusion and surface with all the trepidation I'd felt during those last moments of consciousness.

I sat up abruptly, forcing Lucian to move with me, and surveyed my room. The last thing I remembered was being in the kitchen, but now I was in my bed. "How did I get here?"

"You've been here the whole time," Lucian assured, cautiously.

I stopped my frantic assessment of the room and studied Lucian. I tried to read his expression, but as usual, it was unreadable. "No. There was someone in my house; I got up to find out who it was, and it was him, Lucian. It was the vampire we were just talking about. His name is Malus, and he was telling me that he had a plan, but wouldn't say what it was. And he was rambling about how I can sense vampires and that he was going to turn me, so I could help him achieve his goals."

Lucian interrupted my frantic speech, "Riley, please calm down. You've been in your bed the entire time."

"No, that's not possible! The last thing I remember, I was in the kitchen with him," I paused mid-sentence as the realization of how close I'd come to death sank in. A rush of overwhelming emotion filled my body, threatening to spill out and engulf me. Tears began to trickle down, "Lucian, he almost bit me."

He winced and pulled me close, embracing me tightly with the comfort I desperately needed. I usually resented sympathy for myself, but dammit, I could've been turned into a vampire; sentenced to an eternity of atrocious servitude. And for what—someone's sinister plot? Without a second thought, I surrendered, and relaxed in Lucian's reassuring arms, letting him hold me while I wept into his chest.

I'm not sure how long we stayed that way. Eventually, the tears ceased, but I wasn't ready to let go. Lucian made me feel safe and secure, and after my ordeal, it was just what I needed. So, there we sat on my bed, embraced in each other's arms—Lucian lovingly stroked my back, giving me the silence I needed to process my horrid experience, and I had my face buried in his chest, breathing in the intoxicating aroma of his cologne.

When my usual calm had returned, I broke the silence. "You said I never left my bed, how is that possible?"

Lucian exhaled with angst, "Some of us have extra gifts."

I pulled away, so I could see his face, "What do you mean, 'extra'?" My vision of vampires flying around hypnotizing people came to mind again.

Several emotions swam across his face—from insecurity and fear to uneasiness and dismay. "Sometimes vampires develop an extra ability that others don't possess. We call these extra abilities gifts." Lucian averted his gaze from me, the reluctance to continue evident on his face. "For example, some can invade your mind and twist your thoughts, some can levitate, some can sense when other supernaturals are near, and the list goes on and on."

Even though Malus had mentioned me being able to sense vampires, hearing Lucian confirm I had a vampire ability was surreal. Under normal circumstances, I may have been excited. I mean, how many people could say they had a vampire ability, but weren't a vampire? However, since this particular ability had put me in the crosshairs of a psychotic vampire, I'd much rather be normal. "Do you have a gift?"

Lucian briefly glanced at me, "Yes." After a few more moments of silence, he finally elaborated on his one-word reply, "I can read thoughts."

Without hesitation my cheeks burst into flames as I recalled some of the more erotic thoughts I'd had involving Lucian while in his presence. "So, you know everything I'm thinking?"

"Not exactly," he hesitated again. "Some vampires can listen to everything that crosses your mind, but it doesn't work that way for me."

A sudden rush of calming relief swept over my body, which allowed my face to slowly return to its normal shade.

Lucian continued, "I only receive glimpses of thoughts, and only if it's accompanied by a strong emotion." I raised an eyebrow, and he elaborated, "If you're excited, stressed, or even frightened then your thoughts, along with your emotion bursts into my mind."

"Does that work on other vampires? Can you catch anything from Malus?"

Lucian's face became somber, "Yes, I can also catch glimpses from vampires, but I have to be in close proximity with someone, whether it's a vampire or human, to receive their thoughts. But in his case, as soon as he realizes I'm near, he immediately moves out of my range to pick anything up from him."

"Great, so what's his gift?" I reluctantly asked.

"Malus can, apparently, invade the minds of humans while they sleep."

"Are you trying to tell me I dreamt everything that just happened?" My tone held an edge of defensiveness.

"Not exactly. He was able to penetrate your mind while you were asleep, but he never entered your apartment. Everything that happened between you two, though, was real."

"Could he have bitten me and turned me into a vampire in the dream, like he said he was going to?"

"I don't know. He's simply too powerful for me to judge the range of his abilities. Technically, I don't see how it would be possible. You need the actual exchanging of blood for the process, but if he's powerful enough to hide to this degree, then who knows what he's capable of?"

Lucian's eyes trailed off in thought. "Maybe, if I hadn't shown up to scare him away, he planned on entering your apartment for the turning. He could have used the dream to get information and determine how useful you'd be to him."

"And after scaring the shit out of me, he'd let me wake up and turn me," I finished for him.

He contemplated my assumption, "Yes. At least I hope that's the way it would've happened. I don't like the idea that he's capable of creating a new vampire without the blood exchange."

That actually made me feel better about the situation. Malus was still scary as hell, but at least he wasn't exceptionally powerful. With one piece of the puzzle solved, I moved onto the next one, "How did you know to come back?"

"After leaving you, I returned to the club, so I could speak with Avery. With the new information we learned from Amy, he ordered a handful of the werewolves to prowl the streets to search for any unfamiliar vampire scents. It wasn't long before they called, saying they'd found one in Kensington Estates."

I interrupted, "That's a neighborhood close to here."

Lucian nodded, "I panicked when Avery told me that. I knew it was only a short distance between there and your office. I left straight away to Kensington and began the search for the scent myself. It didn't take long to find, and I followed it right to your doorstep. When I was only about two blocks away, he must have sensed me and fled. I sent the wolves to hunt him down, while I came in here to make sure you were alright."

A torrent of emotions spread through me and threatened to break down my composed façade again. "Thank you," I murmured while barely holding on to control.

He smiled somberly, accentuating his handsome features, "You're very welcome. Now, you should get some sleep; you've had an intense night."

"Are you crazy? I can't sleep right now," I protested. I was wide awake and knew I would be for a while.

"Okay, then let's talk."

We laid on my bed, for what seemed like hours, and discussed everything from my unsuccessful search for a secretary to Lucian's early childhood experiences growing up in 19th century London. He was so easy to talk to, and it had been such a long time since I'd had a lengthy and in-depth conversion with a man, that I found myself almost ready to throw my reservations of him and dating out the window. And since Lucian seemed to have the same feelings toward me, it made the decision that much easier—or harder depending on how I wanted to look at it—to say fuck it and give it a try.

I finally drifted off to sleep sometime after I'd recounted again what happened between myself and Malus and relaying stories from my childhood. I grew up about fifty miles south of Louisville in a city called Elizabethtown. E-Town, as the locals called it, was large enough to have a community college and hospital, but small enough that you had to find your own means of entertainment outside of bowling or the movie theater.

I didn't set my alarm before falling back asleep, so I wasn't surprised when I woke to bright morning sunlight trickling through the curtains. I rolled over to peer at the clock; it was eight-thirty in the morning. Luckily, I didn't have an appointment scheduled until almost noon. Content with the amount of time I had until my first client, I turned back over to find a bare space where Lucian had been. He must have snuck out shortly after I fell asleep. Since I didn't stir the entire night, I had no idea what time he actually left.

I sighed, longing to have seen him still laying there, but I guess that would've been impossible; he was, after all, a vampire. He probably fled sometime before dawn to his daytime retreat. I let out one more sigh before grudgingly rolling out of bed to begin my usual morning routine.

When I returned to the bedroom after my shower, dressed in dark gray jogging shorts and a matching tank top, I was unexpectedly face to face with Lucian. He was still wearing the same clothes from the night before, only now donning designer sunglasses and holding a gas station cup of coffee.

"I wasn't sure how you liked your coffee, so it's black."

Without delay, I panicked. Lucian was a vampire, yet there he was standing right in front of me, in a stream of sunlight. "What are you doing here?"

Lucian stood there expressionless, "Most humans need coffee in the morning. After the night you had, I thought you could use some. If you want me to leave, I can."

"No, I don't want you to leave. I just thought . . . you mean you don't burn in the sunlight?"

Lucian's face softened, and he shook his head as he grinned, "You watch too many movies." He strolled farther into the room, handing me the coffee. It wasn't my drink of choice, but I gladly accepted it.

"Thank you," I paused, "so, you don't die at dawn or burst into flames when the sun hits you?"

"No," he snorted, "most of the rumors about my kind are false. In fact, vampires fabricated most of them, so we could easily prove we're human."

I took a sip of the coffee, making a face as the warmth traveled down my body. I forgot he said it was black. I'd have to drown it down with milk and sugar.

Lucian continued, "The sun does make us feel drained, though. And we can't use our abilities to their fullest during the day since the sun makes us feel exhausted. It also hurts our nocturnal eyes. It's bearable, but wearing strong sunglasses helps a lot."

Intrigued by this discussion on vampire lore, I sat the coffee on the nightstand and settled myself onto the bed, "What else is a myth?"

Lucian removed his sunglasses, placing them on the bed, and seated himself beside me, "Well, crucifixes don't bother us, or garlic. And we don't have to be invited into someone's home to be able to enter."

"What about silver?"

He groaned regretfully, "Silver doesn't kill us, but, like werewolves, we do have a slight allergy to it. If we sustain a wound from silver, it'll take longer to heal versus a wound inflicted by another metal or material."

"So, you do heal fast?" I asked, captivated by this conversation.

"Yes, our bodies heal at a highly rapid rate compared to yours," he faltered, "which brings me to something I'd like to discuss with you."

"And what's that?" I cautiously asked.

He shifted himself on the bed until he had one leg on and one leg off; our knees barely grazed each other. "If you can sense vampires like Malus suspects, then there's something extraordinary about you. No human should be able to do that. A lot of vampires can't even do it."

I flushed with a mixture of embarrassment and confusion. It wasn't every day someone told you you're different from every other human being in the world.

"I'm afraid Malus' interest in you won't fade, especially after I ran him off last night. Riley, he'll come back for you."

My heart leapt for an earth-shattering beat. I didn't want him to come back. If I'd only experienced a taste of what he was capable of in dream-sequence, I didn't want to find out what the real thing could do. I'd give almost anything to spare myself that vile encounter.

"I'm glad you feel that way because I have a possible solution which would rectify, not just this problem, but another one as well."

I raised a quizzical eyebrow.

"Sorry, you felt strongly about that, and I picked up on it."

I sighed, I guess I'd have to get use to that, "So, what kind of solution did you have in mind?"

Lucian reached for my closest hand, engulfing it with both of his. "Just remember what you were thinking, anything would be better than having Malus come back for you."

That made me nervous; the skepticism must have showed on my face.

"You'll need twenty-four-hour protection from him. Just because we're weakened during the day, as you can see, it doesn't stop us from being active. At night, although I can temporarily give some of my responsibilities at the club to others, I'll still have to handle most of them personally. And, being the local Consul, I need to spend a lot of time tracking him down. So, I won't be able to be with you as much as I'd prefer."

I didn't like where this was heading.

"You also need a secretary for your business, right?"

"Yes," I confirmed slowly, not sure if I should answer truthfully.

"Then I want to suggest, and I remind you, this would only be temporary until Malus is caught, that one of the security guards move in with you and work as your secretary."

I was speechless. Was he actually suggesting I let a stranger move in with me? And on top of that, a werewolf?

Sensing where my thoughts were traveling, Lucian swiftly persisted, "It would only be for a short time. The person I have in mind for the job is trustworthy, and I personally know him very well."

"You want me to let a guy I've never met before, and who also just happens to be a werewolf, move in with me?"

"Riley, I promise it's not as bad as you're making it sound. It will be strictly professional; think of it as a live-in bodyguard, nothing else."

I removed my hand from his and averted my gaze elsewhere. He was right, a live-in bodyguard didn't sound as appalling as a strange werewolf living with me. "Is he dangerous?"

Puzzlement showed on his face. My concerns, however, must have filtered through to him, because the bafflement quickly slackened, "no. You won't have to worry about him turning and hurting you. If he's still needed in a few days, during the full moon, I'll take over completely that night."

I needed to think. I needed to clear my head. With Lucian right beside me on the bed, it made it nearly impossible. Without hesitation, I descended from the bed and paced to the center of the room.

Lucian stayed on the bed, but didn't relent in his persuading. "And Aiden has experience as a secretary. His mother owns a flower shop, and he used to work there during the summer. He'd answer phones, schedule deliveries, and perform whatever other office work that needed to be done."

The tempting prospect of a secretary was almost enough to make me give in. I'd desperately needed help for a while, but I'd been so swamped with work I hadn't had time to even post a job opening, let alone conduct interviews.

And it would only be temporary. He could even take enough of the work-load from me, so I could search for someone to fill the job permanently. But to live with me? Could I do that? And with a werewolf? Lucian promised it would be safe, and even though I hadn't known him very long, for reasons I hadn't been able to figure out yet, I trusted him completely.

The familiar tingling crawled over my skin, and my body went rigid. I realized in that instant Malus was right; I knew

Lucian was near, I could sense him. I felt the warm erotic sensation of breath on the back of my neck.

"You just sensed me behind you, didn't you?" he asked, intrigued.

I turned to face him, "Yes."

I couldn't read his expression, but it appeared to be pure enchantment.

Lucian burst into laughter, "Amazing."

I grimaced, "What's so amazing?"

"You can truly sense us. I've never seen anything like this before." He beamed. "I tried to use my vampiric abilities to sneak up behind you, but you still sensed me."

Dumbfounded, I asked, "So, most vampires can't even do this?"

"No. Vampires do get a feeling when they see another vampire, but it's more of a recognition of someone who's like them. There are few of us that can sense other vampires at a distance. And the older you are, the more powerful you are— you develop the ability to hide yourself from others."

"Like Malus," I surmised.

"Yes," Lucian confirmed.

"Can you sense him like that?"

His euphoric smile faded, "No. He's too powerful and can hide his presence from me."

"So, if I can, and I'm just a human . . .," I trailed off.

"You see now why you're so intriguing to him. He's not used to many people being able to sense his presence, least of all, a human. You're a mystery he wants to solve, and unfortunately, I think he'll stop at nothing to figure you out."

"Okay. Then yes."

"Yes?" Lucian asked, confused.

"Yes, I'll accept a live-in bodyguard."

He took a step towards me, closing the distance between us. "Are you sure you're okay with this?"

I let out a long sigh, "No, but I'll have to be. I'll take a werewolf roommate any day over a psychotic vampire who wants to experiment on me."

He studied me intently, as he had during our first meeting, and brought his hand up to touch my face. "I promise I won't let him hurt you. Even if I didn't have these strong feelings about you, I'd still protect you with my life."

His eyes portrayed assurances of that promise, and as I gazed into them, he tenderly adjusted his hand to cup the side of my face. I leaned into it and closed my eyes, allowing the sweet scent of his skin to draw me in closer. When I felt Lucian's warm breath on my face, I opened them again. He was noticeably closer, his eyes heavy with a lustful flame that I knew matched my own.

We slowly closed the distance until our lips met. A flame of heated passion erupted inside me, spilling throughout my body as the kiss passionately evolved. I parted my lips to allow his caressing tongue to explore my mouth.

My body bent and curved into his as I draped my arms around his neck. He mimicked my movements and wrapped his arms around my waist, pulling me even tighter to his body.

"Sorry to interrupt," a voice cleared their throat, "but I've been in the car for a while."

Lucian promptly pulled away from our embrace to address the intruder. A small wave of embarrassment rose to my cheeks as I did the same.

"You have impeccable timing." Lucian's sarcastic tone imitated my thoughts exactly.

Lucian turned to me, "Riley, I'd like you to meet Aiden."

My cheeks burned even hotter. Aiden, who was about to become my roommate and employee, just witnessed me kissing his other boss.

I pushed my embarrassment deep down, stiffened my backbone, plastered a smile on my face, and greeted him. "Hi, it's nice to meet you. I'm Riley." I offered my hand to him.

He grinned and accepted with a firm shake. "Same here, I'm Aiden." He was wearing medium-wash blue jeans with rips in the knees, worn brown work boots, and a red t-shirt. His dimpled smile was genuine as it reached his baby-blue eyes. Covering his short dark-blond hair was a tattered ball cap that had two folded beer bottle caps on each side of the bill. He was slightly taller than Lucian and more muscular.

"I have some obligations to attend to at the club, so I'll leave you two to get acquainted with each other." Lucian looked from me to Aiden.

"So, I take it I'm staying?" Aiden hesitantly asked.

"If that's still alright with you," Lucian offered.

Aiden smiled again. "Yeah. I'll go get my bags from the car." I watched as he turned and left, similarly mesmerized by Aiden as I had been with Avery. Both men seemed to possess the same gracefulness to their movements—it must have been a werewolf thing. Once he was out of sight, I turned to Lucian. "I'll walk you out."

He held out his hand, and together, we walked to the door that led outside. "If you need anything, don't hesitate to call me."

"I won't. Thank you for everything, Lucian."

"You're welcome. And you'll be fine with Aiden, I promise. I'll be in touch soon to check up on you."

"Okay." He leaned down and gave me a chaste kiss before he walked out the door.

I didn't know what to think. I'd only known Lucian for two days, but somehow he'd managed to break through all my barriers. The thing that scared me the most, though, was that I didn't mind anymore. I'd let him get closer to me in those two days than I'd let anyone else in a very long time.

I lingered in the doorway and watched him travel down the steps. I wasn't sure where we'd go from here, as we'd clearly crossed a point of no return with that amazing kiss, but I found myself feeling almost eager to find out. He spoke to Aiden momentarily before he glanced up at me with a grin and a wave goodbye as he climbed into his vehicle to leave.

I remained there until Aiden returned with several bags, carrying them effortlessly. "Are you sure you want to move in here and work for me?" I inquired as he walked into the apartment, and I closed the door behind him.

"I'm positive." He thoughtfully added, "To be honest, I'm kind of getting tired of working at the club. Doing some office work will be a nice change."

"What about protecting me? Are you okay with that, too?"

"I don't mind a bit."

"And living with me?"

He laughed apprehensively, "Are you trying to talk me out of this?"

An embarrassed chuckle slipped out, "I'm sorry. I just don't want you to feel like you have to do anything you don't want to."

Aiden stared at me with consideration. "I appreciate that. But I'm really okay with all of this."

"Okay, then let me show you around." His dimpled smile returned, which caused his already boyishly handsome features to intensify. "How old are you?" I questioned as I directed him through the living room and into the kitchen.

"Twenty-three."

"You're only a year younger than me." I hoped with the small age difference we might actually have some things in common. I continued with the tour and showed him my room before moving on to his, which was two doors down. "And the guest bathroom is the door in between our rooms."

He nodded appreciatively.

"Well, I'll let you get settled in, and then I'll show you the office downstairs and go over everything you'll be in charge of. Sound okay?"

"Sounds good."

I gave him a reassuring smile and left him to it.

CHAPTER 6

E ight hours later, Aiden and I were racing down the road in my Jeep to get to a local cell phone company before six. Bradley Sanders worked there as a customer service representative, and I'd been trying to catch him in the act of cheating on his wife, Ally, for three weeks.

Ever since she came into my office almost a month ago, we'd been working together to capture his infidelity on camera. He worked Monday through Friday, nine to six, but she'd been suspicious for months when he said he had to work late on the occasional Friday. Curiosity finally got the better of her, and she started driving by his work when he had to stay over. Mr. Sanders' car would be there in the parking lot, but he wouldn't answer his office phone and would only call her back after several minutes and always from his cell phone.

Tonight was the first Friday since she'd come to me about her suspicions that he had to stay over. She called me about an hour ago, hoping I could check on him and see if he'd been telling the truth, or if her gut feeling was right, and he was being unfaithful.

"So, how long have they been married?" Aiden asked. He had the file open in his lap, going through the pictures that Mrs. Sanders supplied of herself, Mr. Sanders, and his car. There were also some other miscellaneous documents in there describing her suspicions, where he worked, and their personal history.

"Three years."

"How old are they? They both look so young."

"He's twenty-five, and she's twenty-three."

"Did she say why they got married so young?" Aiden inquired.

I peered over at him, "She got pregnant, so they got married."

He looked up from the photos. "Oh," he considered that for a moment, "that's not the right reason to get married. Then you end up in a situation like this." He went back to combing through the file.

When I was younger I would've argued with that logic, but after witnessing dozens of failed marriages, I couldn't agree more. You had to want to be with each other, not because you felt like you had to or it was the right thing to do. "I completely agree."

I looked at the clock as I pulled into the cell store's parking lot. I had fifteen minutes to spare. I circled around the building to the back where the employees parked and searched for Mr. Sanders' car.

"There it is." Aiden pointed to a silver Ford Taurus and held up the photo for me to compare.

I examined the picture and then looked at the car again. "Yeah, that's it," I agreed and found an empty parking spot two rows back which would allow an unobstructed view of his car and the employee entrance to the building.

I parked the Jeep, turned off the engine, and used the last fifteen minutes before his scheduled time off work to check my camera equipment and get it ready. Any time I went out of the office for a job, whether it was for unfaithful spouses or suspicious insurance claims, I always brought two cameras: one for photos and one for video. I mainly relied on my Nikon camera to take pictures, but if it was dark outside, I couldn't afford for the flash to give me away. In those instances, I switched to my video camera, which had night vision, to capture what I was after.

"All right, all the equipment is on and ready," I said as I laid them both down in between us. I settled comfortably in my seat and waited for Mr. Sanders to make an appearance.

"Do you usually do this every night?" Aiden asked.

"Not every night, but usually at least one evening a week. And sometimes, I have to go out during the day, depending on the person's schedule I'm tracking."

Aiden took out the photo of Mr. Sanders before closing the file and placed it on the dash. He positioned the photo in between us, on top of the video camera.

"So, do you think you'll like working at the office?" I inquired.

"I think so. It won't be as stressful as working at the club. I needed a break from that."

"I don't think I could deal with all of those drunk people every day."

He chuckled, "it definitely gets old after a while. But Lucian is a good guy, and I don't mind working for him."

I quickly glanced over at him before giving my attention back to the door. "He seems like a good guy."

"He's the best vampire I know, that's for sure. Usually they're full of themselves and think they're better than us. But not Lucian, he's different. He actually cares about other people."

"So, what about werewolves?" I carefully began, not sure how sensitive the subject was with him. "What are you all like, in general?"

He had a bemused look. "Usually we're pretty normal. You'd be surprised at how many werewolves you've probably met in your life and never even knew it. There's the occasional jackass, but mostly we're just like everyone else."

"Normal, but just happen to shift into a werewolf during the full moon." I grinned and stole another glimpse at Aiden.

He smiled impishly, "Yeah, I guess that's not exactly normal."

"I'm just teasing. You seem pretty normal to me."

"No, you've got a point. I'm stronger, faster, can hear, see, and smell better than any human, and can shift into a werewolf any time I want. That's not exactly normal."

"Any time? I thought werewolves could only shift during the full moon?"

"We don't have a choice about shifting during the full moon, but any other time of the month we can shift if we want to."

You'd think by now I would be used to all of my assumptions about vampires and werewolves being shattered, but, apparently, I wasn't. It was hard finding out all of your preconceived ideas about supernatural beings you'd grown up with were completely wrong.

"There he is," Aiden exclaimed, bringing me back to reality.

I grabbed my camera, zoomed it in, and took a picture of him exiting the building at five-after-six. I'd already set up my camera to put a date and time stamp on each photo.

We watched as he walked over and got into a black Mustang with dark-tinted windows, parked close to the entrance. I snapped a few more photos of him getting into the mysterious vehicle before it backed out and drove away.

"What do we do now?" Aiden asked.

I backed out of my spot as well, "We follow them."

I stayed at least three vehicles back from the Mustang until it pulled into a hotel about three miles away from Mr. Sanders' work. I entered a restaurant parking lot next to the hotel and parked where I had a good view of the Mustang. I grabbed the camera just in time to capture pictures of Mr. Sanders and an unknown brunette female exit the vehicle and passionately kiss before they walked into the hotel.

Once they were out of sight, I regretfully sighed as I lowered the camera.

"What's wrong?" Aiden asked, concerned.

"I just wish that one time, I could tell my client they're wrong, and their spouse or significant other isn't cheating on them."

"I take it this happens a lot?"

I turned to him. "You have no idea. I've been doing this for almost two years, and I haven't been able to prove anyone wrong when they think their partner's being unfaithful."

"Makes it hard to want to get into a relationship knowing how many people cheat."

"Yes, it does," I agreed as I pulled out the memory card from my camera and placed it, along with the video camera, in their cases. Aiden put them both in the backseat for me, and I put the memory card in my purse. "Now it's time to go to an hour photo store and develop these pictures."

"When are you going to tell Mrs. Sanders?"

"After I get the pictures printed out, I'll call her and ask her to meet me at the office."

"Will you tell her over the phone?"

"No. I made the mistake of telling someone over the phone once, and it wasn't pretty."

"What happened?" he asked, intrigued.

"She insisted that I tell her over the phone; that she couldn't wait until she reached the office to find out if he was really cheating on her or not. After a few minutes of pleading, I caved and told her what I'd found out. She was driving during our conversation and ended up causing an accident. Since then, I've refused to tell anyone what I find out until they're sitting across from me at the office."

"I never thought of that," Aiden admitted.

"People go crazy when they find these things out. Even if they already suspected it and pretty much knew they were being cheated on, having it confirmed with pictures or video makes them flip out."

"Because they still hoped they were wrong," Aiden offered.

I considered his statement, "You're right. They still hold out hope until the moment I show them the evidence. Even after they've seen everything, you can see it in their eyes that they don't want it to be true."

"Do you think Mrs. Sanders will break down?"

I backed out of my parking spot and began our drive to the store. "You never know. It's always good to be prepared for it, though."

We sat there in silence for a moment before Aiden finally said, "This is the hardest part of your job, isn't it?"

"Yeah."

"I guess I'll have to get used to it then."

"Unfortunately, you never get used to it."

CHAPTER 7

As it turned out, Mrs. Sanders handled the news of her husband's infidelity very well. She wasn't one of those spouses who pretended to want to know, but in all actuality, didn't. She had already come to terms with the idea of him being unfaithful and now just wanted the proof of it, so she could file for a divorce and move on with her life.

"Can I have copies of these photos?" she asked. Her tears had ceased already; the only evidence she'd even been crying was the puffy redness of her eyes.

"Yes. These are your copies to keep." I always made two copies of the photos I developed: one for the client if they chose to take them and the other for my records.

"Thank you, Ms. Hunter," she said with a grim smile.

"You're welcome. Again, I'm sorry."

She nodded appreciatively, shook my hand, and then gathered the photos and placed them all back in the manila envelope. As soon as I heard the door ding, signaling her departure, Aiden appeared in my office.

"She took that a lot better than what I would have."

"Me, too," I agreed.

He sat down in the seat Mrs. Sanders had just occupied. "Well, you have no more appointments scheduled for tonight, and it's after seven," he paused, unsure whether to continue. "Can we eat now?"

I laughed. "I'm sorry. Yes, we can eat. You'll have to remind me when it's time to take a break for food. I get so wrapped up in work I usually forget about it."

Aiden nodded, "So, what sounds good to you?"

"Hmm, I don't know. We can go get something, or we can call a pizza or Chinese restaurant to deliver."

His bright-blue eyes lit up. "Chinese sounds great."

"Chinese is it then." After finding out what Aiden wanted, I grabbed my phone and dialed the number for my favorite Chinese restaurant in the area—I may or may not have most of the local restaurants pre-programmed in my phone—and called in our order. "It should be here in about twenty minutes."

"Great, I'm starving," he said as he placed a hand over his stomach.

"Me, too." Mine growled at that precise moment in agreement.

The doorbell dinged, and Aiden and I both looked at each other. I usually didn't have walk-ins this late in the evening, and I had just hung up with the Chinese restaurant, so it couldn't be our food already. We both quickly stood and went into the waiting area to see who'd entered the building.

As soon as I cleared the corner and could see the entire room, my heart stopped. The tingling sensation flared across my body, warning me just before I saw Lucian sitting in the same chair he'd occupied the previous day. Tampering down a bit of jealously as I took in his appearance—every time I'd seen him, he looked impeccable, and tonight was no different. He wore black dress shoes, a dark-gray suit with the jacket left undone, and an off-white button down-shirt underneath. Seriously, did he wake up looking that good? Or did he have to work at it like the rest of us mere mortals.

"Hello." He stood and walked over, placing a gentle kiss on my forehead. I closed my eyes and sighed inwardly; I could get used to that. "I can't stay long, I have to get back to the club. I just wanted to stop by to see how your day went and make sure Aiden's treating you well." He cast a playful warning glance in Aiden's direction.

"Aiden is treating me just fine." I flashed a smirk Aiden's way. "And no sign of Malus, so today was a good day."

"Unfortunately, there hasn't been any sign of Malus since last night. I don't know if he's trying to lay low, or if we just haven't found his scent around the city yet."

"He's probably going to lay low for a while," Aiden surmised as he sat down in one of the three chairs in front of the secretary's desk.

"That's what I was leaning toward. He's not foolish, and he knows we'll be searching for him heavily after his performance last night," Lucian agreed, and we both joined Aiden in the two vacant chairs next to his.

"What do you think he's up to?" Aiden asked.

Lucian answered without hesitation, "There aren't enough facts for me to make any assumptions yet. He's mentioned having a plan, but the possibilities are endless. Is he trying to take over the area? Or are his intentions on a smaller or larger scale? Just because he told Riley it would be world-shattering, doesn't necessarily mean that's true."

"So, how long do you think it'll to take before you can catch him?" I questioned.

"If he's playing games and staying hidden, then who knows how long it could take?" Lucian speculated, "It could take days or even weeks. But don't worry, if we haven't captured him before the full moon, you'll stay with me while Aiden has to be away." Lucian gave me an intense look that I couldn't quite decipher.

I thought about what his look meant and the possibilities that could happen by staying with him, but then remembered Lucian's inopportune gift of receiving them and quickly stopped the direction my thoughts were taking. I cleared my throat, "So, how are things going at the club tonight?"

"It's Friday, so hectic. And it's only the beginning of the night, which is why I should be leaving to get back there. I can't be gone long, but I wanted to see you in person, even if it was only for a few minutes." He stood and faced Aiden. "Take care of her for me."

"You can count on it," Aiden promised.

Lucian turned, wrapped his arms around me, and pulled me into him. I buried my face in his chest and inhaled his sweet scent. "I'm sorry I can't be here with you."

"It's okay. I understand," I said as I enclosed my arms around him as well.

We remained that way for a moment, only withdrawing from each other's embrace when the door alerted us of another visitor. I turned to see the delivery boy from the restaurant with our food.

"I'll leave, so you can eat." He reached in his pocket and pulled out a flash drive, "Before I go, here's a present." I took the drive and looked at him questioningly. "It's the footage from *Silver Moon's* surveillance cameras the night Jessica disappeared. We've already looked through it and confirmed, without a doubt, she's on there. She arrived by herself and left with the same group of humans that security said smelled like a vampire they didn't recognize. Since it's just our cameras, I don't know what vehicles they left in, but I wanted you to have it, so you could go through the videos yourself."

I didn't know what I would be able to discover on the videos that Lucian and his team couldn't, but I appreciated the gesture all the same. I'd go through them in between appointments and write down anything I could about the group of cult members she left with. "Thank you so much, Lucian. I really appreciate this."

His eyes bore into mine, "I gave you my word I'd help you however I could, and that's what I'm doing." Lucian turned away. "I'll see you tomorrow," he promised before he walked out the door.

Aiden had already taken the food from the delivery guy and checked to make sure our order was correct. I stuffed the thumb drive into my pocket as I ran to my office and grabbed some money out of my purse. When I returned, Aiden nodded, signaling all our food was there. "Here you go," I handed the delivery guy the money. "Keep the change."

"Thanks." He nodded appreciatively and swiftly left.

I locked the door behind him. "You want to take it upstairs?"

"Sure. I'll take it up, while you lock up down here," Aiden offered.

"Thanks. I'll be up in a minute." He grabbed the bags and headed down the hallway, toward the door that led upstairs. I stood there for a moment before following him, feeling almost drunk. Lucian had a way of intoxicating me with the slightest effort—but I wasn't complaining. It had been a long time since anyone had stirred those kind of emotions in me, and I liked it.

I groaned, expelling the drunk stupor out of my body and walked down the hallway, turning out the lights as I went. I was hungry, and food was waiting.

CHAPTER 8

T he night of the full moon came with no progress on the search for Malus, so as Lucian promised, I would spend the evening in the basement of *Silver Moon*, while Aiden and his fellow werewolves rendezvoused in the woods somewhere outside of Louisville. The basement, as it turned out, had several living quarters, the largest of which resembled a one-bedroom apartment and belonged to Lucian. The other rooms were more like dorms and had a bedroom, mini-kitchen, living room combo and a separate bathroom for whoever needed a place to stay for the night, or even for a short period of time while in between homes.

Lucian picked me and Aiden up from my building and explained all of that to me on the way to the club. He also filled me in on how the roster for the club normally worked; it consisted of Lucian, the security team—which were mostly werewolves, along with a few vampires, the bartenders— exclusively reserved for vampires, and humans—who held office positions, general staff, and were available as donors. But during the full moon, for obvious reasons, the club was entirely void of werewolves, which left the responsibility of the entire security detail to the few vampires who were employed by the club. Lucian said there were a few other vampires who were willing to work on those nights, but sometimes, depending on the crowd size, they still experienced a shortage of security per drunken-stupidity ratio.

Conveniently, there was such a shortage that night. At least that was the way it looked so far. Lucian left me at the bar while he took my overnight bag to his room and tried to call in some extra help. If it'd been any later, I would've protested and went with him, but since it was still early the club wasn't busy yet, so I didn't mind waiting for him out there. The only people walking around were the workers who were getting the last-minute preparations for the night's customers taken care of.

The music was on, but barely perceptible; they wouldn't amplify it to its earsplitting volume until another hour or so. It was so quiet you could even hear the chairs scraping the floor from across the room as employees removed them from the tables and placed them neatly underneath.

With nothing else to do, I seized the unique opportunity to take in the ambiance of the club, without the distraction of an inebriated crowd. The wooden dance floor took up the majority of the lower level, which spanned about two-hundred feet from the steps that led to the main entrance toward the focal point of the room, which was the enormous stage, framed with midnight-black curtains. The rest of the space was filled with short pub-style tables and the bar area that I was at. My gaze drifted to the left of the dance floor—lining the wall were two rows of the mundane ebony tables, each with four chairs to match. The two women who were getting that area ready for the night already had all the chairs down and were wiping them, along with the tables, down with wet rags.

Behind them, was an employee's only door that I knew led to the hallway where Lucian's office was, and in the corner closest to the stage, were the entrances to one of the sets of bathrooms. Occupying the other corner beside the stage was the DJ booth, an entrance to a VIP area—that I assumed held the donor rooms—and spanning about 20 feet along the wall to the right was the bar. Between the two was a large, obtrusive gray door that appeared to be made of steel. More of the same four-seated tables were on either side of the bar. There was a waist-high metal guardrail that enclosed the raised section, which the stairs from the dancefloor led to; it was nestled in-between the dance floor and the entry room.

After walking through the front doors of the club and past the security guard checking IDs, there was a large open entry room with more of those black leather couches and matching armchairs. There were restrooms to the right, a door with 'employees only' written on it to the left, and an open double doorway leading to the raised area of the club straight ahead.

The entire club was painted a charcoal gray, and there were paintings of nighttime scenes decorating the walls. There was even a large tapestry hanging above one couch that depicted a pack of wolves howling at a full silvery moon.

It was a completely different experience with the music almost muted and most of the lights on. In another hour or two, the music would pick up to its deafening roar, and the overhead lights would dim. I knew from my limited experience there that black lights hung over the bar and there were bubble and smoke machines underneath the stage and the elevated area that led to the entrance. They also had dozens of strands of patio lights strung across the ceiling above the dance floor, which gave the illusion of a starry sky.

"You know they're all jealous of you."

Startled, I almost fell from my barstool. I turned toward the bar to see who had spoken. I'd been so engrossed in checking out the room, I hadn't noticed that the bar, which had been empty when I first sat down a few minutes ago, now had two people tending to it.

One was a twenty-something male with short, styled, blond hair and slightly chiseled features, giving him that 'All-American' look. He wore a long-sleeved black button-down shirt that hugged his very muscular arms, which were cleaning glasses at the far end of the bar.

The other one, who had spoken, was directly across from me, leaning toward me with a bar towel in one hand. She had long, wavy brown hair, dark eye makeup that framed her easy honey-brown eyes, high cheekbones, a small nose, and lips as full as mine that were turned up in a mischievous grin.

I had been so lost in thought, I hadn't noticed them behind the bar, or knew who or what she was talking about. I also realized I'd ignored the prickling tingle trying to warn me these two were vampires. "Who are you talking about?" I asked, genuinely confused.

She shifted her eyes to the right and nodded her head, "All of them."

I followed her direction, which steered to the workers who were finishing arranging and clearing tables. I knew they were there, but only now, having it brought to my attention, did I notice the not-so-friendly glares they were sending my way. I quickly turned back around to the bartender. "Why are they glaring at me like that?" Lucian hadn't introduced me to any of them; he just said they were some of the human employees that worked there. So, to the best of my knowledge, I hadn't had time to piss any of them off yet.

"Because they're all dying to get their hands on Lucian." She paused and smirked, "Or should I say the other way around? But as a rule, he doesn't drink from humans, unless it's an emergency."

Sensing my confusion, she added, "He drinks bagged blood."

"Really?" I asked.

"Most of us do . . . to an extent. There's not always a willing donor around, and sometimes you just don't want to deal with one. But he prefers to only drink from bags." She leaned forward farther, supporting herself with her elbows on the bar. "Since he's taken such an interest in you, all of them assume he's chosen you as a donor."

I blanched at that. I hadn't thought about letting Lucian drink from me. He seemed so human most of the time, so things like that hadn't crossed my mind. I wondered what it would feel like—would it hurt? Would I let him if he asked me? I cleared my head, I'd worry about that later. "So, can you read minds, too?"

She shook her head. "No. Unfortunately, I don't have any gifts." She raised back up and wiped the bar down where she'd been leaning. "I'm just your standard issue vampire," she winked.

I grinned, I liked her. "So, how do you know what they're thinking?"

"Easy. You can read it all over their faces."

"She's not trying to intimidate you, is she?" Aiden came up beside me.

"No." I drew out the word. I couldn't tell if Aiden was serious or asking in a joking manner.

"Like you could do anything about it if I was." She grinned, extending her fangs for a more threatening effect.

"Is that an invitation to finally see who would win in a match?" he retorted playfully. Ah, he'd only been joking. It seemed this back and forth retort was a long-standing thing.

"Anytime, Wolfman," she teasingly snapped back.

"You two cut it out already," an unfamiliar voice chimed, thick with a southern accent.

I turned to see who the voice belonged to. He came up to stand on the other side of Aiden. He was about the same height as Aiden, around six-foot, but where Aiden was a thicker, well-pronounced muscular frame, he was a slimmer, solid build. They were both dressed similarly, wearing brown work boots, distressed jeans, and t-shirts. Aiden's was a plain white shirt, while the other guy sported a gray one with a college basketball logo.

"And what are you going to do about it?" she countered him.

"I'll tell you what I'll do," he cocked a crooked smile as he pulled out a stool and sat down. "I'll go get you two a room, so you can finally work things out." He wiggled his eyebrows.

She burst into laughter and retracted her fangs. I looked at Aiden, who had a blush on his face. "Okay," she began, throwing her hands up, "I'll play nice . . . for now."

The new guy didn't give Aiden a chance to respond. He leaned over toward me. "Hey," he extended his hand. "I'm Jimmy. You must be Riley."

"Yes, I am." I shook it. "So, you're the Jimmy Aiden's told me about?" Aiden had mentioned his best friend, Jimmy, during some of our downtime over the last few days. I knew they'd grown up together, were interested in almost all the same things, spent a large amount of their free time together, and were both werewolves.

He glanced at Aiden. "You haven't been telling lies about me, have you?" he impishly asked. Even though most of the lights were on, it was still hard to see all of his facial features. He had on a ball cap similar to the one Aiden wore, with matching beer caps on the bill, but it was pulled down and casted a shadow over his face. From what I could see, he was just as attractive as Aiden. His features were more chiseled, accompanied by a strong jawline, and the hair curling out from underneath the sides of his hat was so dark, it was almost black. I couldn't tell what color his eyes were, but they were inviting, nonetheless.

"I've only told her the truth," Aiden mischievously promised.

"Oh, no," Jimmy somberly said, "That might be even worse."

The four of us laughed. "I don't doubt that," the bartender playfully added.

"Well, I hate to leave, but we'd better get going if we're going to make it on time," Aiden warned.

Jimmy pulled a cell phone from his pocket and checked the time. "Yeah, you're right." He slid it back in his jeans as he rose from the stool. "I guess we'll see you all later." He smiled and walked toward the exit.

"Bye," Aiden said to the bartender.

"You guys have fun tonight," she sincerely replied.

"We always do." He grinned before turning to me. "I'll see you tomorrow morning. I'll leave as early as I can."

"Okay. Be careful." I wasn't really sure what to say. I felt like Aiden and I had bonded during our few days together, but I was still at a loss for words. What did you say to your werewolf bodyguard when he left you to shift in the woods?

"Thanks. You too." He hesitated for a moment, I think also feeling the same as I did—not really sure how to handle the situation—before he left, following Jimmy out.

I watched him walk away until I saw Lucian approaching. He was dressed to match the security team tonight, donning an all-black outfit—from his shoes and slacks to his button-down shirt with the sleeves rolled up to his elbows. I didn't think anyone would mistake him for security, though, because even though he was in all black like them, his clothes were too stylish to be confused with the security detail.

"I see you've met Ellie." He nodded toward her as he approached us. He sat down on the barstool next to me. "Well, I called everyone that should've been available tonight," he sighed. "But I only managed to get two people to come in."

"So, this should be an interesting night," the male bartender said. He'd eased his way over to us when Lucian had approached.

"Yes," Lucian absently agreed.

"You really need to get more people on the emergency list," Ellie pointed out.

He looked at her. "I've been meaning to hire more people for a while, I just haven't gotten around to it. We're usually fine on workers, it's just around this time of the month that we experience these shortages."

"Yeah, and it seems like it's getting worse each month." The guy snorted.

"Yes, it does," Lucian acknowledged. He focused his attention on me, "If you're ready, I'll escort you down to my room before the crowd begins." He rose from his seat.

"Lucian, if you need me to help out tonight, I don't mind."

"That's very thoughtful." He took my hand and helped me down from my stool. "But we'll be fine."

"Are you sure?"

"It's only a weeknight, so we should be able to manage. But, I'll have to stay up here and help all night."

I nodded my understanding, but my heart sank. I'd hoped we would have been able to spend the night alone together. I still wasn't sure how far I was willing to go with Lucian, but if the sinking feeling of disappointment I had meant anything, then I already knew the answer to that question.

He gave my hand a gentle squeeze and led me away from the bar. I glanced back at Ellie, "It was nice meeting you."

"You as well." She smiled warmly and went back to her prep of the bar area.

We walked hand in hand through the employee's only doorway and into to the hallway where his office was. We walked past that, to the end of the hall and stopped in front of another door.

"This leads down to the living quarters." He opened it, revealing a stairwell like any other you'd expect to find in a large building.

When we reached the bottom and exited the stairs, we were in a large open room that reminded me of a man cave. The walls were dark red and covered in various framed movie posters. Several couches and recliners circled around a media center, which boasted one of the largest flat screen televisions I'd ever seen. On the other end of the room, there were several sets of small black kitchen tables and chairs. In the corner was a decent-sized kitchen area with black counters and cabinets, a stove, a couple of microwaves, and a refrigerator.

"This is a break area for all the employees," Lucian explained as we passed through the area and into another hallway. "And these rooms," he gestured toward the black doors lining the hall, "are for people to stay in."

One door, in particular, caught my attention. It was the same heavy duty steel like the one upstairs by the bar. "What's that room?"

He didn't pause to look where I was pointing. "That door leads to the tank."

"So, is that another tank upstairs by the bar?"

He stopped at the last door on the right. "Yes. We have one upstairs for easy removal from the dance floor and one down here. A lot of times it's impossible to get a shifting werewolf from up there down here before someone sees them."

"Then why have one down here?" I asked.

"Occasionally some of the wolves have nowhere to go, or just don't want to go anywhere. I let them use this room on those nights." He pulled out a set of keys from his pocket and unlocked the door. He reached in and turned on the lights before he motioned me to enter first.

I admit, even though I'd been looking forward to this moment, I was a little nervous about going into his apartment. I took a deep breath and walked in.

What I'd imagined his place looking like—and I may or may not have spent a fair amount of time doing so—was something that resembled his bare office, but what I saw astounded me. The focal point of the living room was a soaring antique carved mahogany fireplace. The carvings depicted leaves trailing up both sides and continuing along the mantle, toward the center where they wrapped around each other until you could no longer decipher where one ended and the other began.

Seeing where my focus was directed, Lucian came up beside me and softly said, "I'd never seen anything like it when I purchased it from an estate sale about thirty years ago."

"It's beautiful." I could barely take my eyes from it.

"That's the same reaction I had when I first saw it. I had a gas line installed when I moved into this apartment, so I could place this here and enjoy it."

I knew I could remain lost in its beauty for quite some time, but I also knew Lucian had to be leaving me soon. I reluctantly tore my eyes away from the fireplace and took in the rest of the décor. Above the fireplace was a large oil painting of a crumbling castle perched on the edge of a grassy cliff. The scene was colorless, apart from rays of light shining down from rolling storm clouds, illuminating pieces of the castle and the shadowed landscape.

Surrounding the fireplace were two mud-brown loveseats and an oversized matching arm chair, positioned just outside a large decorative rug and framed an empty coffee table. I broadened my view of the room to see miscellaneous night-time paintings and aged metal artwork adorned the dark-beige walls. There were several bookshelves made from the same wood as the fireplace, filled with books—everything from the tattered and old to the pristine and new.

Lucian gave me a moment to look over the room before saying, "The kitchen is over there." He pointed to the left.

I shifted my gaze toward where he was pointing. There was a long bar that separated the kitchen from the living room with four swivel high-back bar stools. The cabinets were a rich dark wood with weathered brass knobs and what looked like moonlight granite countertops. The black stainless steel appliances contrasted nicely with them.

"I stocked a variety of drinks and food for you. I wasn't sure what you liked, so I got an assortment of different things." He led me into the kitchen. "You can help yourself to anything you see. I placed everything that didn't need to be refrigerated in the cabinets. There are plates and glasses in there as well, and the silverware and utensils are in the drawers. You can go through them when you get hungry. You should be able to find everything you need."

"Thank you." I was surprised at how much thought he'd put into me staying there for the night. "I appreciate that."

"You're welcome. Just please don't be alarmed when you get into the refrigerator," Lucian hesitantly continued, "I keep bags of blood in there. I shoved them all in the back," he quickly added, "so you wouldn't have to see them as soon as you open it, but they are in there."

"That's fine," I promptly replied, trying to keep a neutral face. I didn't want him to feel bad or guilty about having the food he was required to consume in his apartment. And I really didn't mind. Blood had never made me squeamish, and it would be in bags, so there wasn't any way it could get mixed into the food I'd be eating.

"I'm glad it won't bother you." Lucian regarded me intensely. He seemed to shake off whatever he was thinking as he said, "Follow me, and I'll show you the rest of the place."

Anxious to see the rest of his apartment, I eagerly trailed behind him. There were only two doors in the hallway, he pointed to the first one and said, "This is the guest bathroom." We walked past it without peering in. "And here," he said, halting in front of the last door and motioned for me to enter first, "is my bedroom."

A wave of emotions flooded through me, which I quickly struggled to suppress, for fear he'd receive them—everything from nervousness to excitement, and even a hint of arousal. When I walked in, I was again drawn to the focal point of the room, the ornately carved king size bed.

"I loved the carvings on the fireplace so much, I had the bed and furniture made to replicate it," Lucian explained.

I was speechless. The bed was a four-poster and carved with the same scrollwork of the trailing leaves as the fireplace. The headboard rose halfway to the posts with the leaves tracing the top edge and meeting in the middle in the same fashion as the mantle.

The walls were the same color as the rest of his apartment and held similar oil paintings and metal artwork. On top of the long dresser sat a flat screen television with two decorative vases on either side.

"I placed your bags on the bed," Lucian said, moving further into the room. "And the double doors to your left open to the bathroom, and the single door to the right is my closet."

I looked from the doors to the bed and saw my bags laying there, just as he'd said; I hadn't even noticed them until then. My attention drifted from my bags to the bed again, and a yearning spread through me—one for a night alone with Lucian in that bed. Many scenarios played themselves out in my head, and each one ended with both of us exhausted.

"I'm sorry I won't be able to be here with you. But, know you're safe down here, regardless of whether I'm here with you or upstairs."

I quickly ended my thoughts. I'd have to start being more careful, unless I wanted Lucian to know what I romanticized about. Besides, I had all night to fantasize after he left. "Thanks," I said, trying to keep the disappointment out of my voice.

"And," he continued, "I'll check in on you every chance I get."

"Sounds good."

He leaned forward, gently kissed my cheek, and spoke softly in my ear, "Make yourself at home. I'll be back down as soon as I can." He left with one brief glance back—one I thought held longing and regret, but I wasn't sure if it was really there, or if it was just me wanting to see those emotions on his face.

I sighed and sat down on the bed by my bag. Ever since Aiden had interrupted our first kiss the other day, Lucian hadn't made another attempt to pick up where we'd left off. He chose instead to place soft whisperings of kisses on my face. I knew it was better than nothing, but I'd never wanted more in my life. Being in his presence affected me in ways I'd never experienced before.

It'd been almost a week since our first meeting, and even though I'd seen him every day since then, it was never for more than a couple of hours at a time, and I craved more with every ounce of my being. I was in unchartered territory with Lucian, and although I was profoundly attracted to him, I was also confused by that attraction.

But after a few restless nights, I decided to just go with it. I knew despite him being a vampire, I was safe with Lucian, and I was now almost certain he'd been truthful when he said he didn't have an ability that caused the pull I felt toward him. I'd avoided men and relationships for years, so when I did finally find a guy that I wanted more with, why not give in and give it a try?

I would move forward with Lucian as slow or fast as he wanted to go. If he didn't want to take things further at all then I'd be okay with that as well. Not saying I wouldn't be frustrated, but I wouldn't be the first girl who was turned down by their crush; I'd be fine.

My stomach noisily protested it was time to eat. I still had to unpack all of my toiletries and pajamas first, so I allowed myself one more look around his bedroom before I reluctantly took out everything I needed for my long night alone.

CHAPTER 9

I usually enjoyed performing criminal background checks; they were easy and didn't take much time. But, I'd been staring at Justin Nall's application for employment at a local security agency for every bit of twenty minutes. I had ten of them I needed to get through, before I could finish examining the surveillance videos Lucian had given me, but so far, I'd only managed to finish four of them— needless to say, my mind was elsewhere.

When Lucian was near it was hard to concentrate on anything else besides him, but apparently, that was now the case when we weren't even together. My thoughts kept drifting to him while I tried to concentrate on Justin's employment history. Lucian had only been able to sneak away from the club long enough to go down to his apartment twice while I was awake. Each visit was only for a few minutes and didn't even warrant a kiss on the cheek, or a touch of any kind. In fact, it seemed like he tried to stay as far away from me as he possibly could.

Even that morning, after I'd showered and was ready for the day, I walked into the living room and found Lucian asleep on one of the couches. When I sat my bags down, he immediately woke up and explained that he'd come down around five in the morning and hadn't wanted to disturb me because I was sleeping so soundly.

The drive back to my office held little conversation, outside of the events that had occurred in the club the night before. When we pulled up to the front entrance to the office, Aiden was already waiting outside the door for me. Jimmy had dropped him off only a few minutes before we'd arrived.

I felt bad he had to wait for me to get in. I'd only known Aiden for a week, but like Lucian, I felt an overwhelming sense of trust when it came to him. When my thoughts hadn't drifted to Lucian, they'd been mulling over whether to get Aiden a key made for the office and apartment.

Lucian had taken my bags out of the vehicle and handed them to Aiden while I unlocked the door and disengaged the security system. Once inside, I watched Aiden disappear down the hallway to take my bags and his backpack upstairs to the apartment. I turned, expecting—and secretly hoping—that Lucian would take advantage of that opportunity to finally play out a small portion of what I'd spent the past week fantasizing about.

But to my dismay, he never came any closer than the doorway. He told me he had to leave; that he had some things he needed to take care of. After that, he would go home and get a few hours of sleep before he opened the club for the night's wave of partygoers.

I knew he hadn't had much sleep since Malus made his grand appearance outside my apartment several days ago. And I knew he had to be exhausted; you could see it in his eyes when he thought no one was looking. I didn't know how much sleep vampires needed, but it was obvious he wasn't getting enough. I just hoped his worries about the club and Malus were the reasons for his sudden distance.

I sighed heavily and placed my head in my hands. I was way overthinking the situation. Of course, he was tired and worried. I mean, who wouldn't be in his position? I was just trying to find unwarranted reasons why he wouldn't be interested in me.

I'd made up my mind that if he didn't want more I'd be okay with that and wouldn't sulk or push him on the matter. But now that I was faced with it, I couldn't stop thinking about it. Now that I'd taken the leap from single by choice to ready for the next step with Lucian, I was scared and trying to find his disinterest in everything he did—or didn't do. I took a deep breath and slowly exhaled while I told myself I needed to stop acting like a teenager with her first boyfriend.

I actually grinned a little with the thought of that comparison. If I was being honest with myself, I had to admit that was exactly how I felt with him. The last few years of my life had been so dedicated to college and my career that I did feel like I was starting over in the romance department from scratch.

I simply wasn't use to how normal relationships naturally progressed, just like a teenager. And also just like a teenager, I couldn't stop thinking about him. But, if I wanted to *really* be honest with myself, then I also had to admit that I liked that. I *had* been so engrossed with school and my career over the last several years, that I was wholeheartedly welcoming the change.

I just needed to find a happy medium, so I could enjoy spending time with Lucian, while still getting my ever-expanding workload finished.

"Are you okay?" Aiden asked. "Or have I finally caught you napping during work hours?"

I lifted my head from my hands and saw him standing in the doorway smirking. I grunted, "You know better than that."

"Oh, I'll catch you not working every waking moment one of these days," Aiden joked. He strolled into my office and sat down in an empty chair. He somberly asked, "Seriously, what's wrong?"

"Nothing," I lied as I leaned back in my chair. I tried to keep a straight face. I'd always been a terrible liar and gave myself away every time with a sneer or hint of laughter.

"I don't believe you." His stare was penetrating. "Your scent and body language suggest otherwise."

I raised a quizzical eyebrow. Great. Now it didn't matter if I could keep a straight face or not—he could smell if I lied.

"Look, if you don't want to tell me what's wrong, that's fine. I know we haven't known each other very long, and there's a lot of things that aren't my business. But, I just want you to know that I'm here for you if you need me."

He got up to leave. "Wait," I said as I exhaled a heavy breath and leaned forward. He slowly sat back down. I stalled, not sure how to say what had been on my mind, or if I should say anything at all and just let him walk out. I finally blurted out, "I'm just worried about this whole Malus thing."

He stared at me questionably. I tried to put forth every ounce of energy I could into making sure he wouldn't recognize my dishonesty. I hated lying to Aiden, but my juvenile train of thoughts concerning Lucian was just not something I felt comfortable talking to anyone about, especially him. I didn't want him jumping to the conclusion that I was some crazy-obsessed person after only a week of . . . well, I didn't really know what term to define our relationship.

I knew we were more than friends, but I didn't know if we would officially be considered dating. My lack of certainty on the status of our relationship was just one more reason I didn't want to confide in him about my immature concerns. It was simply a fleeting moment of female emotional weakness—one that most women had in new relationships where they feared the man's interest wasn't at the same level as their own.

And I *was* worried—hell, I was even terrified of Malus and what he could do, so technically, I wasn't lying. Aiden just didn't have to know Malus wasn't what I'd been concerned about at the precise moment he walked in.

His face eased, "It's going to be okay. We'll catch him, I promise."

I relaxed, "I know you all will." I smiled, in an attempt to show I had confidence that they would. I truly did believe they would catch him eventually. My only concern was how many people he'd kill or kidnap before that would happen. Make that two concerns—and I would be one of them. "I just hope it's soon."

"Me, too," he sighed. Aiden started to say something else, but was cut off by his ringing cell phone. "It's Jimmy," he said, before answering.

"Hey, what's up?" he asked, placing the phone up to his ear.

I couldn't hear what Jimmy said, but from the expression on Aiden's face, I knew it wasn't good news. He sat there for a while, just listening. He finally looked up and met my eyes, his own heavy with worry and despair.

"No, I don't have any questions. You've pretty much covered everything." He paused to listen to a response before adding, "Okay, I'll talk to you later." He hung up and slumped back in his chair.

"Let me guess," I whispered, hoping what I thought wasn't true, "Malus struck again last night?"

He nodded. "That spineless coward waited until all the wolves were out of town to come out of hiding. He knew the other vampires would be busy with their jobs, so he could come into the city unnoticed." He was getting angry. He stood up and began pacing back and forth across the room.

"How many did he take?" I asked.

Aiden stopped pacing and turned toward me. I froze. His beautiful baby-blue eyes were now amber. It was a little unnerving to see that color staring out from a human face.

"I'm sorry," Aiden said, as his eyes slowly bled back to their natural color. "That bastard just pisses me off. You don't have to worry, I'm not going to go all wolf on you."

"It's okay. I didn't think you would, I was just surprised to see your eyes like that. I've never seen that before."

He walked over and sat back down. "I guess it is a shock to see for the first time. I grew up with it, so it was never anything special for me. But, I still remember the first time I saw a vampire's eyes change." He smiled faintly, calming back down. "I'd been so used to the way ours looked, I wasn't prepared for how different theirs are."

"Their eyes change?" I asked, remembering Malus' icy cobalt stare.

"Yeah. Like us, when they get pissed or have some other kind of strong emotion, whatever color their eyes are fades into something lighter and becomes almost translucent."

That definitely explained why it seemed like Malus' eyes were glowing in the streetlamp the other night.

"But to answer your question, so far they've only heard of one disappearance last night."

"Well, at least it was only one." I said, trying to find something good about the development. We sat there for a moment in mutual silence, contemplating. I finally broke it by asking, "Do you think he's trying to take over the area?"

"No," Aiden said immediately. "It doesn't work that way with vampire laws. He would have to go to Lucian's boss and challenge him to take over this region. Lucian's position is appointed, not won. And it's not exactly a position very many vampires are waiting in line for."

"Why not?"

"It's kind of like a police officer and counselor all in one. He has to hold all their hands and take care of all the needs of every vampire in the area. Any issues they can't resolve themselves—which, trust me, is a lot—he has to help out with and make sure they all stay in line. There's a lot of bullshit, and it's a lot of work. The only reason Lucian even accepted it was because his Sire is the Dominus of this state, and he asked Lucian personally to accept the position of Consul."

"Sire . . . meaning the one who turned him?" I asked.

"Yeah. Lucian couldn't tell him no, so he accepted it. I'm glad he did, though, because he actually cares about everyone else and not just the vampires. A lot of vampires have actually moved here because of that; because they feel the same way

Lucian does." Aiden thought for a moment before adding, "Most vampires think they're better than the rest of us and are more like Malus. But that's not the case with a lot of the vampires you'll meet living in this area; they're more like Lucian."

So, Lucian wasn't just a nice guy, he was also a nice vampire. And, apparently, that was saying a lot. "Okay, so any other suggestions about his intentions?"

Aiden shook his head. "I guess this could be his way of challenging the Dominus. Even though this is Lucian's region, it's still under his Sire's jurisdiction." Aiden considered that scenario. "But, I don't think that's it. There would be so many other ways to challenge the Dominus, and the pieces just don't fit."

"You know more about this stuff than I do, so I trust your judgment. I just hope he's doing all of this for some kind of power-trip, because I don't want it to be the other option."

"Other option?" Aiden asked, unsure what I was talking about.

I took a deep breath before saying it out loud. Since I'd first met Malus, I'd had a growing fear of what I thought his intentions were, and I was desperately hoping it wasn't the case. I referred to it in my head as the *other option*. "That he's psychotic, and this is just the beginning of a major vampire meltdown."

Aiden sat still, contemplating my theory, his unwavering gaze set straight on mine. "I've heard about that happening before." He stood up, unnerved by the possibility. "But it hasn't happened since before my father's lifetime . . . that we know of." He turned to leave. "I'm going to go finish up my appointment confirmation calls."

"Wait," I pleaded as I stood from my chair. "What happened? Do you think that's what's going on now?"

He turned back toward me. "All I know is the human death toll reached the hundreds before they finally brought him down."

I felt the blood drain from my face. I knew the devastation would be considerable if Malus did suffer from a mental break, but I didn't realize it could be that drastic.

"The good news, though, is that I don't think he would take just a few at a time and only when he knew we were at our weakest. He's obviously sane enough to know he needs to stay undetected. Every case that we've seen of vampbreak, as the wolves call it, they didn't care. One day they just woke up and snapped, killing everything in their path."

I relaxed a little with that information. Malus was certainly calculating his every move and not making any rash decisions. That still left the option of a serial killer, though. Just because he hadn't snapped and gone on a killing spree didn't mean he still wasn't a killer. Usually the most successful human serial killers were cunning and sly; why wouldn't a vampire one be any different? "So, then all we can really do is just wait for him to slip up?"

"You aren't going to be doing anything," Aiden smiled weakly. "But, I think that's all that can be done . . . for now, anyway. Lucian is already doing everything he can with the daily and nightly patrols. And so far, there hasn't been any sign of him."

I snorted, "Trust me, my one encounter with him in dream form was enough to last me a lifetime. I'm not one of those girls that goes looking for trouble and likes to get rescued. I'm perfectly happy staying right here under the protection of more powerful people."

"Well, that's a relief," Aiden sighed playfully. "I was getting worried that you'd seen too many of those vampire movies where the human girl always wants to be the hero and tries to go after the bad guy."

I blushed, "Well, I do like those movies, but I only like to watch them. It's not on my bucket list to act any of them out."

He gave a short laugh before turning serious again. "Hopefully, whatever his plan is, we can take him down before more people disappear. And I promise I'll do everything in my power to keep him from getting you."

I didn't know what I'd do without him and Lucian. "Thank you, Aiden."

"You're welcome." He left to finish his work.

CHAPTER 10

O nly one person was reported missing from the night of the full moon. We had no concrete evidence Malus was behind it, but all the signs pointed to him. A young man went out for drinks at a bar with his friends, and he never came back from a bathroom trip. According to the news report, the security cameras showed him leaving the restroom and instead of returning to his friends, he walked out of the building and into the street. No one walked out with him, and there weren't any cameras outside the building, so they lost track of him from there.

Over the next two weeks I poured through all the footage Lucian had given me and tried to track down as many more videos as I could from local establishments. I made a few phone calls to Mrs. Greenwell giving her updates—which were vague and lacking any mention of vampires. I was buying time by telling her I was still waiting for permission to review the surveillance from *Silver Moon* to see if she'd left with a man.

Lucian spent most of that time convincing more vampires to work, not only at his club, but several of the other local bars as well. The group of humans who were abducting partygoers hadn't entered *Silver Moon* since the night of Jessica's disappearance and were abducting them from other establishments instead, so Lucian wanted to have as many lookouts as possible all over the city.

Now that he had a substantial work force helping out in the club and on the hunt for Malus, he hadn't been as distant as he'd been around the full moon—which completely eradicated all those unwarranted adolescent fears that had crept up the morning after. However, between his Consul responsibilities, handling the club, and the search for Malus, his schedule was still filled with little room for me, but he always managed to squeeze some time in every chance he got. I added him, Aiden, and Aiden's friend Jimmy to the list of people allowed in the back parking lot, so Lucian could come and go as he pleased without the security guard having to call me every time.

Mondays were when I got to spend the most time with him and were fast becoming my favorite day of the week. He'd come over in the evenings, and we would spend the night snuggling on the couch watching movies, or playing games with Aiden and Jimmy. Friday through Sunday were his busiest days, and he usually couldn't spare any time away from work-related matters. *Silver Moon* kept him busy Friday and Saturday because of obvious reasons, and Sunday was dedicated to his Consul obligations.

All the vampires in Lucian's region depended on him to take care of everything they felt like they couldn't do themselves. Mostly, he listened to their personal issues and gave advice.

Aiden was right, he was like a counselor—I thought the more appropriate term should be babysitter, though—to the vampires.

Curious about what they could possible need guidance about, I asked. He laughed and said I'd be surprised at how similar we were; that vampires were once human and still retained their personality and insecurities even after being turned into a vampire. A lot of them were newly turned and needed advice and help adjusting to their new lives. It was technically their Sire's responsibility to guide the new vampires, but sometimes they either didn't like their Sire, or their Sire refused to help.

Most of his Sunday was spent settling feuds and passing out bagged blood to those who needed it. Since it would raise suspicion if vampires continuously flocked to local vampire-owned blood banks, they delivered blood in anonymous trucks to the club for Lucian's appointed handlers to distribute. The vampires could go to the club any day of the week for a handout, but most of them chose to wait until Sunday, so they could also discuss any issues they were having with Lucian.

Silver Moon was closed on Sunday nights, but by the time he was finished with his Consul obligations, it was well into Monday morning. He would catch up on his sleep during the day, and since Monday nights were slow at the club, he would come over to my apartment once Aiden and I closed the office.

Unfortunately, Mondays were one of my busiest days. I usually didn't get to lock the doors until well after seven in the evening. I had started opening the office early, though, to try and get a head-start on the workload, so Aiden and I could close up as early as possible.

Luckily, that Monday hadn't been too bad. Jimmy didn't have to work at the club, so he hung around the office and provided some much-needed comedic relief from the stress of a dozen walk-ins and twice that amount in phone inquiries about my services. Since I knew it was a Lucian night, I didn't schedule any stake outs for after hours, and somehow, we managed to see every one of our potential clients and return all phone calls by five.

Two pizzas and three games of Yahtzee later, we were dressed down in shorts and t-shirts and were preparing for a popcorn and movie night. Lucian was going to be a little late because of a Consul emergency, but as soon as that was settled, he'd be joining us. Aiden and Jimmy were cleaning up the pizza and board games from the coffee table in the living room, while I heated up an entire box of popcorn. Both of them assured me they could easily devour two to three bags a piece, even after consuming two pizzas between the two of them. Apparently, an insatiable appetite was the result of an extremely high metabolism from their lycanthropy—I guess the movies got a few things right.

It took me a while to find bowls large enough to accommodate their hefty portions of popcorn, but once I did, I handed them over to eagerly awaiting hands. I threw away all the empty bags, grabbed my much smaller bowl, and headed into the living room to join them. "So, what movies did you all pick out?" I asked, before stuffing my first handful of delicious extra buttery popcorn into my mouth and slouching down on the couch. I tossed my favorite throw blanket over my legs and raised them up to rest on the coffee table.

They both grinned. "It's going to be an *Underworld* marathon."

I laughed, "Seriously?" Not that I was complaining, because I fucking loved those movies, but out of everything they could have picked out, they picked a vampire and werewolf film?

"What?" Aiden asked slyly. "I thought with all the bullshit we've been through lately, it was appropriate."

I rolled my eyes. "You'd better be glad I actually like those movies."

"I told you!" Jimmy proclaimed with a Cheshire grin planted on his face. I threw a small handful of popcorn at him as he stood to retrieve the remote. Before he sat back down, he picked up every piece that I'd thrown and shoved them all in his mouth.

"Yuck! I can't believe you just picked those up off the floor and ate them." Actually, I could. I learned very quickly after the full moon that Aiden and Jimmy were a two-for-one deal. They were always together, and since Aiden had moved in with me, Jimmy had also unofficially moved in as well. And a few pieces of food off the floor, wasn't the worse thing I'd seen him eat over the last couple of weeks.

"Five second rule," Jimmy replied, as he kicked back on the couch and turned the movie on.

"Five second rule?" I questioned.

"Yeah, you know . . . if it's been on the ground for under five seconds then it's still good," he answered nonchalantly.

Aiden also came to his defense, "And if that's not good enough for you, then remember . . . werewolves over here. We don't get sick."

I snickered and rolled my eyes again, "Touché."

We all relaxed back into the couch, the only sounds filling the apartment were the beginnings of the movie and the crunching of popcorn. It was amazing how different my life had become compared to this time last month. I thought I'd enjoyed my solitude; that I preferred it, but now, on nights like this, I didn't think I wanted to go back to that. I'd had more fun hanging out with these two in less than a month than I'd had in the last couple of years.

As I tried to focus on watching the vampires do their thing, I started to wonder what it would be like to be a vampire. I'd actually wondered that a lot recently. I wasn't sure how personal those types of questions were to them, so I'd been hesitant to ask Lucian about what happened when a human became a vampire. Or how the whole being born a vampire thing worked. He briefly mentioned it during the night after we'd first met, but there'd been so much going on with Malus, that I hadn't really had time to bring that one up again—but I did plan on bringing that topic up. I wanted to know what the differences were between the Born ones and the Made ones. I'd assumed vampires could only be created, so I was very curious to know more about how they're born.

I also hadn't brought up the issue with my eyes. It wasn't like I hadn't thought about it, because honestly, it had been on my mind a lot—probably more than anything else. The only time I'd mentioned Malus' comment about how certain vampires would like to know I existed to Lucian, he'd quickly brushed it off. And he hadn't brought it back up, either. I did, however, in a round-about way, ask Aiden and Jimmy about it. But since they only had limited experience with vampires—meaning they'd only met the local ones, they had no idea what I was talking about.

They did say it could have something to do with a particular House, but since there weren't any vampire Houses near Louisville, they didn't know much about them. They'd met a few Housed vampires doing business in Louisville, but that was about it. And they assured me that I should hope I never met one of them, because as Lucian had implied, they were very stuck up. I believe Jimmy's exact words were, "They walk around like they have a stick shoved up their ass, and they think they're better than everyone else."

I grinned. Jimmy had a way with words. But that still didn't give me any more clues as to why my eyes were a big deal. The only conclusion I could come to, just didn't make any sense. I kept trying to push those thoughts out of my mind, but it just wouldn't go away. Something about it felt right—felt like it had a ring of truth to it. And no matter how hard I tried, I couldn't shake it. I knew my mother's lineage, but my father's was a complete mystery, even to my mother's parents.

And if my eyes, which I had gotten from him, did belong to a particular family— one that were vampires—then what did that say about my father? There was no way he could've been a vampire. Wouldn't I have known? Wouldn't there have been signs? I wasn't very old when they died, but surely I would've remembered odd behavior, or blood bags in the fridge, or something? And I didn't see how he could've died on a hike. Vampires are supposed to be near immortal, so how the fuck could he and Mom have died, if that were the case?

So, was he only part vampire, full vampire, or was it all just a coincidence? And if he was, what did that say about me? I did have a gift only vampires had, but last time I checked, I didn't have fangs and didn't crave blood. Blood didn't bother me, but I'd never felt the need to drink it. I didn't have any kind of aversion to the sun; actually, I *liked* being in the sun. And last time I checked, I didn't have superhuman speed, agility, sight, or hearing. I still cringed when I thought about gym in high school; I never finished last, but I was definitely closer to the bottom half of the class for everything we did.

There were just too many what-ifs, whys, and hows when traveling down that rabbit hole. That's why I kept trying to brush it off, and think of some other explanation for the cryptic comments and strange coincidences that had come up. But it was the reason why I'd been wanting to ask more questions about the Born vampires. I particularly wanted to know if a vampire and a human could have a child. And if they could, was that child a vampire or a human?

My now familiar tingling sensation erupted along my body, pulling me from my thoughts. I smiled. "Lucian must be here," I told the boys excitedly.

Aiden had a confused look on his face, "Are you sure?"

"Well, this spidey-sense thing hasn't failed me yet," I pointed out.

He snickered, "True. I just wasn't expecting him so soon. He was supposed to be meeting with Samuel tonight."

Jimmy chuckled, "I'm so glad I'm not there tonight."

"What am I missing?" I asked. "Who's Samuel?"

"He's like the most annoying vampire I've ever met," Jimmy replied. "He asks for a meeting just about every other week."

"Yeah," Aiden added, "and it's always over dumb shit."

"And it takes forever."

127

"It takes forever." They both said at the same time. They laughed at their inside joke and stood from the couch. "I'll go open the door," Aiden said, while Jimmy grabbed both of their empty popcorn bowls and took them to the kitchen.

I shook my head. They were a mess.

I reached over to get the remote, with the intentions of pausing the movie, when I saw it. Two icy cobalt eyes were in the window by the television, and they were looking right at me. "Shit!" I screamed and half jumped, half ninja-crawled over the back of the couch. I was surprised I was able to move that fast. Through the sheer terror that had taken over my body, I'd somehow managed to vault over the couch faster than I'd ever been able to move in my life. It was amazing what fear could do; why couldn't I move like that all the time?

Aiden and Jimmy ran back in the living room. Jimmy got to me first and crouched down beside me, "What happened?"

"It's him." I managed to whisper. I cleared my throat, trying to get my next words out stronger. "Malus, is in the window next to the TV."

Aiden, still standing, strode over there in an instant. I stayed hunkered down behind the couch, afraid to see those eyes again. Jimmy stayed with me, one hand on my back, rubbing small circles, the other reached into his pocket to grab his cell phone. He made a few swipes and placed it next to his ear. "He's here." A pause. "Yeah, I'm with her, Aiden's investigating. I'm not sure what happened." Another pause. "Will do." Then he hung up.

I heard the window open, and I somehow managed to crouch down even lower, squeezing my eyes shut. I was scared for Aiden, but seriously, how the fuck could I help him? Rationally, I knew I couldn't, but the unselfishness in me made me cringe at how weak I was being. I shouldn't be okay with him potentially sacrificing himself for me. It was me that Malus wanted, so it should have been the other way around—I should be sacrificing myself, so no one else got hurt. If something happened to Aiden, or anyone else, I'd never be able to forgive myself.

Jimmy raised his head to peer over the couch, "Aiden, he said not to go after him."

"Are you fucking serious?" Aiden yelled.

"He wants both of us to stay with Riley. He's afraid it's a trick to lure us away from her. And he'd rather that douchebag get away than to leave her unprotected."

I heard him curse again as the window slammed closed. A moment later, I felt the air shift as he knelt beside Jimmy. "Hey. It's okay. He won't get you with us here. Come on, Riley, let's get back up on the couch. I closed the blinds, so even if he's still out there, he can't see you, and you won't be able to see him."

I exhaled the shaky breath I didn't realize I'd been holding. I opened my eyes and raised my head. Both of the guys were almost eye level with me. I could see flecks of swirling amber battling to take over both of their baby-blues. I nodded and let Aiden help me stand. I was a little shaky at first, but managed to walk around and sit down on the couch.

We didn't talk much until Lucian showed up. When the tingles came, I tensed, fearing it was Malus again, but it was Lucian who walked through the door. I jumped up and ran into his outstretched arms. The tears burned my eyes, wanting to escape, but I was able to hold them back. I'd already embarrassed myself enough by cowering behind the couch like a chicken shit, so I didn't want to add crying, hysterical lady to my *'things I wish I could do over today'* list.

When I heard more people enter my apartment, I reluctantly let go of Lucian to see who'd come with him. It was Avery and Ellie, who both wore their *Silver Moon* black outfits. They must've been working at the club that night and came to help Lucian hunt Malus. "Hey," I said, trying to regain my usual calm demeanor. "I hope you all aren't leaving the club short-handed."

"Naw," Ellie said as she came farther into the apartment. "It's been a slow night, so far. And Eric can handle the bar by himself. If not, then oh well. He'll deal." She grinned, flicking her long wavy locks behind her. "Trust me, catching this asshole is way more important."

"Speaking of," Avery said, as his imposing form stepped closer, "what happened?"

I gave them a quick run-down—after all, it happened so fast, there really wasn't much to tell. Avery nodded and began barking out orders.

"Aiden, Ellie, you come with me. We'll circle around the building and track his scent. Jimmy, you stand guard outside the apartment door in case he's creeping around out there." He turned, not waiting for anyone to follow him, and bounded out of the apartment. Aiden followed close behind, giving me a reassuring smile before he disappeared into the night.

Ellie wasn't far behind Aiden. She looked back before exiting, "Don't worry, if he's out there, we'll find him." She paused, "And don't do anything I wouldn't do while we're gone." Ellie gave us a devilish grin, winked, and vanished outside with the others.

Jimmy cleared his throat, as he came up beside us, "Um, yeah. Please don't, because that would be really awkward for me."

"Oh, shut up, Jimmy!" I punched him in the arm. It wasn't hard, but he acted like I almost broke his bone as he playfully whimpered all the way to his position outside the door.

Once he closed it, Lucian took me back in his arms. "I'm so sorry, Riley."

"Lucian, there's nothing for you to apologize for. He made it very clear that he wants me, so I knew this was going to happen sooner or later." I'd just been secretly wishing it was going to be later—or preferably not at all.

He pulled back and led me to the couch. We sat down, facing each other, before I continued, "I'm just thankful I've got Aiden and Jimmy here. If it weren't for them, I know he would've already tried something."

"I think so, too. I'm afraid he's going to start getting desperate since you're never alone. Riley, I can't tell you–" He broke off and looked away. I wasn't sure what he was going to say, so I just sat there, letting him gather his thoughts. Finally, he focused back on me. Lucian placed a hand on the side of my face, "I can't tell you how scared I was when I got that phone call. You're so fragile being human, and I don't want to lose you. I promise we're going to get him. Maybe not tonight, but we will."

I tried to analyze what he said, but I couldn't concentrate as his hand slowly moved around to gently cup the back of my neck. Lucian leaned into me, as he pulled me closer to him. "I know," I managed to murmur, before our lips softly met. I placed my hands on his chest, feeling the muscles underneath his shirt. I wished I could rip it off to finally see Lucian without clothes on. I'd spent a few nights snuggled up to his body and feeling it through clothing had made me devote a considerable amount of time imagining what he looked like without it.

He groaned against my mouth and used his other arm to pull me closer, deepening the kiss as he did. I felt his tongue slip past my lips, and I allowed my own to meet his. Lucian pulled me even tighter to him, as I slid my arms around him and pressed my chest against his. I'd already taken my bra off for the night, and the friction against my breasts was going to drive me crazy.

Between that and Lucian's skillful tongue making me wonder how well he could use it in other places, I was straddling him before I even realized what I was doing. It had been quite a while since I'd gotten off by anything other than my vibrator, so my body was a little too eager for the prospect of the real thing.

My breasts, heavy with need, brushed against his chest, as I sat fully down on Lucian's lap. His hardness seemed quite impressive through the thin cotton of my shorts and underwear, and my body betrayed me again, rubbing against his length on its own accord, sending a rush of pleasure through my body.

Lucian stilled instantly. I broke the kiss, panting slightly as I looked at him. He was breathing heavily and had his eyes closed, but he didn't release his hold on me. "Riley," he began, "as much as I would love to continue this—and believe me, there's nothing I want more—we can't. The others will be back any moment."

The lust rushed out of me as I slowly slid off him. I blushed shamefully as I realized what I had been about to do; what I was willing to do, not even ten minutes after the exchange between Jimmy and myself. I guess it really had been a long time if my body was so willing to pounce on Lucian with a werewolf right outside the apartment door and the others due back any minute.

"I'm sorry, I don't know what came over me," I lied, because I knew exactly what had come over me, I just didn't want to admit it to Lucian. And I silently promised my still lightly throbbing clit a date with that vibrator later—with the shower running and music streaming loudly from my phone. I didn't want those sensitive werewolf ears to hear that. A girl has got to have a little privacy.

He opened he eyes, "You have nothing to be sorry about. If anything, it's me that should be sorry. I started this, and it's my fault we haven't been able to be alone longer than a few minutes."

I teased, "Well . . . when you put it that way, I guess it is your fault."

Lucian smirked, "With your permission, I'd like to rectify that . . . soon."

"Oh, yeah? What do you have in mind?"

He was about to answer me, when we were interrupted by everyone strolling through the door. I inwardly groaned. I really wanted to hear what he'd been about to say.

"So?" He smoothly rose from the couch, discreetly adjusting himself as he did, and walked toward everyone.

"We followed the trail a couple of blocks over, but it disappeared. I assume he had a vehicle waiting," Avery relayed.

"I figured that would be the case," Lucian replied with an exasperated sigh.

"So, what do we do now?" Jimmy demanded. "Just keep waiting until that dick comes back and catches her alone? What the fuck are we supposed to do?"

"Jimmy," Avery barked his name in warning.

"No, it's fine," Lucian waived it off. "He's right. Malus is going to keep testing us until he finds an opening. And I have to be honest with you all . . . I'm at a complete loss on what to do. I don't think we have any other options at the moment other than to continue guarding her and to keep searching for him."

Ellie waltzed by the guys and sat down next to me. "Personally, I'm betting this guy is a Born."

"You think?"

"Yeah, it's the only thing that makes sense. A lot of power, breaking vampire laws, and the conniving *'I get what I want attitude',*" she rolled her eyes, "that's the average Born in a nutshell"

"So, are Born vampires stronger?" I asked.

"Yeah, unless a Made has some age on them, or a really powerful Sire, then a Born is just naturally stronger and more powerful. But, that also means they come with a much larger ego."

I could hear the guys in the background continuing their conversation, but I wasn't listening anymore. Ellie had my full attention. Maybe I could get some of the questions that had been bothering me answered. "So, how does that work, exactly? The whole being born a vampire thing?"

She stared at me blankly, "Well, when a man and a woman love each other very much, they usually decide to become intimate . . ."

"I know that!" I quickly and embarrassingly interrupted. "I mean, does it have to be two vampires to make a Born?"

She grinned, "I knew what you meant, I'm just fucking with you." She propped her legs up on the coffee table, crossed them, and leaned back into the couch. "We're not very fertile . . . which is weird, when you think about it, since we have accelerated healing. But for whatever reason, it's hard for a vampire to get pregnant, and it can take decades to have a child. Not that I'm complaining, though," she quickly added, "I'm grateful I don't have to worry about pills, shots, or," she shuddered, "those insert things, like humans do.

"But I digress," she sighed, "a vampire can get a vampire pregnant, a vampire can get a human pregnant, and a human can get a vampire pregnant. Some ways are just harder than others." She paused and chuckled, "Ha, get it . . . *harder* than others."

I snickered. Ellie had a different sense of humor, but I liked it. Ever since I'd first met her, I had a feeling we would get along well together, and I was thankful she was giving me a much needed distraction from my most recent Malus encounter.

"Anywho, it's *easier*," she winked, "to get pregnant with some combinations than it is with others. It's too much to go into right now, because there's so many other variables such as a Made versus a Born and blah, blah, blah, but it *can* happen either way. And just because it can happen between a human and a vampire, it doesn't mean that each child will go through their Becoming. Some of them remain human and live out their lives, or get pissed since they didn't get the vampire gene and have someone turn them."

My confusion must have shown on my face because she hastily added, "A Born is basically a human with slightly enhanced senses until they go through their Becoming and turn into a full-fledged vampire. That can happen when they're at an age anywhere from sixteen to twenty-five." She shrugged, "It just depends. I've seen a Born with two Born parents go through their Becoming closer to twenty-five and a Born with one human parent have it happen at seventeen. But, no matter when it happens, it's a painful process. That's something that doesn't discriminate—whether you're Born or a Made, the process of Becoming is similar and just as agonizing."

She had a far-away look and a scowl on her face. I wondered if she was remembering her own Becoming. I shuddered. I might have been interested in the process of turning into a vampire, but that didn't mean I wanted to experience it.

"Thanks for explaining all of that to me. Since I kind of got thrown into this world, I'd like to know as much about everything as I can."

She smiled sincerely, "No problem. And if Lucian doesn't have time to answer any questions you have, feel free to hit me up." She stood up. "I don't mind at all."

"I may take you up on that." I stood with her. Now that I knew a vampire could get a human pregnant, I would definitely have more questions.

We walked next to the guys. "I really think I should stay," Lucian was saying.

"Dude, you know Samuel isn't going to leave." Aiden pointed out.

"Yeah, I would put money on the fact that he's still sitting there waiting for you to get back." Jimmy laughed.

Lucian groaned, and I think I actually saw a hint of a smile on Avery's face. "Lucian, he's right." Avery checked his phone. "He's still sitting in your office."

Lucian looked back to me with the weight of his decision etched on his face. I could tell he wanted to stay, but was torn by his Consul obligations.

"It's fine, Lucian," I tried to ease his mind. "You need to go, and I've got these two guys here to protect me."

Jimmy spoke up, "Yeah, I'll stay here tonight. I'll sleep on the couch. Or not sleep at all, if that's what it takes. I doubt he'll be back tonight, though."

"And you know Samuel will have a shit-fit if you don't go back," Ellie added.

Defeat shone in his eyes as he relented, "You're all right. I'll go back and deal with Samuel."

Avery nodded with approval. "I'll be waiting in the car."

"I guess that's my cue to leave as well," Ellie mused. "See ya, girlie. And don't forget, you know where to find me if you need me."

"Thanks, Ellie."

"Well, here it is that I'm once again having to cancel our plans."

"Lucian, really, it's fine. I get it, you're a busy guy." I grinned, "And Samuel needs you."

Lucian smirked, "Regardless, I promise that one day we'll have a proper date, and *nothing* will come between us and those plans."

"That would be nice," I agreed.

He wrapped his arms around me and gave me a gentle kiss before reluctantly pulling away. "Goodnight," Lucian said, before walking out of my sight.

Disappointed in how my night ended up, and still shaken at my most recent encounter with Malus, I turned around to face my two werewolf guards, "So, what are we going to do now?"

CHAPTER II

L ucian had finally come through on that date. Well, I guess it wasn't technically a date, since we weren't going anywhere, but he did kick everyone out of my apartment, so we could be alone for the night. And after the last few weeks that we'd had, I'd take any kind of a *date* I could get.

"So, what are we going to do now?" I asked, once everyone had left.

A predatory smirk spread across his face. "I can think of a few things." He advanced in a blur, our lips meeting instantly, and our bodies pressed together. He walked us backwards, never breaking our contact, until my back met the wall with a not-so-gentle thud.

His hands roamed under my t-shirt, his skin sending a blazing warmth along their searching path. I was startled at his sudden aggressive behavior, it was such a drastic difference from the sweet, gentle Lucian that I'd experienced over the last several weeks. But, we hadn't really been alone either, so maybe this version of him was another side I just hadn't seen yet. Whatever the reason, I was so not complaining. I don't think I'd ever been that turned on before.

We broke apart just long enough to shed both of our shirts, and I wrapped my arms around his neck and pulled his mouth back down to my own. His fresh hold on my waist lowered, until I could feel him unbuttoning my jeans. With his help, I shimmied them down and pulled my legs out. Next, it was his turn. I reached to return the favor, only to find his own hands there, already taking care of the job.

His heated mouth left mine, and began to make a trail along my neck, sending fiery shivers throughout my body. I moaned and wrapped my arms back around his neck and shoulders, encouraging him to do anything but stop. I felt his hands grip my ass, kneading it as I arched my back and leaned my head against the wall, giving him more access to my throat. Maybe not the smartest thing to do with a vampire, but at that point, I really didn't give a fuck. I wanted—scratch that, I *needed* Lucian in me so badly, that was all I could think about.

Suddenly, his grip became tighter as he hoisted me up. Taking the hint and needing no further encouragement, I wrapped my legs around his waist, bringing my hot center directly against his extremely hard length. The friction it made against my clit—even through my panties—was almost enough to bring me over the edge into a much-needed orgasm.

He growled against my throat, and I simultaneously felt the pressure of the wall disappear and a subtle breezy movement, before a falling sensation. Shocked, I opened my eyes and saw my bedroom walls, then the ceiling, as I landed on my bed. I looked down the length of my body, to see Lucian smirking as he removed his boxer-briefs, freeing his manhood and finally giving me a full view of what I was about to get.

There was a predatory look in his eyes as he slowly climbed on the bed and crawled over the top of my legs. Heat pooled in my core as he pulled my underwear down and then spread my legs open, baring me for his viewing pleasure.

"You have no idea how long I've waited for this," he softly said before leaning down to kiss and lick his way down my thighs.

I stifled another moan and closed my eyes, trying not to squirm under his touch. It was all almost too much. I was normally down for foreplay—actually, I usually needed it to get in the mood—but right then, I don't think I could have become anymore turned on. All I wanted was Lucian inside me.

When I felt his hot breath between my legs, I bit my lip and tried to hold myself together. If he so much as did one small swipe with his tongue, I knew it would send me into an orgasm. I'd always been a one-hitter-quitter, never able to have more than one orgasm during intimacy, and I desperately wanted it to be with him inside me. Then again, maybe it would be different with him? Maybe I could finally have those elusive multiple orgasms I'd always read about?

That would be amazing, but I didn't want to take that chance, so I opened my mouth to beg him to come up and have sex with me, but whatever I was about to say died on my lips as I opened my eyes and stared down my body. Where Lucian had been, Malus now crouched. Those icy blue eyes burned bright as he grinned wickedly.

I opened my mouth and screamed as he lunged for my throat.

I braced my arms up, in an attempt to protect myself—more out of instinct than really thinking it would do any good. When he grabbed my arms and started to shake me, instead of just plowing through them to get to my throat, I panicked and started to thrash, trying anything I could to throw him off me.

I was vaguely aware of my name being called, but I was so focused on trying to keep Malus from sinking his teeth into me, it took a few minutes to realize it was Aidan saying my name. I stopped my struggle, and the grip on my arms immediately eased. I cautiously opened my eyes and was relieved to see a pair of amber ones staring back at me.

I released a shaky breath and tried to sit up. Aiden eased back on the bed, no longer hovering over me. I avoided eye contact as I scooted back against the headboard and tried to move my damp hair from my face. I was drenched in sweat—not sure if it was from the first part of my dream with Lucian, or from the latter with Malus . . . probably a little of both. I made a mental note to strip the bed, before I went down to the office, and wash it all.

"Are you sure it's not really him?" Aiden questioned.

I cleared my throat and braved a glance in his direction. His eyes had bled back to their usual blue. "Yes, I'm positive." And I was . . . mostly. "It feels completely different than that first time."

His unwavering gaze was almost too much, but I didn't want to look away, afraid if I did, he wouldn't believe me. And if he didn't believe me, I knew without a doubt he'd tell Lucian, and I didn't want Lucian worrying about the stupid dreams I'd been having. He had enough on his plate without adding more to it.

Something in my steadfast resolve must have resonated with him because he nodded his head in acceptance. "Okay, if you're sure."

"Aiden, I promise I'm one hundred percent sure about this. If I wasn't, I would tell you."

"I think you would," he raked his hand through his hair, "it's just . . . it's been three nights in a row that I've had to wake you up from these nightmares."

I shamefully looked away. "I know." Ever since I'd seen Malus in the window, I'd dreamt about those eyes each night, and Aiden always managed to wake me up right before he bit me. Usually, I'd been alone in the dream when Malus attacked me, but this time I wasn't. Of all the dreams that could've morphed into a nightmare, I was pissed this one was one of them.

I guess dreams really did imitate real life, because Lucian and I just couldn't be alone without getting interrupted, whether I was awake or asleep. If I couldn't have him while I was awake, why couldn't I at least get him in my dreams?

"Look, I'm not trying to make you feel bad. I'm just worried. Even if this isn't really him and it's just dreams, it's clearly taking a toll on you. And it's only a matter of time before Lucian realizes something's off."

I gave him a pointed look. "I'll be fine. And like I said, I'm positive it's not him. I don't know how to explain it, but I can *feel* the difference. This is just a reoccurring dream where he pops up. That's it. So, please don't say anything to Lucian. Not yet."

He sighed in defeat, "Fine. But if this keeps up, either you tell him, or I will."

I could handle that, because I'd make sure the dreams stopped. I had already decided that if it happened one more time, I would take some sleeping pills. I still had some leftover from college when I used to have trouble sleeping because of stress. One pill and an hour later, I'd fall into a dreamless sleep and wouldn't wake up for about eight hours. I'd be so zonked out, I wouldn't move the entire night and wake up in the exact same spot the next morning. So, with a gleam in my eye, I gladly accepted Aiden's challenge. "Deal."

CHAPTER 12

"**T**hank you so much, Ms. Hunter. When the owner notified us about an employee witnessing the plaintiff club-hopping, we knew she was faking her injuries." He had a devilish grin, knowing he was about to get the case against his client dismissed.

"It was my pleasure, Mr. Cane." And it was. I'd worked my ass off my entire life, so I always got a little bit of satisfaction when I was able disprove injury cases. Not saying the woman didn't get an injury when she slipped and fell at a restaurant, but it was probably only a bruise—not the debilitating and near-permanent damage to her hip she claimed and was trying to get a four-hundred-thousand-dollar settlement for. Basically, she was trying to lie about an injury and get a huge payday for it.

An employee from the restaurant saw her out clubbing a couple of weekends ago; they weren't a hundred percent sure it was her, but he was suspicious enough to get a video of her dancing, just in case. The video was too blurry to be allowed as evidence in a courtroom, but good enough that the lawyer hired me to follow her around.

Aiden and I got footage on the first day of her jogging in the park, despite the severe hip and lower back injuries she claimed she had in the lawsuit. I was surprised she'd been so careless. This wasn't the first insurance or injury fraud claim that I'd investigated, but it was the first one where it only took one day of surveillance to disprove a claim.

"So, are the files you emailed the only copies I will receive?"

I glanced at my watch, it was almost five. Mr. Cane was my last client meeting of the day, and I was getting anxious to wrap it up. The front door was already locked, and Aiden was out picking up dinner. Mr. Cane was a busy lawyer and opted to do a video call versus meeting with me in the office.

"No," I gave my full attention back to the computer screen. "I sent the video in an email, so you could have instant access to the footage. I've already uploaded a higher resolution copy on a flash drive, along with several photos that were taken of the woman. My assistant, Aiden, dropped it off with your secretary around the time our video call began. So, it should already be waiting for you."

"Perfect. Another outstanding performance, Ms. Hunter. I may just have to switch from paying case by case to keeping you on hand with a retainer."

I smiled. "That's definitely something we can discuss further when you're ready, Mr. Cane."

We ended the call after the usual good-bye pleasantries, and I stretched, yawning. I shouldn't have been tired since I'd taken the sleeping pill the night before, and it had worked like a charm.

I'd been dead to the world until my alarm pulled me out of my dreamless sleep that morning.

I shut my computer down, and checked my notepad where I'd written down all the buildings around Louisville that I wanted to get access to their surveillance footage. I'd started with the ones close to *Silver Moon,* so I could try and see the vehicle Jessica and the others left in, but as more disappearances happened, I'd added several more to the list. My goal was to find the group who were kidnapping people on some of the footage and get a license plate or anything else helpful.

Lucian had footage of the group inside the club and leaving, but since there wasn't a parking lot close by, the cameras didn't capture the vehicle they were using. The still photos of the individuals weren't that great, but they were good enough that we could possibly identify them on other footage.

Most of the names were scratched off, but there were still a few we hadn't been able to get a hold of. I made a mental note to tackle those names again first thing in the morning and set the notepad in the middle of my desk, so I would see it and not forget.

I turned off all the lights downstairs and made my way up to the apartment. As soon as I walked through the door, a delicious smell wafted all around me. My stomach growled in response. "It sure smells good!" I called out.

"Roadhouse food always does," Aiden agreed as I walked around the corner to the kitchen. He had pulled the styrofoam boxes out of the takeout bag and transferred his steaks to a plate. He usually ordered two or three steaks every time we got food from a steak house and that was in addition to his sides. Werewolf metabolism was no joke.

"So, where did you say Jimmy was?" I asked, as I rounded the bar to start loading my food to a plate as well.

"He's at the club working. Someone called in, so he had to go in early."

"Gotcha." I busied myself with the task of mixing the dressing into my salad. It wasn't like Aiden and I hadn't been alone in the last month, but usually in the evenings, Jimmy was also there. If he did have to work at *Silver Moon*, he would go in later, once I was already in bed.

It would be fine, though; I'd become completely comfortable with Aiden. He was quiet, sweet, and protective—but in that older brother sort of way. He seemed like he was one of those all-around good guys that rarely existed anymore. I didn't know how he was still single, he'd be the perfect catch for any girl.

Jimmy, I'd learned, was completely different from Aiden. They were both attractive and protective by nature, but Jimmy wasn't the quiet, sweet type—he was more of a cocky smartass. But he was funny and managed to always make me laugh. I'd gotten used to having both of them there in the evenings.

I stiffened, the tingling shooting up and down my body. I discreetly grabbed the knife Aiden had used for his steak and prepared to turn around and use it. It was Friday, so there was no way Lucian would have been there instead of at the club preparing for the night's rush, especially since it was the night before the Kentucky Derby. The Derby was a major local event and there was always an influx of people in town for the annual race, and they all wanted to get drunk and celebrate.

Aiden must have noticed my sudden stillness. He peered at me out of the corner of his eye, then down at the knife in my hand. He sniffed the air and grinned, but then tossed a worried expression my way.

Confused, I turned around. Stunned didn't even begin to describe what I felt as I took in the sight of Lucian. He had his usual black dress slacks and shoes, but he'd added some color with a light lavender button-down shirt. He was always so swoon-worthy, and I was over here in my band shirt, black skinny jeans, and my hair thrown up in a messy bun. He seriously made me consider swapping my comfortable clothes out and try to dress better. I always felt underdressed and unattractive next to him.

He gave me a tight smile. "So, is there anything you want to tell me?"

"Huh?" I wasn't sure I understood the question; I was still shocked at his sudden appearance in my kitchen. I set the knife down and cleared my throat. "Anything I want to tell you?"

He nodded his head. I had no idea what he was talking about. I sifted through the events of the last several days, but nothing came to mind. Unless . . . I jerked my head toward Aiden, who avoided eye contact with me.

"Why didn't you tell me?" Lucian asked softly.

I continued to glare at Aiden until he finally looked up. He shrugged unapologetically, before dumping all his sides into one box. He grabbed his plate, box of sides, and walked past us. "I thought he needed to know," he called out behind him as he disappeared around the corner.

Recognizing I may as well get this over with, I faced Lucian. "I didn't want you to worry about me." He began to talk, but I held up my hand, "And before you say anything, I want you to know that I'm absolutely positive it's not him. If it was, I would've told you the first night it happened. It's only normal dreams that I'm having." I paused, contemplating what I'd just said. "Well, I guess they're not really normal, but you know what I mean . . . it's just regular dreams, but he's in them."

His eyes softened, "I believe you, Riley."

"You do?"

"Of course. Aiden already told me Malus wasn't invading your dreams."

"Um, then why all the dramatics?"

"Dramatics?" His lip twitched.

"Yeah, you know," I waved my hand around, "coming in here, questioning me like I did something wrong, acting like you're mad, and just being here in the first place. Aren't you busy?"

He chuckled, which made his eyes sparkle. I held back a sigh and tried not to get distracted. "I just wanted to hear it from you. And I'm never too busy to see if you're alright. Why? Would you rather I hadn't stopped by?"

"Seriously?" I huffed, trying to hold back a grin. "This is exactly why I didn't want to tell you about this. You're way too busy to be taking time out to stop by over something like dreams."

"I'd rather know what's troubling you, than be kept in the dark. I care about you, Riley." He closed the distance between us, taking my hand in his. I had a flashback to my dream, before Malus so rudely interrupted it, but tried to quickly bury it. "Please tell me next time it happens. I just want to make sure you're okay."

I looked into his emerald eyes and wondered, not for the first time . . . "Why me?"

149

His brow wrinkled in confusion, "I don't think I understand what you're asking. Why did Malus choose you?"

I blushed profusely as I realized I'd said that out loud and quickly looked anywhere except at him. The damage was done, though, so I might as well put my big-girl-panties on and elaborate on my two-word question. I stalled for a moment before sucking in a deep breath, "Why did you choose me?" I risked a glance at him. "Why are you doing all of this? And why do you care so much about me?" There I'd said it.

Enlightenment flooded his eyes. "Riley, you are the kindest, most caring, loyal, and most beautiful creature I've ever seen. I won't lie, I've dated many others in my past, but they were all different; they didn't care about anyone but themselves, and none of them come close to comparing with how amazing you are." My cheeks burned even hotter. "I consider myself lucky that you gave *me* a chance, knowing what I am."

"But that didn't matter to me," I interrupted.

He nodded knowingly, "That's exactly my point. You saw past what I was and gave me a chance. I don't want anything to happen to you, and I will protect you with my life," he promised with a blazing heat in his eyes.

We'd spent quite a bit of time together since that fateful night when I walked into *Silver Moon* seeking information about Jessica, and we'd grown close in the process. The attraction was mutual between us, we were comfortable with each other, and things were just easy with him—when we weren't worrying about Malus. I knew he liked me, but I had no idea his feelings were that strong.

I didn't know how to follow that confession. I wasn't exactly ready for my own yet, so I settled on, "Okay. Next time, I'll tell you."

His smile lit up his entire face. "Good. Now, you'd better eat your food before it gets cold."

As if in response, my stomach growled loudly. He gave me a knowing grin before stepping closer and placing his lips on mine. He deepened the kiss, but instead of the wild, scorching moment we had in my dream, it was slow and sensual. Somehow, that managed to turn me on even more.

After what seemed like an eternity, but in all actuality, probably wasn't even a minute, we ended the kiss. He gently leaned his forehead against mine and whispered, "I'll see you soon." He then squeezed my hand and left.

I slouched back against the counter. I didn't know how much more teasing my body could handle. Something was going to have to give soon. And just like with Aiden, I often wondered why Lucian was still single. I mean, hot guys who were actually nice . . . why the fuck hadn't they been snatched up yet?

I pushed those thoughts away and finished getting my food ready. I grabbed a glass of sweet tea and joined Aiden in the living room.

"Are you mad at me?"

I set my stuff down on the coffee table next to his, but instead of sitting on the couch, I opted to sit with my legs crossed on the floor. I waited until I was completely situated before I answered him. "No. I know why you did it, and I don't blame you."

He nodded, "Good."

We sat there in a comfortable silence enjoying our meal for several minutes before I gave in and turned on the news. I'd always watched it in the mornings, and I followed most of the local stations on social media, but since I'd learned about Malus, I had taken the habit of watching it every evening as well.

I set my fork down and looked at Aiden when the first story finished; about three new disappearances the previous night in the Louisville Metro area. He rubbed his hands up and down his face and let out an exasperated sigh.

"It just doesn't make sense." He leaned back on the couch. "We can't figure out how he's sneaking around under our noses and doing this. The more we look into it, I think what that girl told you was true. He can't be operating inside Louisville, he's got to be sneaking in or sending someone else into the city to do his dirty work for him. And the sad truth is . . . we just don't have enough manpower to search outside the city for him."

I didn't really know what to say to that. I knew very well the lengths they were going to in order to search for him. "There's not really much more you all can do."

He leaned forward and picked up his fork. "Lucian even went as far as requesting additional help from his Sire. Hopefully, he'll send a request up the line to get a BloodGuard unit stationed here."

"Is that a good or a bad thing?" I asked.

He thought about it for a moment. "Like I've said before, most vampires are dicks. I've never met the guy, but I'm hoping that if he's Lucian's Sire, then maybe he's got some of the same qualities as Lucian. And being this area's Dominus, I hope he'd be concerned enough to help, if for that reason alone.

"And as far as the BloodGuard goes . . . it's always been relatively peaceful around here, so there's never been a need for anything more than a Consul. But, they're supposed to be good at what they do, and there's no question we could use the help right now. So, I guess we'll see."

CHAPTER 13

T he next several days passed by swiftly and were rather uneventful . . . not that I was complaining. Aiden had solidified his place as a much-welcomed addition to the office a hundred times over. He caught on promptly to every task and seemed to always be one step ahead of everything. I was even considering offering him the position permanently. He liked working at *Silver Moon,* and all his friends worked there as well, but he was about to begin taking online classes at a local community college. Those long nights were going to be tough to juggle with schoolwork. If he stayed working with me, he could do schoolwork in between his responsibilities during the day and have every evening to finish what was left.

It had been a little over a month since he first moved in with me, and it was hard to imagine how uneasy I was about the situation at first. Not only had Aiden been an immense help with the office, he'd made improvements in my life in general, as well.

I had become lonely by absorbing myself in work. I thought I'd been content, but now I recognized it was just a façade I'd foolishly let myself believe. Looking back, I could easily see that it evolved from deceiving my grandmother. She was already apprehensive about me being alone in a big city, so the last thing I wanted was for her to worry about me also being miserable. I'd put on a happy-face for her benefit for so long that it stuck with me, and I eventually believed it myself.

It was so frustrating when you were blind about certain things until after the veil had been lifted. Then you could see everything so unmistakably—what led up to it, how it happened, and even what you could've done to prevent it. It wasn't fair when life was so infuriatingly exhausting, but then again no one ever promised life would be easy.

Aiden's ringtone floated from the guest bathroom, interrupting my epiphany and brought me back to reality. I knew it was Jimmy calling to discuss their plans that night. I smiled faintly as I removed the sizzling bacon from the frying pan.

I was a good cook . . . when I decided to actually fix food. My grandmother taught me early on the importance of greasy, but absolutely mouthwatering southern cooking, and she taught me to enjoy cooking it. But when you were cooking for one, it just didn't seem worth the hassle to prepare a full course meal every night of the week.

Even though Aiden had been living with me, we'd been so busy with my ever-expanding clientele and trying to hunt down building owners to get permission to access surveillance footage that I'd been too exhausted to stray from my usual take-out routine. Just tracking down those owners had been a time-consuming challenge.

We finally managed to get through my entire list, but when we were able to reach them, most of the owners refused to give me access since I wasn't affiliated with the police department and didn't have a court order. Apparently, looking for a missing girl wasn't important or worth their time. The few that had allowed me access, either ended up being the wrong angles, or didn't have anything on them that helped.

And in contradiction to my constant pleas not to, Aiden had been helping with the grocery and take out bills. Or should I say, since I wouldn't accept money, he went out and bought stuff on his own, knowing there wasn't anything I could do about it. As if working for me and living with me, all while protecting me against a psycho vampire wasn't enough, he also cleaned the apartment and bought food. I figured the least I could do was push through my exhaustion and start giving him some home-cooked meals as a small token of my appreciation.

Crazy Bitch emitted from my cell phone, and I groaned, knowing the ring tone belonged to my best friend, Hattie. I knew she was mad at me, and I couldn't blame her. If our roles were reversed, I would be upset with her as well. Since all of this began a month ago I'd been avoiding seeing her, which luckily, was easy to do since she still lived in E-Town. Despite both of our busy work schedules, we usually tried to get together at least once a month for a lunch date, but out of fear for her safety, I'd cancelled on her this past month and evaded each attempt she made to reschedule it.

I desperately wanted to tell her everything that had happened and to have someone that wasn't supernatural to talk to about it with, but I knew she would insist on being with me, and I couldn't risk that. I pulled the last piece of bacon from the skillet, swiped the talk button and braced for the impact, "Hey, Hattie, what's up?"

"What's up?" She was pissed and made no effort hiding it. "I should be asking you that question."

"What are you talking about?" I knew my attempt at playing coy wouldn't work, but I had to try.

"You know exactly what I'm talking about. Why have you been avoiding me?"

"I'm not avoiding you," I protested. I tried to sound believable, but the truth of the matter was . . . I had been. It was bad enough that I was in danger from Malus, there was no way in hell I was going to put a target on her back as well. I would never forgive myself if something happened to her on my account.

"Bullshit," she began, "you're barely answering my phone calls, you rarely call me back, and you cancelled our lunch date. And if that isn't bad enough, you couldn't even do me the decency of standing me up on the phone, you had to do it by text." She took a breath. "So, stop lying and start spilling about what I've done to piss you off."

"Hattie, I promise you haven't done anything to piss me off." I laid the plate of bacon on the counter next to the rest of the breakfast I'd cooked, turned off the stove and went into the living room to sit down for this conversation.

"Then what's wrong?"

"Nothing," I continued to protest. "I've just been really busy. I've been working on a missing person's case." This was partly the truth. She couldn't accuse me of lying about that.

She sat there a moment in silence. I knew what she was doing; she was debating on whether or not to believe me. Finally, she spoke, "I've heard about the disappearances up there. But I've known you since third grade, and you've never been a good liar."

"I really am working on a case," I interrupted as I sat down on the couch and pulled my legs up underneath me.

"Oh, I believe you about that, but there's more to it that you're trying to hide from me. So, what is it?"

It was almost scary how well she knew me. I tried to think of what I could possibly say that would appease her curiosity and keep her at bay . . . for now.

"You're taking too long. Stop trying to think of a lie to tell me. Sooner or later I'll find out, so you might as well be honest about it now."

"Hattie, the truth is . . ." I hesitated, I knew she wouldn't accept what I was about to tell her. "The truth is that I can't tell you the truth."

More silence. I knew that wasn't good. She was right, we had known each other since we were eight, and we knew almost everything there was to know about each other. There were no secrets between us, until now. I'd hoped to evade her until all of this was over, but Hattie was persistent and stubborn by nature, and it was taking much longer to catch Malus than any of us had anticipated.

"Are you in some kind of trouble?" Sometimes I wished her intuition wasn't so right on. Over the years, it had gotten a little eerie at times.

"Hattie, I'm sorry, but I can't let you get involved. As soon as all of this is over, I promise I'll tell you every insignificant detail of what's happened over the last month. But until then, I can't risk you knowing anything."

"You're joking, right?" Great, she was *really* pissed.

"No."

"Do you really think I'm going to sit down here and wait while you're up there in some kind of trouble? I don't think so. I'll be up there in forty-five minutes."

"No!" I almost screamed into the phone. "Hattie, please don't come up here. You're my best friend, and I would never forgive myself if anything happened to you . . . especially if it was because of me."

"Riley, what the hell have you gotten yourself into?" Her anger had dissipated into concern.

"I can't tell you yet."

"Does it involve your case?"

I answered slowly, "Yes."

Another moment of silence. "Okay. I'm not happy about not knowing what's going on or not being able to help you, but if you're this freaked out about it, I won't get involved."

I sighed heavily with relief. Usually she didn't give up that easily.

"But you have to promise me that the moment all this is over, you'll spill everything."

"I promise."

"Now, I'm assuming the police are involved, right?"

"Not exactly." I heard Aiden, now finished in the bathroom, rustling around in the kitchen.

"What do you mean, not exactly? Either they are or are not." Hattie was becoming aggravated again.

"You won't understand, but I can't involve them."

"Fuck that, I'm coming up there."

"No." I protested once again.

"If you're in danger then who's going to protect you?"

I glanced back at Aiden in the kitchen. He was piling up a plate of food. "Let's just say I have it under control."

"And what's that supposed to mean?"

"I can't really say."

"Look, if you don't want me to get involved, then I at least need to know you're safe."

I sighed again and silently debated about whether or not to tell her about Lucian and Aiden. Finally, I decided it wouldn't hurt, just as long as I omitted some obvious details. "Okay." I took a deep breath. "When I started working on this case, I had to go to *Silver Moon* on a lead. I met with the owner, Lucian, and he's been helping me ever since. When we realized I could be in danger, he sent one of his security guards from the club over to stay with me for protection."

"So, you have a bodyguard?"

"Something like that. His name is Aiden, and he's been living with me and working at the office."

Aiden cleared his throat behind me. I turned my head to see him standing there in between the kitchen and living room, holding his plate of food. He whispered, "Who are you telling that to?"

I placed my hand over the phone and whispered as well, "Hattie. I'm giving her just enough info, so she won't try to come up here."

He nodded knowingly and walked back into the kitchen to eat. I'd already told him and Lucian all about my best friend, her quick-trigger temper, and my concerns about her rushing up here if she knew I was in danger.

"Are you okay with him living with you?" Hattie questioned.

"Yes. It's actually kind of a nice change."

She chuckled, "I get it. You must like him."

"I do, but not in the way you're thinking."

"Sure." She snickered.

I laughed with her, more in relief than anything else. If she had switched her concerns from my safety to discussing the new men in my life, then the worst was over, and she was satisfied enough that she wouldn't come barging up here on a white horse to try and save the day.

"I swear! Aiden and I have become good friends, and that's where it ends."

"So, is he single?"

I grinned. "Yes."

"Is he cute?"

Hattie was always on the lookout for a new potential man, despite the fact that her relationships never lasted long. It wasn't because of her, even despite her famous temper. To most men she was a catch, with her beautiful shoulder-length, naturally wavy brown hair, rich brown eyes, and a petite figure. Guys never dumped Hattie, but she *always* found a reason to ditch them. She wanted the perfect man and wouldn't settle for anything less. And since there was no such thing, she was still actively looking. "Very cute," I confirmed.

Ding Dong.

The tingling sensation flooded over my skin, and my heart fluttered knowing who that was. Lucian had just been over the night before, so I wasn't expecting him back already. Actually, he'd been able to come over for the last two nights in a row. He, Aiden, Jimmy, and I'd had a nineties movie marathon one night and spent the other one playing card games. It was so relaxing to be able to forget about all my problems, and I'd managed to not think about Malus at all these past few days—well, until my phone call with Hattie.

"Hello. Riley. Are you still there?"

"I'm sorry, Hattie, but I have to go. Lucian is here."

"Oh, I see. The reason you're not interested in Aiden is because of Lucian."

I drew out the word, with an obvious smile in my voice, "Maybe."

"You'd better tell me all the details about him soon. You can at least do that without jeopardizing my ignorance of what's going on."

"I will. I'll talk to you later, okay?"

"Alright. Good luck and remember if you need anything, call me."

"Thanks." I hung up the phone, raced to the door, and opened it. My breath caught in my throat at the sight of Lucian; his tousled, but always stylishly messy hair glinted in the sunlight, and his dark sunglasses, which were an almost permanent fixture during the daylight hours, upped his sexiness level a couple of notches. Areas low in my body ached, reminding me of just how attracted I was to that sexiness. Tearing my focus from his face, I took in the plain white t-shirt that hugged his chest and threatened to tear with a miniscule flex of his biceps.

Suddenly, the memory of our sensual kiss the other day burst forward into my mind, causing the harmless ache to evolve into a passionate need. Lucian smirked knowingly, which caused my cheeks to highlight my embarrassment. The memory was evidently strong enough for him to receive. I stepped aside to let Lucian enter, and so I could also avert my mortified gaze elsewhere. His seductive smile was too much for me at the moment, and I didn't want him to inadvertently learn about all the fantasies I'd been having of him as well. As it was, it took everything I had from tackling him where he stood.

Lucian casually strolled in with Jimmy right on his heels, nose turned up to sniff the air.

"What's for breakfast?" He gave me an approving smile.

"Bacon, biscuits and gravy, fried potatoes, and scrambled eggs." I gestured toward the kitchen, "I just finished, so it's all on the counter. Help yourself."

"Thanks." Jimmy said as he immediately bounded to the kitchen to start piling up his first plate.

"As you know, tonight is the full moon," Lucian's statement took me by surprise. Somehow, I'd forgotten all about it.

I nodded, "I'll close up early. That way I'll have plenty of time to pack my bags and head straight over to the club."

He sheepishly smiled, looking absolutely adorable. "Actually, I had different plans. Would you like to accompany me to dinner this evening?"

Did he just ask me out on a date? As I struggled to keep my jaw from landing on the floor, I flushed and blurted out the wrong thing—as usual. "You don't have to be at the club tonight?" Only I would, instead of graciously accepting an offer to go out with the hottest and sweetest guy I'd ever met, try to talk him out of it.

Thankfully, he didn't seem put off by my question, "I've hired more employees over last few weeks and enough of them are vampires, so while the wolves are away, I'll be taking the night off."

I pretended to think about it for a minute. "Well, since you're taking the night off, I guess I could go to dinner with you."

He grinned, "So, it's settled, then. Tonight, we'll go to a restaurant, eat, talk, and finally have a chance to get an evening to ourselves."

The thought of *finally* being completely alone with Lucian, with no interruptions, caused my heart to skip a beat. I'd wanted that for so long, and now it was actually going to happen.

"Unfortunately, though, I can't stay right now. I've been out all night tracking, and I need to get some rest before our date tonight."

It was official then—a date. My already flustered heart went into hysterical overdrive hearing the confirmation. It stopped altogether as he leaned in and softly kissed my cheek.

I couldn't move or breathe while Lucian's lips touched my skin. I felt like an unsuspecting deer trapped in a passing vehicle's headlights. The difference though, I enjoyed my entrapment. His lips left my cheek and brushed against my ear, "Until tonight." He pulled back with a smug look on his face, pleased with the obvious effect he continued to have over me.

As he headed for the door, I watched him leave, knowing the next time I saw him would be for our date. After the door closed, I stood there for a moment, digesting what had just happened. I was elated at the thought of my night alone with Lucian, and I knew nothing could get me down today. If only every day could be like that. And maybe it would, once Malus was captured. With that joyous prospect, I headed to the kitchen with a small bounce in my step to see if there was any food left.

CHAPTER 14

After what seemed like hours of trying on, searching, and trying on again, I finally settled on a low-cut, but not low enough that I'd have to worry about my boobs falling out, navy-blue dress. It had a cascading sleeve with the longest length just touching my elbow, a cinched waist with a matching ribbon to extenuate my waistline, and a modest length coming down right above my knees, because let's face it, I didn't wear dresses often, so forgetting I had one on and flashing everyone was a very real possibility.

It was May in Kentucky, which meant the temperatures in the evening could range anywhere from the forties to the eighties, but luckily it was going to be in the low seventies that night, so I wouldn't have to worry about freezing, needing to find a jacket to match the dress, or all the hair growing back on my freshly shaved legs before dessert.

I slipped into my black high heels—which I may or may not have been practicing walking in the entire time I'd been getting ready—and gave myself one final look-over in the floor length mirror. To accompany the dress and heels, I'd styled my long blonde hair and applied more makeup than I usually wore. I had to admit, it wasn't the best smoky-eye I'd ever managed, but for being out of practice, it wasn't bad. Satisfied it couldn't get much better, I grabbed my clutch and went into the living room where Aiden and Jimmy were waiting for the final verdict.

"Wow," They both uttered simultaneously.

I grinned. That was just the reaction I was hoping for. "So, you like it?" I already knew the answer based on their near speechless response, but sometimes a girl just needed a little more of a boost to the ego, especially tonight. It was our first date, and I already knew Lucian was going to look unquestionably divine as usual, so I wanted to make sure I was almost in the same league. Or at least get enough compliments, so I'd feel like I was.

"Are you kidding?" Jimmy asked, "You look amazing!"

"Yeah," Aiden added, "you look incredible."

They would have continued with their praiseful gushing, and I was so not going to stop them, but before they could say anything else, Lucian arrived, ringing the doorbell. I flashed a nervous glance at the boys. Was I ready? Yes and no. Jimmy, sensing my faltering uncertainty jumped up to let Lucian in.

As soon as I laid eyes on him, I felt severely underdressed, as usual—despite my best efforts. He wore designer brown dress shoes, dark denim jeans, and a light weight long-sleeved deep-blue sweater with the sleeves pushed up to his elbows. I knew it was all in my head, but I couldn't help but feel mediocre every time I was in the same room as Lucian. I didn't think there was a single item of clothing he wouldn't be able to pull off and

166

manage to look better in than almost any other person in the world.

"Riley, you are absolutely stunning." Lucian beamed.

I tore my eyes away from his captivating body and focused on his face. He'd taken his sunglasses off, allowing me to see those sparkling emerald eyes, which were crinkled from his glowing smile. He had that, *'I'm the luckiest fucking man in the world'*, look on his face. My cheeks flushed as I said, "Thank you."

Seeing his genuine in-awe expression, and knowing it was all directed at me, erased most of my inferiority fears. For the first time that day, my eagerness for the night was overpowering the nervousness I'd been feeling all day.

Thirty minutes later, Aiden and Jimmy were on their way to meet up with the others, and Lucian and I were pulling into a well-known Italian restaurant. I'd always heard the food was mouthwateringly delicious and had wanted to try it, but I refused to eat alone in a sit-down restaurant, and all the guys I'd went on dates with, so far, hadn't wanted to go somewhere quite so expensive on a blind date.

The restaurant itself was beautifully decorated and had that romantic, someone's getting lucky tonight vibe—but in a classy way. From the endless trailing greenery and strategically placed wisps of lavender to the candlelit tables, strings of white lights adorning the ceiling, and the stucco walls painted in hues of clay and mud-brown, it all came together beautifully.

"Would you like to see our wine list?" The waiter had a thick one-page menu stretched out toward Lucian.

Lucian, never faltering his gaze from mine, asked, "Would you like to look over the selection?"

The waiter shifted his stance, now holding the menu closer to me. "No thank you. I'm not a big wine drinker. Water is fine with me."

Lucian nodded, "Water for her then. As for me, I'd like a glass of Venae."

He glanced up at the waiter, whose shocked expression matched my own. I had a feeling there was still so much I didn't know about vampires. They could eat and drink? And what the hell was Venae? I wasn't a wine expert, but I'd never heard of it before.

"Yes, sir. Excellent selection, sir." The waiter tossed a resentful glare in my direction as he placed our dinner menus in front of us.

When the waiter walked away to fetch our drinks, Lucian spoke, "He's very jealous of you."

"Is that what that look was for?" He nodded. Based on his statement and the amused expression that went with it, I assumed he'd picked something up from the waiter's mind. Curious as to why the waiter would feel that way, I probed, "Why's he jealous of me?"

I didn't bother whispering since Lucian hadn't, either. I didn't think anyone would hear us anyway since we were alone in the room. When we first entered the restaurant, Lucian discreetly slipped money into the host's hand and requested something a little more private. The host graciously slid the bribe into his pocket and led us through the restaurant's crowded dining area and into one of several separate smaller rooms. The room we were placed in was large enough for eight scattered tables, but were all currently vacant except for the one we sat at.

He seated us in the middle of the picturesquely decorated room, which matched the wistful décor of the main dining area. On each table were two pillar candles on either side of a crystal vase that held a single freshly cut red rose. The overhead lighting was dimmed, allowing the majority of the illumination to come from the twinkling strings of white lights and tabletop candles.

"He's jealous because you're with me. He wishes he was in your place."

I sat back in my chair, stunned. "I've never had a guy envious of my date before. Plenty of girls, yeah, but never another man. At least that I know of."

"He's not gay," Lucian stated.

Confused, I asked, "Then why would he be jealous that I'm with you?"

He leaned forward, "Because I'm a vampire."

Intrigued, I mimicked his movement and leaned toward Lucian as well, "How does he know that?"

"Because of the drink I ordered."

Maybe blood was the only option on the menu for vampires. With as much time as I'd spent with Lucian over the last month, I'd never seen him eat or drink. "So, that wasn't wine you ordered . . . it was blood?"

"Yes. This is one of several restaurants in Louisville where you can order it. Milo is a very smart entrepreneur. He owns every restaurant in town that serves blood for their vampire patrons."

"That *is* very clever. Serve it in a wine bottle and we unsuspecting humans would never know the difference." I contemplated that opportunity, "You should do the same at your club."

Lucian flashed a prideful grin.

"You already do, don't you?"

"Yes. We serve it in a dark-red motif cup to disguise the contents."

"So, what if one of us sees the drink and thinks, 'Hmm . . . I've never had that before. I think I'll try it.'?" We had unconsciously continued to lean toward each other, both of us now leaning over the table, our faces not far apart.

"Then they get one. Minus the blood, of course." He reached out with both of his hands to embrace mine. "That's why I only hire vampires as bartenders, so they'll know who to give the blood to and who gets the imitation drink."

I only heard a portion of what he said. His thumbs were tracing small circular patterns on my hands, which sent currents of heat throughout my body. Mischievous thoughts began to swirl inside my head involving the table—and for once, I really didn't care if Lucian knew them.

"Lucian, darling, how have you been?"

Startled by the voice, I jumped, inadvertently wrenching my hands out of Lucian's. I twisted in my seat to see the source of our intrusion and the sudden explosion of tingling throughout my body. A fairly short, slim man waltzed toward us carrying one empty glass, one filled with water, and a wine bottle tucked under an arm. He had shoulder-length curly dark-brown hair and soft, almost feminine facial features. Like most of the vampires I'd met so far, he was exceptionally attractive. Not my type, but attractive nonetheless.

Lucian, who was facing the man, smiled broadly. "Milo, it's good to see you. I wasn't expecting to be served by the owner himself."

He reached the table and placed my water in front of me and the empty glass in front of Lucian. "Please. Any time a good friend comes in, I have to stop by and say hello." He opened the bottle and poured a thick dark substance into Lucian's empty glass. I wrinkled my nose as the smell of blood hit me. It wasn't repugnant, but it was strong, and that surprised me.

Lucian stared at me with concern and shock. I wasn't sure why and was about to ask him when Milo continued, "And speaking of hello, who is this gorgeous woman you're with?" He finished pouring and set the bottle down on the table. Milo took my hand, just as Lucian had on the first night we'd met, and laid a kiss on the back of it.

Milo was bursting with enthusiasm, accompanied by southern charm and a thick Louisiana accent. "I'm Riley. It's a pleasure to meet you, Milo."

"Oh no, darling, the pleasure is all mine." He let go of my hand, and placed both of his on his hips. "Now you have to tell me where on this Earth did Lucian find such a gorgeous woman as yourself?"

His good humor was intoxicating. "Well," I looked at Lucian, hoping he would explain. I didn't know how much the other vampires knew, or were supposed to know about the ordeal with Malus.

"Riley is the private detective I've been working with over the disappearing humans," Lucian answered for me.

I looked back to Milo in enough time to witness a dark cloud pass over his face, devouring the playful spirit for a split second, before slipping away and allowing the flirtatiousness to return. "Well, that's a shame. I thought you finally had a girlfriend."

"Well, old friend," Lucian stole my attention back to him, "tonight is not about business." Lucian's eyes stayed fixed on mine.

"Oh, I see," Milo said slyly, "well then I'll leave you two alone, just as soon as you tell me what you'd like to order."

I had completely forgotten about the unopened menu lying next to my arm. I quickly picked it up, opened it, and chose the first thing that looked appealing. "I'll take the mushroom ravioli."

"Excellent choice." Milo beamed as he relieved us of both the menus. He gave me a quick wink as he grabbed the bottle of blood and silently stalked out of the room.

"Milo is an interesting character." Lucian smiled.

"Yes, but I like him."

"As do I."

"I'm glad we're in a private room, or this would look odd—me eating and you not," I confessed.

"If we hadn't lucked out with this privacy, then I would've ordered something."

"But don't you think someone would notice you not eating?"

He smirked, "No, because I'd be eating."

"You can eat food?" I asked incredulously.

Lucian chuckled at my astonishment. "Yes, I can eat food. Most of us just choose not to."

"Why? Does it make you sick?" Why didn't I already know this? I'd been around vampires for over a month, and I was still finding new things out about them.

"No, but it doesn't taste the same as it does for you. We can taste the flavors, but they're bland. If we find ourselves in a situation, however, where blood is out of the question, eating food will sustain us for a short while."

"But not for long?"

"Unfortunately, no. Restricting our diet to only food will weaken us, and over time, the effects would be devastating." Lucian considered his explanation, "Think of a human surviving on water alone. It would keep them alive for a while, but it wouldn't be long before they'd begin to weaken without the nourishment their body needs from food."

"But in your case, food is blood," I stated the obvious.

"Precisely. Plus, there's one other reason we don't like to ingest food often." A flush rose up in his cheeks as he paused to take his first sip from the glass—was he blushing? "Are you familiar with the old saying, what goes in must come out?"

I burst into laughter, "So, you don't have to use the bathroom unless you eat food?" Lucian hadn't ever excused himself to go to the bathroom in my presence, but I hadn't really noticed or thought about it until that moment.

His laughter joined in my own, "All the blood we consume goes directly to keep our bodies nourished and in top condition. Nothing is wasted. So, there's nothing for the body to expel."

"So, what about drinking other liquids, like water?"

"Same as food, we don't need them. I occasionally drink at the bar for show, but not very much."

"You mean alcohol?"

"Yes," Lucian confirmed.

Intrigued, I asked, "Can you get drunk?"

"Not from drinking alcohol. Our bodies are constantly healing themselves, whether it's from aging or injuries, so we can't get drunk from ingesting alcohol. Our bodies won't allow it."

"But . . .," I added for him.

"But . . . if a human is intoxicated when we consume their blood, then we can feel the effects."

"How can that be possible?" I asked, fascinated.

"Blood is our food, and when we ingest it, it automatically flows throughout our body to sustain and heal it. If that blood is saturated with alcohol, then it flows throughout our body as well, giving us the same effect as humans when they drink it."

"A drunk vampire doesn't sound too safe."

"Depends on the vampire," he said somberly.

"So, if vampires heal so fast, is it impossible for you to die?" We'd touched on this subject briefly, but never in depth. I wasn't sure how resilient their bodies were, and since Malus wanted me, it seemed like a good thing to know.

"No," he confirmed. "Not all vampire lore are myths. Fire will kill us, a beheading, or sometimes, if the vampire is young enough, something punctured through the heart will do the trick."

"Like a stake through the heart?"

"Yes. It is cliché," he took another sip of his drink, "but if it's a young vampire, they won't be able to heal that kind of an injury quickly enough."

"So, do I need to start sharpening some stakes to keep with me?" I asked playfully.

Lucian replied with a smirk, "Depends on who you're planning on staking."

"You know I could never hurt you," I confessed. I knew he was joking, but I wanted to make sure he knew how I felt.

He studied me with his penetrating gaze, "I know."

We continued the conversation with some playful banter, discussing Aiden and his quirky habits and my conversation with Hattie until the food and another refill for Lucian arrived.

It was slightly awkward being the only one eating, so I tried to finish my plate as quickly as possible without appearing to be a pig. We kept up our conversation throughout the meal and when I'd consumed the last bite I could possibly manage, without feeling bloated, I wiped my mouth and leaned back in my chair.

"Can I ask you something?" I asked Lucian. The look he'd given me when Milo brought his blood out bothered me for some reason.

"You can ask me anything, Riley."

"When Milo came out and poured your drink . . ." I hesitated. I wasn't sure how to word what I wanted to say. "You gave me a weird look. I just wanted to know what it was for."

Lucian shifted in his seat. "I thought I picked something up from you, and it confused me a little."

I tried to remember what I'd been thinking about. Milo was talking, so I was taking in his character and determining what I thought about him. "I was deciding whether I liked Milo, but I wouldn't think I was concentrating hard enough for you to pick up any of that."

He shook his head, "No, it wasn't about Milo."

I raised an eyebrow, "Well, then what was it?"

He fidgeted with his glass, "Riley, could you smell the blood when Milo poured it into my glass?"

I wasn't expecting that. I'd had a reaction to the blood, but I didn't think it was a strong one. Lucian regarded me with curiosity in his eyes. "Yeah," I admitted. "Why, was I not supposed to?"

"It's unusual," Lucian began, "humans wouldn't normally—"

Milo walked into the room, interrupting Lucian. "Was your dinner satisfactory?" he asked.

I was irritated at the interruption, but it wasn't Milo's fault. I tried to hide my frustration as I answered, "Absolutely delicious."

"That's wonderful." He picked up my plate and turned to Lucian. "Do you need a refill?"

Lucian held up his hand, "No, thank you."

Milo placed our check face-down on the table in front of Lucian.

Lucian cleared his throat, "Milo, you seem to be acting differently since I mentioned the disappearances. Why is that?"

Milo shifted uncomfortably, "Have I?"

"Yes," Lucian continued to hold Milo's gaze as he placed money under the ticket, "you have."

After a moment, Milo broke his stare to look at my not quite empty plate. "Would you like a box to take the rest home with you?"

"No, thank you." It was evident whatever Lucian hinted at made Milo uneasy. The vivacious charismatic persona from earlier was gone, and it was obvious he was trying to avoid conversation altogether.

"Well, you two enjoy the remainder of your evening." He turned to walk away, but before he could take a step, Lucian was already in front of him, blocking the way.

"He's been here, hasn't he?" Lucian questioned accusingly.

Milo took a small step back, "Why would you think that?"

"Because you're avoiding the question, and I've heard rumors he's been paying a few of the locals a visit." That was news to me. I didn't expect Lucian to keep me informed of *everything* that went on regarding Malus, but something like that? That was an important piece of information that I felt I should've already known.

"Now, Lucian," Milo stammered, "I think you need to drop this business with him."

Lucian's eyes transformed. Still the dazzling emerald hue, but now beholding a florescent luminosity as he closed the gap Milo had intentionally created between the two of them. When he spoke, his fangs were protruding menacingly. "I will not back down. He is killing innocent humans in my territory, and I will not sit back and allow it to happen."

Lucian was furious. I'd never seen him like that before. Every word he spoke was careful, deliberate, and filled with the conviction he spoke of. He was every bit an alpha male right then and it was so fucking hot.

Milo backed up until he fell into Lucian's vacated seat. He placed his face in his hands and began to sob, "I'm sorry, Lucian. I know you can't let him do that, but you have no idea what you're going up against."

As Lucian kneeled in front of Milo, the fury softened from his face. I watched spellbound, as his fangs retracted and the luminescence slowly left his eyes. "I know what he's capable of."

"Then you know why I was scared to tell you about it. Why all of us are scared to even mention it."

"Why don't you tell me about it now?"

Milo nodded, inhaled a deep breath and began, "He came to me one night after work. I didn't know he was there. You can

177

imagine my shock. No one has snuck up on me in two hundred years."

"He's quite powerful," Lucian agreed with a nod of his head.

Milo continued, "He told me he was recruiting vampires. When I asked him for what, he just grinned and said I would find out soon."

A shiver ran through my body. Malus had confessed something similar to me during my unfortunate encounter with him.

"What did you tell him?" Lucian questioned.

"What do you think?" Milo tore his face from his hands to peer at Lucian. "I knew he was rogue. It was written all over him—the sneaking around, clearly not belonging to a House, and he had the crazy vibe going. I told him he needed to clear any recruiting with you first."

"And?" Lucian coaxed.

"He laughed at me," Milo fumed. "That rogue bastard laughed at me and said you didn't matter—that you'd be out of the picture soon." He paused, "He never even waited for an answer from me; he just assumed it was a yes. He said when he was ready for me, I would know. Then he left."

Lucian contemplated for a moment, "You said the others were afraid as well. Did he do the same thing to them?"

"Yeah. Exactly the same to at least three others . . . that I know of. He just appears in front of you, assumes you're going to help him, and then leaves."

Lucian stood and place a hand on Milo's shoulder. "Thank you for your honesty."

"I'm so sorry I didn't tell you sooner. I've just been so shaken up by the whole thing."

Lucian removed his hand from the other man's shoulder, "That's alright. All that matters, is that you did." Lucian walked to me and stretched his hand out for mine. "Are you ready?"

"Yes." I took his hand, stood, and told Milo, "it was very nice meeting you."

He bounced out of the seat, with a somewhat renewed gusto. I think he felt much better getting that off his chest. "No, dear, the pleasure was still all mine." He made a small bow before departing, leaving us alone in the room once again.

Lucian started to lead us out, but I hesitated. He turned to me, "What's wrong?"

While their conversation was still fresh in my mind and we had the privacy the room permitted, I had to ask him, "Do you think Malus is building an army?"

Lucian frowned, "You keep surprising me on how clever you are."

"So, you think that, too? It would explain all the disappearances. If he's building an army, he needs victims to feed them."

"Now," Lucian said, "the question is, what is he building an army for."

CHAPTER 15

T he journey to *Silver Moon* held little conversation. Lucian and I were deep in our own thoughts, both of us contemplating the new development in the slowly unraveling mystery.

The only conclusion I could come to was that Malus was indeed trying to lead a revolt. But against who? The High Council was in Europe, so it didn't really make sense that it was his target. The Low Council for the U.S. was in New York, and there weren't any Houses near enough to Louisville for them to be a target either. Unless, that *was* the plan—being that far away, he could amass his army undetected and then pounce before anyone would even realize what was going on.

There were a lot of *ifs* in that, but it would make sense. And with the way Lucian said Houses and the Domini basically operate on separate systems, and no one shares any information, he could use that against them. He could take out a local Consul or two, and unless someone notified the Dominus, he could operate and build his army undiscovered. There wasn't a BloodGuard unit in this region, so he wouldn't even have to worry about them.

It did make me wonder if he was capable of pulling something like that off. If he managed to intimidate enough vampires to follow him, he might be able to. And even though no one had said as much, a fear was creeping inside me that Malus was more powerful than Lucian. If that was true, would Lucian even be able to defeat him on his own?

I quickly buried that thought. I didn't want Lucian to know how frightened I was about his safety. Maybe having a BloodGuard unit come to the area wouldn't be such a bad idea. I just hoped they could get one here before it escalated any further.

"Here we are." Lucian pulled into the employee parking lot behind the club. He refused to let me carry my overnight bag into the building and thought my attempt to appear aggravated about it was cute.

Lucian turned and went into his office instead of immediately downstairs. He set my bag on the couch. "If you don't mind waiting here for a few minutes, I have to check on a couple of things first."

"No, that's fine."

He left, and I sighed as I settled down on the couch next to my bag. I decided to pass the time by browsing my social apps. I was only a few scrolls in when my vampire radar sent the familiar signals up and down my skin. I looked up from my phone, expecting to see Lucian framing the open doorway, but my smile faltered as I stared into the hazel eyes of a woman.

She was leaning against the door frame with her arms crossed. She appeared to be about my height, with dark hair that trailed down her back, resting just above her hips, and she was wearing the signature black of the bodyguards, only instead of pants, t-shirt, and military style boots her outfit consisted of black jeggings, knee-high lace up boots with a three inch heel, and a black halter top showcasing an impressive amount of cleavage and sculpted arms.

"So, you're Riley?" She spat my name as if it were venom.

I ignored the tone, got up, and walked over to her with my hand held out, "Yes, and you are?"

She looked at my hand with disgust. Even with revulsion underlying her features, she was still beautiful. She had unblemished olive skin, lashes that threatened to reach her eyebrows and full lips which were curled into a sneer, exposing her fangs.

"I don't shake with humans."

I lowered my hand and gave her my best, *'I'm not bothered by you'* smile, "That's okay, I don't mind. So, what's your name?" She was obviously trying to unnerve me, but it would take a lot more than that, and even if she did manage it, I'd never let her see it was working.

"Brianna. I'm one of the new security guards." She grinned, "Lucian tracked me down and asked if I would come here." She paused, her grin widening even more, "How could I tell him no, we are, after all, old lovers." Her faint Spanish accent was more pronounced when she said *lovers*, making me wonder if she'd thickened it on purpose, for my benefit.

My smile quickly mimicked hers, widening as genuinely possible as I could manage, "He is irresistible."

"You have no idea," she said teasingly. "Or do you?" she asked in a mocking tone. "I think not, but regardless, you're right." Brianna knew the intimidation wasn't working, so she was going for the jealous card—which was beginning to work. Staring at the vampiric beauty who had just confessed Lucian had tracked her down personally and that they used to be together, how could it not? I must've done a good job at hiding it, though, because her grin faded.

"Why is this Malus after you anyway?"

I opened my mouth, but then closed it. I didn't know what to say. Obviously, Lucian hadn't told her, and I wasn't sure if there was a reason for that.

"Now, Brianna," Lucian came through the door startling her and me at the same time. I inwardly sighed in relief at his perfect timing. "I've already told everyone, including you, that it's best if you don't know."

He bypassed her without so much as a glance and placed an arm around my waist. I tried to hold back a triumphant smirk, but I'm fairly sure it slipped out a little.

Her eyes narrowed and her nose flared as she spoke, "I just don't see what's so important about a human that someone as powerful as Malus would stop at nothing to have her."

"You wouldn't. You don't see humans as anything more than cattle. And don't forget, it's for your own protection that you don't know. I explained all of this to you before you came. If you're having trouble dealing with this, then you're more than welcome to leave at any time."

After a prolonged moment of silence she replied, "No. I will stay. You're right, I knew the situation before I came and made a promise to you that I'd help." She turned to leave, but stopped

183

midway, "But know this, my loyalties lie with you and no farther." With that said, Brianna stalked out of the room.

Lucian looked at me apologetically, but I waited until we were alone in his underground apartment before I inquired further. Lucian had already placed my bag on his bed, and I'd begun to remove my toiletry items to place in the bathroom. With my eyes occupied on my task, I decided it was the opportune moment to ask. "So," I began, unsure how to phrase my question, "you and Brianna used to date?"

Lucian was seated on the antique fainting couch at the end of the bed, removing his shoes. He was still in my peripheral vision, though, and I could see him tense out of the corner of my eye.

"I should have known that was why she was speaking to you." He stood and came over to me. I kept with my chore, though, seeming not to notice. "She doesn't approve of dating humans, so she was probably trying to make you jealous."

"So, you did date then?" I asked, my voice carrying a nonchalant tone, trying to act like I wasn't as interested in the answer as I actually was.

"Yes, but that was almost fifty years ago and very briefly. Once I discovered how negatively she felt about humans, I couldn't be with her anymore."

I stopped my efforts at pretending to be interested in my belongings and turned to him. "Sorry," I began apologetically, "I know I'm being silly, but she tried to insinuate more than what you said . . . more like you still had a thing for her."

He chuckled, "I can assure you that the relationship I have with Brianna is no more than an old friendship."

I nodded, but still felt unsure about the situation. I believed Lucian when he said there wasn't anything between them, but I was nothing more than an ordinary, mundane human, while she was a stunningly beautiful vampire like him. How could I not feel inadequate in comparison, whether it was warranted or not?

Lucian frowned, "What are you thinking?"

"You don't know?" My smile faltered.

"No, it's a jumble, and I can't decipher it."

I sighed, "It's just . . . I would understand if you wanted to be with her." I returned to my tedious task of unpacking, "And it's not like we're technically dating anyway. You're just helping me out with my case and protecting me from Malus."

Lucian's uncontrollable laughter broke my concentration. "You think I would want her over you?"

"Well, yeah, she's so beautiful." Despite what he'd said before, I still had a seed of doubt. He was a vampire, so why wouldn't he rather be with someone like him?

"But not as beautiful as you are." The laughter had vanished from his lips. I knew I was attractive to a lot of men—with my long blonde hair, unusual gray eyes, a sun-kissed complexion, full lips, and a curvy figure—but I still felt ordinary compared to other women, especially ones as beautiful as Brianna. Deep down, I felt like I simply couldn't compete.

I looked at him now, as he continued. "And I can assure you that you're much better company than she could ever be. Like I told you before, no one can compare to you." A smile slowly formed once more on my lips, hearing his words. "And as far as us technically not dating . . . I thought we were." He moved forward slowly, until there wasn't more than a breath between us, and placed his gentle hands on my waist. I rested mine on his arms, and we kissed as we had the last time, but now with the confidence that there would be no interruptions.

My hands began to explore the detailed muscles underneath his thin sweater, traveling from his arms to his chest. Lucian's lips left mine as he moved back far enough to pull the sweater off, revealing the perfection underneath. He tossed it aside, and his mouth found mine again in enthusiastic desperation; his kiss filled with a fervent need, no different than my own.

I reached behind me to pull the zipper down on the back of my dress, but stopped when I felt a sharp pain sear through my lip. Lucian instantly jerked away, causing me to almost fall, "I am so sorry."

"Sorry for what?" But as soon as the words left my mouth, I saw the blood on his lip. I realized instantly that his fangs must have slipped out, accidently nicking me in the process.

He turned away, panting. "We shouldn't do this, it's too dangerous."

"No." I firmly demanded. I'd waited, what seemed like an eternity for this moment, and I was not going to allow something stupid, like an insignificant nick, to hinder it. "It's fine, Lucian," I managed to say in a calmer tone.

"You don't understand." He faced me again, "I can't control them during moments like this."

I could see them now. Whether Lucian was intentionally allowing me to, or if he didn't really have a choice at the moment, I wasn't sure, but it didn't frighten me. At all. Oddly, it had the opposite effect—it was turning me on even more than I already was. "I don't mind a few nicks."

"But you still don't understand, I might do more than that. Taking blood and intimacy is closely related for vampires, and it's been a long time since I've been intimate with a woman, and I may—"

"Lucian, I don't care," I interrupted. And I didn't. "If you bite me then so what? That's what you do."

I'd actually already thought about it. Ellie had brought it up about a month ago, so I had plenty of time to outweigh the pros and cons. I finally decided that it wouldn't bother me.

"Do you really mean that?"

"Of course." It was getting difficult to concentrate with Lucian and his half-naked splendor standing in front of me. "I've had plenty of time to think about this. If we're going to be together then I want you to."

Lucian once again closed the distance between us, his bare chest brushing against my still-clothed breasts. "How do you know you want me to?"

Looking up into his mystifying eyes, I fought the urge to pounce on him, "I don't know. I just do."

"What if you don't like it, or it makes you feel uncomfortable?" He slowly inclined his head toward mine.

"Then we won't try it again." My voice was thick with lustful promise.

"You are absolutely amazing, Riley." That was all he managed to say before enclosing his lips on mine once more.

A carnal delirium engulfed me entirely, and the next coherent moment where I could focus on anything other than his hands and sultry lips enthusiastically roaming my body, showed me we'd somehow ended up on the bed.

Lucian's pants were undone, and my attire only consisted of my lavender bra and matching bikini-cut lace underwear. Lucian had his back against the massive ornate headboard, with me straddling him. I had one hand on his flawless chest, the other entwined in his sandy hair. I felt his searching hands on my back, followed by my breasts spilling out of my bra. I allowed it to slowly fall off of my shoulders before removing it and tossing it aside. His caressing hands soon found them, as I leaned in for another kiss.

When I pulled back his eyes were filled with the same luminosity as they had been with Milo, only instead of anger saturating them, it was a fiery passion. "Are you sure you're okay with me doing this?" The blatant need in him was as obvious as the amount of restraint he was bestowing by not biting me.

"Yes." I whispered, unable to utter it any louder; I was intoxicated with an overpowering need of my own.

He grinned, showcasing his fangs and leaned forward to take my breast in his mouth. I closed my eyes as he twirled his tongue around my nipple, sending twinges of pleasure throughout my body. I drove my hips down on his hardness, unable to stay still.

"Are you sure?" Lucian asked once more around a mouthful of breast.

"Yes." I whispered again, without opening my eyes.

He began to caress my other breast as I felt his lips open wider and then two sharp pricks. Pleasure erupted from them, drowning everything else out in hypnotic waves. I moaned with desire and satisfaction as I ground my hips onto his pelvis even harder, desperately wishing there were no pants in the way of reaching the hardness I could feel through them.

When Lucian's mouth left my breast and the momentous euphoric grandeur ceased, I opened my eyes to see Lucian's piercing radiant emerald ones. There was a small drop of blood on his lip and without thinking, I leaned forward and licked it off. His eyes widened as he promptly placed either hand on each one of my butt cheeks, hoisted me up, and threw me on the bed. As I landed on my back, I could hear the ruffling of clothing and the clinking of a belt before my panties were stripped off as well.

Lucian was suddenly above me, propping himself up with his arms, careful not to touch me just yet. I slid my hands up his sides and onto his back, pulling him closer to me, forcing him to forgo any teasing. He smirked as he succumbed, pressing his bare body slowly and seductively against mine. Another small moan escaped my lips as his hardness pressed against me. I spread my legs to allow easier access.

He playfully taunted me, however, threatening to slide in at any moment, but never quite accomplishing the task. My surging need swiftly evolved into an ample necessity. I ground my hips up to meet his in an attempt of provocation.

He halted his agonizing teasing and pulled back, ready for penetration. I looked into his illuminated eyes, causing my breath to catch once again. In this moment, all worries involving Malus, or anything else for that matter, were long forgotten—all that existed were me and him.

The delirium was threatening to take hold again as he carefully began to enter me. With each inch he delicately inserted, moans of unimaginable pleasure flowed from my mouth, and my resistance was hastily crumbling. With one final shove, all of Lucian was inside me, propelling my back to bow and allowing the breathtaking delirium to crash through all of the barriers once again and swallow me up in desire.

CHAPTER 16

I blindly searched for my phone, which was stealthily hiding somewhere on the nightstand. At least that's where I thought I left it. It was pitch black in Lucian's bedroom, so I had no idea what time it was or how long we'd been asleep.

My search was frenzied now, trying to answer it before it stopped ringing. I knew more than likely it was just Aiden, but regardless, I didn't like missing a phone call. There it was, "Hello." I promptly answered, my voice coming out groggier than I expected.

"And where are you at this time in the morning?" I hastily cleared my throat to respond, but the stern voice continued. "I already know you're not at home, or at the office. I've tried both numbers." She paused, before continuing with a more subtle, enthusiastic tone. "So, tell me, who is he, and why haven't I heard about him?"

I laughed. She never failed to put a smile to my face. "I can't hide anything from you, can I?"

She replied with laughter of her own, "No. That's what grandmothers are for."

"Well, I can't really talk right now, but I promise I'll call you later with details." There was a moment of silence, which was too long for her. "Mamaw, are you there?"

"Oh, yes, dear, I was just thinking . . . how about you and this mystery boy come down here for dinner tonight?"

"Um, I don't know if that would be a good idea."

She interrupted, "Now you listen to me, anyone who can date my granddaughter can come down here and meet me."

She said it with unyielding finalization, but I wouldn't give up just yet. "I'm sure he would love to meet you, but he has work obligations."

"Nonsense," she snapped. "Who works at night? I won't take no for an answer."

And she wouldn't. My grandmother was notorious for her resolve; once her mind had been made up, that was it. I sighed heavily with defeat, realizing there wouldn't be a way around this. I just hoped Lucian wouldn't mind. If nothing else I could take Aiden with me instead. "Alright, what time do we need to be there?"

"Dinner will be at six. And if you can manage to close up early, you can get down here and visit some before the food's ready."

I smiled at the pure satisfaction her voice held. "Okay, I'll see what I can do."

"Good, I'll see you then."

"I love you, Mamaw."

"I love you, too, dear."

When I hung up the phone, the lights turned on. I squinted for a moment, allowing the blinding brightness to gradually soften. Once my eyes adjusted, I saw Lucian laying on the bed. He was on his side facing me, with his head propped up by his hand.

And he was still completely nude. I realized then, so was I. But that thought quickly vanished as I admired the perfection which was displayed in front of me. My thoughts wandered to the night before. I never knew sex could be like that. I'd always enjoyed it, but what I experienced with him was beyond enjoyable . . . beyond anything I'd ever felt before in my life. Especially the bite. I wasn't sure what I'd expected, or if I even had any expectations, but what I felt in that moment when his teeth pierced my skin and he drank my blood surpassed anything I could've anticipated.

My breasts suddenly ached with the thought of it. I wanted to look down at the marks—to see them on my skin, but I forced my eyes to stay focused on Lucian. "Does it always feel like that when you bite someone?"

He impishly grinned, "Humans usually feel some kind of pleasure, if they want to. It can also hurt, if they're unwilling. But what you experienced, was to a degree I didn't know could happen."

Great, yet another thing that made me different from everyone else. At least this difference was one I could enjoy.

"What time do I need to have you back?" Lucian, sensing my uneasiness, changed the subject.

I checked my phone to see exactly what time it was, eight-thirty. "Shit."

Lucian sat up, "What is it?"

I quickly rolled off the bed to begin picking up my carelessly scattered clothes from the floor. "I need to get home, so I can take a shower."

"You're more than welcome to take one here."

I halted my brash pursuit as my mind began to cultivate devious thoughts.

Me. Lucian. Shower.

The possibilities were delightfully endless. My body ached with need just thinking about it.

"I did hold off on scheduling my first appointment until noon. I didn't want Aiden to have to rush up here after last night."

"Good, then can I join you?"

I looked up at him. He was leaning over the side of the bed grinning, but then so was I. "Sure. Give me a minute, and then you can join me."

I quickly finished collecting my belongings and carried them to the adjoining bathroom. I placed my clothes, toiletries, and other miscellaneous items on the double sink vanity and looked at myself in the mirror. My eyeliner was smudged underneath my eyes, and the eye shadow I'd carefully applied last night was almost completely gone. I took out one of my makeup remover cloths from the travel bag and tediously began to remove what little still remained.

Usually if I wore makeup, I always washed it off before falling asleep, but during the whirlwind events of the night before, washing my face was the last thing on my mind. It wasn't until after I'd finished getting my makeup off and dried my face with a hand towel that I finally noticed the bite marks. I looked at them, intrigued at how the two abrasions appeared on my bare breast. I smiled with the remembrance of how they got there. Places low in my body responded to the memory, impulsively wanting an encore of last night.

I pushed those thoughts away. More would come soon enough and right now, I needed to brush my teeth. Thankfully, Lucian gave me the privacy I asked for while taking care of my human needs and waited until I turned on the water in the shower before he entered the bathroom.

The shower was enormous, boasting more than enough room for two people comfortably. I stepped in, having just enough time to let the soothing warmth of the cascading water envelop my body before Lucian joined me. We stood there for a breath, gazing at each other, both of us well aware and eager for what was about to transpire.

I went to him, placing my arms around him, and pulling him down, so I could kiss him. I didn't stay there long. Eager to explore, I left his lips and leisurely made my way down to the contours of his chest, while my hand found the girth between his legs and began stroking my hand up and down. It had felt large inside me last night, but now that I was able to feel it with my hand and see it, I had to admit he was quite impressive— easily one of the largest I'd been with.

He moaned in pleasure as he forced me to stop, and his lips frantically found mine again. When I felt his hand roaming between my legs, I willingly opened them. He carefully slid two fingers in, triggering the same breathtaking delirium as the night before to resurface, threatening to consume me completely at any moment.

Lucian backed me up against the shower wall and withdrew his fingers. I was only empty for a moment before I was pushed farther up on the wall and felt him entering me with what my body was craving. I was more than ready for him, and he slid in with one quick motion. I wrapped my arms and legs around Lucian and trembled with the feeling of him driving in and out of me.

I leaned my head against the tiled wall and got lost in the ecstasy. Lucian captured my breast in his mouth, intensifying the pleasure. My orgasm was coming fast, and when I felt him bite down, I embraced it.

After our intimate shower and now sporting a new set of matching bite marks for my other breast, I'd spoken to Lucian about dinner. He actually seemed excited to meet my grandparents and a little anxious to pick me up at five to make our trip down to Elizabethtown. I just had to figure out why I wasn't excited about it.

"Hello, beautiful."

I looked up from my computer to see Aiden standing in the doorway. I smiled warmly, genuinely glad to see him, "Well, it's about time." I pretended to glance at an imaginary wrist watch. "You're going to have to get this up-all-night partying under control."

He leisurely strolled into the room, "I know. I promise I'll join a help group."

We both chuckled as he sat down in the chair in front of my desk. For work, he shed his usual t-shirt, distressed jeans, and slip-on boots for a polo, boot-cut jeans and dress boots. I insisted that he didn't have to change his appearance since I didn't, but he swore he didn't mind and actually wanted to dress up a little while working.

No matter what he was wearing though, he was still adorable. Those sky-blue eyes, clean-shaven baby face, and blond hair made him irresistible to the female clients, and I had to shoo most of them out of the office when they started lingering.

"So, did you have a good time last night?" he questioned with a mischievous smirk.

"Yes, I did. What about you?" I changed the subject before the flushing cheeks syndrome I was prone to endure for all matters involving Lucian came creeping up.

"Always do, don't I?"

"So you say." I asked him once what it was like to shift into a werewolf. He said it was exhilarating to be in the wolf-form they turned into; that no words could describe the freedom they felt running through the woods without the limitations the human body had. "Where do you guys go, anyway?"

"Our pack heads down to my grandpa's farm between here and E-town. He's got several hundred acres that our pack can run free on."

"So, your family are werewolves, too?" I asked, surprised. We'd discussed his family and werewolves in general, but I'd never thought to ask how he'd become one.

"Yep, runs in the family."

"So, if you have kids, will they be werewolves, too?"

"More than likely. If the mother isn't, then it slims down the chances, but it's a pretty dominant gene that carries it, so you never know."

Interesting. "So, what if you bite or scratch someone?"

He snorted.

"I'm sorry." I quickly added. "I'll stop asking questions. I didn't mean to pry, I'm just curious."

"No," he responded, the laughter fading. "I'm just surprised you haven't asked these questions sooner."

I averted my eyes. "I wanted to. I just didn't want to pry or make you feel uncomfortable."

"You can ask anything you want."

I looked back to him. "Are you sure?"

"Yeah. I don't mind a bit. Actually it's kind of nice talking about it to someone who isn't a werewolf or a vampire."

I leaned forward in my chair, "So what happens to the person if you bite or scratch them?"

"Well, nothing if they're scratched. But we have a secretion in our mouth when we turn, and if we bite someone it has a chance of getting into their bloodstream. When it does, it bonds with their DNA and alters it."

"So, what about Jimmy? Was he bitten, or does it run in his family as well?"

"Runs in the family, like mine. That's actually how we grew up together. Our families belong to the same pack."

"If you're gonna talk about me, at least wait until I'm not here," Jimmy announced in his southern drawl as he sauntered through the doorway. He grinned his crooked smile, and I thought, not for the first time, how attractive he was as well. His features were more chiseled, with by a strong jawline and hair so dark it was almost black, but as usual, covered by his signature ball cap.

"I didn't know you were here."

"I had to drop him off," he motioned toward Aiden, "since he refuses to get a vehicle. And I had to use the bathroom, so I figured I'd use yours before heading home."

"I'm working on it," Aiden protested. "I almost have enough money saved up to buy my dream truck."

"And what's that?" I asked curiously.

His face lit up, eager to tell me about it. "A buddy of mine has an all original seventy-two truck that's in perfect condition. I've had my eyes on it for a long time, and I've been saving up to buy it from him."

"I don't know why you're bothering," Jimmy playfully said. "Everyone knows those trucks are over-rated." He looked at me, "Eighties models are the way to go."

"Bullshit." Aiden jumped out of the chair. "The seventies are classics."

I was shocked. There was actually something they didn't agree on. I knew they were only teasing each other with playful guy banter, but I wanted to change the subject, regardless. "Are you guys hungry?"

They both looked at each other, then at me, "We're always hungry," they chimed together.

I shook my head in amusement as I picked up my cellphone to order pizza for lunch. It was going to be a short day at the office, but as I began to feel exceedingly nervous about Lucian meeting my grandparents, I knew it would end up being a long day, altogether. At least I had Aiden and Jimmy there to keep my mind occupied until tonight.

CHAPTER 17

"**A**re you sure you want to do this, because you don't have to?" I felt like a broken record. I'd asked him the same question, in different variations, during the entire trip down to E-Town. But as I neared the exit ramp from the interstate, my attempts became more frantic.

"Riley, I'm starting to feel like you don't want me to meet your grandparents."

"No, I just don't want you to have to do this if you don't want to." That was part of the truth. The other was that I'd only brought one other boyfriend home to meet them, and that had been my high school sweetheart.

"Are you sure that's the only reason, because I would be honored to meet them." I glanced over at him as I reluctantly merged onto the exit ramp for E-Town. I decided to be truthful. "You're only the second guy I've ever brought here, so I'm a little nervous."

"If you'd rather wait for me to meet them, that's fine. I don't want to do anything that'll make you feel uncomfortable."

I thought about it for a minute. Despite being anxious about how the evening would turn out, deep down, I did want him to meet my family. I focused my attention on the familiar scenery passing by until I turned onto my grandparent's road. It wasn't far from the interstate, but had somehow managed to stay mostly untouched compared to other parts of the town.

On the north side, mini strip malls, supercenter department stores, and big chain restaurants had taken over. On their side of town, there were gas stations, the occasional fast food restaurant, and subdivisions all snuggled in between farms, untouched wooded land, and aged picturesque farm houses.

I sighed, "It's fine. I'll get over the nerves. I want you to meet them."

"Then it's settled. We'll go through with this, and hopefully, we'll both survive the night."

I chuckled. He had no idea, even though I'd tried to explain, just how true those words might be. He'd be facing down the scrutinizing eyes of both my grandparents, which wasn't an easy thing to do. My older cousin, Jeremy, still hadn't brought home a girlfriend who'd been able to meet all their expectations. And the expectations they held for whoever I dated, were much higher.

I slowed down to pull in the driveway. It was almost a quarter mile ride down the tree-lined gravel drive until it opened to a large clearing where the house sat. The driveway kept going until it reached a distant weathered barn that housed the few tractors my grandfather still kept. Right behind the barn was a small pond where Jeremy and I often fished as children.

I pulled up next to my grandfather's pickup truck and studied the old two-story farmhouse poised in front of us. The cracked and peeling siding had recently been replaced, stripping it of some of the rustic appeal it had acquired over the decades and inadvertently transformed it from the familiar seasoned home of my youth. The front porch hadn't been touched, it ran the length of the house and was covered in a blanket of roving ivy. Supporting the roof were round columns with a carved, detailed railing surrounding them and enclosing the porch.

I heard the wooden screen door slam shut. I looked up and saw my grandparents standing on the porch anxiously waiting for us. My grandmother was in her plain beige blouse and cotton Bermuda shorts, and my grandfather wore his usual short sleeved button-down plaid shirt tucked into his navy pants. I smiled. I hadn't seen them for over a month, and I was glad to be here. I turned to Lucian, "Are you ready?"

He gave my hand a gentle squeeze, "Absolutely." We got out of the car, Lucian wearing dark wash jeans, a gray Henley shirt with the top buttons open, and black sneakers. It was the first time I'd seen him wear casual shoes, and I actually didn't feel underdressed in my faded jeans, t-shirt, and Converse. We got out of the car and barely made it to the porch before I was tackled by my grandparents. It was a whirlwind of hugs, merciless threats of not waiting so long until my next visit, my grandmother embarrassingly proclaiming to Lucian how handsome he was, and her wiggling her eyebrows at me the moment she thought Lucian wasn't looking.

"Well, come on in," she gestured toward the house proudly. My grandfather held the door open, and we walked into the family room.

The main family room still had the original fireplace, ceilings that seemed to endlessly rise, carved moldings along the top of the walls, doorways that were engraved to match the fireplace, and a massive staircase that led upstairs to the bedrooms. To the right of the fireplace, was a television which sat on a small stand. It looked oddly out of place among the old fashioned character of the room, but this was where they spent the majority of their time, and my grandmother rarely missed her soap operas. Scattered about the room were various antique pieces that had either been passed down from generation to generation, or my grandmother, being a lover of anything antique, had bought over the years.

"I'm just so glad you're here." Mamaw gave me another hug. "Dinner's not quite ready yet, so go ahead and have a seat." She motioned toward the furniture. "Make yourselves comfortable." We all congregated to the arrangement of chairs and couches positioned around the fireplace and television. Lucian and I sat on one couch, and my grandparents chose the loveseat opposite from us.

"So, Lucian, how old are you?" my grandmother questioned, eager to learn any and every thing about him.

"Twenty-eight," Lucian answered, with an amused smirk.

"Four years difference." She lovingly looked toward my grandfather. "That's the same age difference between us."

Papaw nodded his head, "Now Lucian," he chimed in on the conversation before my grandmother could continue her questioning. "What line of work are you in?"

Where my grandmother's initial concerns for someone I was seeing were age, looks, and manners, Papaw was more interested in how they earned a living. He was old-fashioned and worried about me finding a man who could financially support me. It didn't matter to him that I was doing fine by myself, he was set in the old ways where a man should be the primary provider.

"I own my own business."

My grandfather's eyebrows rose in interest, "What kind of a business?"

I had hoped we could avoid this conversation. My grandparents were not the biggest fans of clubs or bars. They'd been to a few in their time, but that was long ago, and they didn't agree with what most of them had evolved into.

"I run a nightclub in Louisville called *Silver Moon*."

I braced for the backlash as I watched my grandfather's smile falter. Silence ensued upon us as he contemplated Lucian's profession. Finally he spoke, "A smart and profitable business owner will always follow one rule," he paused, "supply and demand. I reckon there's plenty of need for those clubs up there, and if you're not going to profit off of it, then someone else will." Papaw may have been old-fashioned, but I'd underestimated his practicality.

"Yes, sir, I couldn't agree more," Lucian replied. Both of my grandparents were smiling broadly and seemed content. So far, despite the fact he owned a club, he'd passed. I sighed with relief.

A faint ding sounded in the kitchen. Mamaw promptly stood up. "I hope you're hungry. Dinner's ready."

Dinner was interesting, to say the least. I had been around Lucian for over a month, and it was the first time I'd seen him eat food. I tried not to stare, but it was hard not to. I was genuinely impressed at how naturally he appeared to eat his food. He even made sure to compliment everything he sampled, flattering my grandmother in the process. I kept waiting for my grandparents to notice something different about him, but they never did, and dinner was a complete success.

"I like him a lot," she whispered.

I stopped drying the plate that my grandmother had handed me and looked at her. We were in the kitchen, cleaning up the dishes, while the guys went off to discuss guy things.

"I'm glad." I hesitated before adding, "I do, too."

"I have an inkling it's more than that." My silence and ever widening lovesick smile confirmed her assumption. Pleased with her intuition, she took another plate from the stack and began washing it. "Now listen, you leave the dishes to me, and you and Lucian go outside for a nice stroll before the rain sets in."

I'd forgotten about the storms. It was still May, which meant we were right in the middle of storm season in Kentucky. The last fragments of the bitter winter were being pushed out by the warm advances from the south, which produced our yearly spring thunderstorms. "Are you sure?"

"Oh, yes, dear. Go on and enjoy yourselves."

"Thank you for dinner." I gave her a big hug. "Where did Papaw take Lucian?"

"Where do you think?" she said smugly.

"Oh, no." I muttered as I ran out of the kitchen, through the dining room, and into the family room. I paused in the doorway as my fear was confirmed—Papaw was showing Lucian his prized gun collection.

"It's important to protect your home from intruders of all sorts," my grandfather explained, as he carefully unlocked the cabinet that held his prized possessions. Lucian was patiently standing there with an amused expression.

"Excuse me. Sorry to interrupt, but Mamaw wanted me to show Lucian around outside before it starts to rain."

Papaw went from blissful to disappointed in a split-second. He looked from Lucian to the gun cabinet and back. "Oh, alright." He sighed in defeat and hesitantly locked it back.

I motioned for Lucian to follow me, and I led him outside. The wind had already picked up, and the temperature had dropped. Menacing clouds replaced the clear radiant sky we'd enjoyed on the drive down. There was about an hour left of daylight, but with the murky storm clouds obstructing the sun's last rays of light, it seemed closer to dusk than it really was. My grandmother was right, it wouldn't be long before it would begin raining.

Once we were a safe distance from the house, I spoke, "I'm sorry about the gun thing."

He smiled warmly, "Don't be. Your grandfather loves you very much and was only making it clear that he'll protect his family at all costs." Lucian leaned down for a kiss, but stopped halfway as a strong gust of wind swirled around us, twisting and whirling my hair in its path. He started to panic and frantically glanced around us.

"Lucian, what is it? What's wrong?"

He hesitated his frenzied search, giving me the full extent of his worried stare. "Malus is here."

CHAPTER 18

O n my drive back to Louisville, I went over the events that had just occurred numerous times. I was still in shock; Malus had followed us down to my grandparents' house, and now he knew where they lived. As long as he was still alive, they'd never be safe. At any given moment, he could kidnap and use them as leverage, forcing me to do his bidding. Lucian promised he'd have people go down and watch their house until they could capture Malus.

Unfortunately, my grandparent's home was in an area where there was little to no cell signal available, and Lucian was adamant that he should stay there to lessen the chances of Malus escaping again. After much persuading, I finally managed to convince him to let me drive back home by myself, on the condition I called Avery as soon as I was able to get a signal and explain what happened.

I also had to call Aiden and drive straight to my apartment where Aiden and Jimmy would be waiting in the parking lot to protect me. So far, the plan had gone smoothly. The hardest part was leaving my grandparents. I was worried about them and didn't want to leave.

I used the weather as an excuse for our early departure. I told them I didn't want to drive through the storm and needed to get home before it hit. They reluctantly agreed that leaving early would be for the best but made me promise I'd return as soon as my schedule would allow it.

Lucian left with me for appearance's sake, but once we reached the end of the driveway, he got out of the car and circled back around to begin the hunt for Malus. I made him promise he wouldn't try to take on Malus by himself.

Avery, several werewolves, and a few vampires were already on their way to Lucian's aide. Aiden and Jimmy were completely filled in on what happened as well and were waiting on me. I was only about fifteen minutes away from my apartment. It had already began to sprinkle, but I should make it there before the heavy rain began.

My cell phone rang. I picked it up, desperately hoping Lucian had somehow gained a signal, but it was a number I didn't recognize. I sighed with disappointment as I swiped, accept. "Hello?"

"Riley Hunter?" a girl asked.

"Yes."

"It's Amy, Jessica's friend. We met at the game store."

"I remember. What can I do for you, Amy? Did you remember something useful for the case?"

"No, but I have better news." She barely contained her excitement.

"Okay, what is it?"

"Jessica called me!" she shrieked.

"What?" I had to have heard her wrong.

"Yeah." She giggled. "It turns out she did run away with that guy, Ben. But she got tired of him and came back."

"Back to Louisville?" That sounded suspicious. If Jessica really was back, she had to escape from Malus first—which seemed doubtful.

He *was* preoccupied with me at the moment, though, and not anywhere near Louisville, so I guess it was a possibility. It would make sense that she wouldn't tell Amy where she'd really been the past month over the phone, if she'd even tell her at all. Being held prisoner by an unstable vampire wasn't exactly something to share with just anyone.

"Riley, are you there?"

"Yeah. Sorry, what did you say?"

"She's in Louisville right now. She's actually on her way to my apartment. She said she needed a place to stay for a few days."

"Where do you live?" She relayed the location of her apartment, which was only five minutes from where I was on the interstate. "Listen, Amy, I want you to be careful, okay? I'm going to pick up some friends, and we'll be over there as soon as possible."

"Why would I have to be careful? It's just Jessica."

"Look, if she gets there before us then watch for anything strange. And you call me, do you understand?"

"I guess. I don't see why you're freaking out, though." She paused, "Oh, she's here. I've got to go."

She hung up before I could say anything else. I hoped Jessica's sudden appearance was because she escaped from Malus and needed someplace to hide for a while. Obviously, he knew where her grandmother lived, so she'd want to go someplace else to stay.

But what if she hadn't escaped? It'd been over a month since she disappeared. If she was meant for food, wouldn't she be dead by now? I'd stayed hopeful of finding her, but I had often felt the chances of finding her alive would be slim at best.

I'd spoken to Mrs. Greenwell several times since our first meeting, but I'd never told her what I really believed—that Jessica was dead.

I tried to call Aiden to tell him about the new development and to propose the three of us investigate the situation, but he didn't answer. Neither did Jimmy. Shit. I tried the house phone, the office, and Aiden again—still no answer.

What was I supposed to do? What if Amy was in danger? What if the reason Jessica was still alive was purely because Malus had turned her into a vampire and she was a part of his malicious plan?

I had no choice. The exit to Amy's apartment was approaching. I knew Lucian would be pissed, but I had to check on Amy. Jessica was already there, which forced me to make a quick decision and didn't give me enough time to contact Aiden and Jimmy first. If Jessica had managed to escape from Malus, still human, she was going to need medical attention. I exited the highway at the exit before mine—the one that put me on a direct route to Amy's apartment.

I tried Aiden's cell, the house phone, and Jimmy's cell numerous more times until I reached Amy's apartment complex, but they still didn't answer. Frustrated and worried about why they weren't answering, I finally left a message on Aiden's voicemail before stuffing my cell phone in my pocket and getting out of the Jeep.

Luckily, the rain had subsided for a moment, but the gloomy clouds overhead were saturated, threatening to downpour at any moment. I just hoped my luck didn't run out with the weather.

Only a few rays of light were escaping through the clouds, signaling the onset of night once they swallowed them entirely. If Jessica truly was a vampire, there wouldn't be any aid from the sun hindering her abilities. I paused outside Amy's door. What if she was a vampire? What could I do to stop her? I'd witnessed a sampling of their strength and agility from Lucian and Malus, and I was no match.

With realization of the danger I could be in, I suddenly second-guessed my decision in coming alone. I wanted to help Amy, but I was no match for a vampire. I needed to get the boys first. I hadn't seen werewolves in action yet, but I knew they'd be a much more suitable opponent for a vampire than I could ever dream of being.

As I debated my dilemma the warning tingling sensation urgently spread throughout my body. Without hesitation, I turned to run back to the Jeep, but the door to Amy's apartment opened. Before I could turn back around to see who was there, something struck me on the back of my head.

My vision swirled, and I saw the ground moving closer to me. A shrill laugh filled the night as I fell. I tried to brace myself for the impact, but the whirling darkness took my vision over completely before I hit, and I knew no more.

CHAPTER 19

An excruciating headache consumed me when I woke up, causing a crushing wave of nausea to engulf me. Through the pain and queasiness, however, I could tell I was laying down. I tried to sit up, but realized instantly that was a mistake. I immediately began vomiting.

Once I finally managed to stop heaving up my dinner, I opened my eyes, thankful to see I managed to miss myself entirely. I looked around briefly to see it had landed in a pile of straw next to me. With my head still spinning uncontrollably, threatening to make me sick again without a moment's notice, I closed my eyes, waiting for the wooziness to diminish.

I wasn't sure how long I stayed there with my eyes closed, but when I slowly opened them again the dizziness had mercifully subsided. The pain, unfortunately, was still there, but it had lessened enough, so I wasn't having surges of nausea, and I was able to fully take in my surroundings for the first time.

It was a small enclosed area that I found myself in, completely surrounded on all four sides by aged lumber. Three of the walls traveled all the way up to a low ceiling, while the fourth wall was only around four feet high. Light from somewhere outside my room trickled through the open area, giving enough visibility for me to see.

I was in a barn stall. Straw was strewn across the dirt floor and there were two sleeping bags unrolled side by side on the opposite end of where I sat. Several food wrappers and trash were scattered everywhere.

I knew I'd been taken to the hideout Lucian and his men had been searching for—the one that belonged to Malus. It was a vampire who knocked me unconscious at Amy's apartment, whether it was Jessica or a vampire who was after her, I wasn't sure yet. Either way, I knew I had to escape from there and fast.

After a few unsuccessful attempts, I finally managed to get up to my feet. Fearing I'd get sick again, I stood there a moment, letting myself adjust to the new position. Once I was certain I could walk, I checked my pocket for my cell phone. It had been removed. I figured as much, but I had to make sure. I walked over to the stall door and slowly poked my head out and peeked around.

I was in an old horse barn, and it looked oddly familiar, but I discarded that thought. There were hundreds of horse barns in the state of Kentucky, and I bet most of them looked similar to one another. I'd been in several myself, and other than small differences, the interiors were basically the same.

I looked across the barn at the other row of stalls and saw a loft overhead. The area in between the stalls was about twenty feet across, and without a loft in the center, was open all the way to the top of the barn. There was a row of light fixtures hanging down the center of the ceiling, but only the one in the middle of the barn was on, casting just enough light for me to see.

A table and four chairs sat in the center of the barn directly under the light. I looked to my right and counted ten stables to the end of the barn, to my left were four until the open doors which led into the night.

Relief swept through me when I saw it was still night. It gave me hope I hadn't been unconscious for too long. I focused on the wall next to the doorway where I could see an array of miscellaneous objects hanging. There were horseshoes, a pitchfork, and several other items I couldn't distinguish with the limited lighting, but seemed like they could be potential weapons.

With a developing plan forming, I looked around again and listened for any noise that would indicate I wasn't alone in the barn. Nothing. I carefully hoisted myself up and over the gate, trying to be as silent as I possibly could. Just because a vampire wasn't within range of triggering my radar, didn't mean I was out of their hearing range.

Crouching, I crept toward the prospective weapons, while also trying to listen for a sign someone was in the barn with me.

"Ugh." A faint moan to my immediate left startled me. I froze, not sure what my next move should be. When another agonizing moan sounded, I suspected it was coming from someone else who'd been dumped there. Not wanting to leave another victim behind, I peered over the stable door. A gasp caught in my throat as I saw Amy laying in the middle of the stall. It looked like she'd been knocked unconscious as well, and was beginning to wake up.

I silently cursed. I knew I needed to get out of there as quickly as possible, but I couldn't leave her there. I was in this predicament because I wanted to protect her, and I wasn't about to stop then. I started to unlock the gate, but stopped. I needed a weapon first.

I was vulnerable, and would be even more so once I had Amy in tow. I crouched back down and apprehensively approached the wall where the prospective weapons hung. Other than the pitchfork and horseshoes, there were several other farm tools, some of which were familiar to me, but I couldn't remember their names.

I quickly glanced over all the possibilities, but once I spied the machete, my decision was made. All the other items were hung from hooks, except for it. The machete rested on a board that was littered with small antique oil cans and spanned the length of the wall.

I carefully picked it up and examined it the best I could with the faint light. The lamp from the barn ceiling wasn't bright enough to light that area very well, but it looked like it had been recently sharpened. Just the feeling of holding a weapon in my hand boosted my confidence. I knew I'd probably never win against a vampire, but having the machete made me feel like I had a fighting chance.

With my newfound optimism, I went back to the gate and checked the latch for any rust. There wasn't any, so I was able to slide it open without making much noise. I left the door ajar and swiftly ran over to Amy.

"Amy," I whispered, as I knelt beside her. "Can you hear me?"

Her only response was another moan. I reluctantly laid the machete down next to my feet and gently shook her shoulders.

Her eyes popped open and frantically searched around until she focused on me.

"Shh," I warned her before she could say anything. "Can you sit up?"

She nodded, and with my help she sat up.

"I'm so sorry," she whispered. "I should have listened to you. And now because of me, you've been dragged into this." Tears welled up in her eyes.

I didn't even bother explaining I would've been in the situation sooner or later, with or without her help. "It's okay. Don't cry." I grabbed the machete and stood up. "We're getting out of here, but in order to do that, you have to stay calm. Can you do that?"

She nodded and stood.

"Good. Now listen carefully. Right beside the door are old farm tools. We're going to walk right by them. I want you to pick one quickly, then we'll get out of here."

"Where are we going to go?"

"I don't know. I don't even know where we are, but it looks like this is where they've been living. So, we need to get as far away from this place as possible. We'll keep going until we find a house and I can use the phone to call for help."

I didn't wait for a response. I turned to exit the stall and expected Amy to follow. Before walking out, I peeked around the gate to make sure we were still alone.

"Riley," Amy hesitantly whispered.

I glanced back at her.

"What Jessica said about vampires is true, isn't it?"

215

She was frightened. I couldn't blame her, so was I. At least I'd had the last month for the knowledge that supernatural beings existed to sink in. She was having to process it in a matter of minutes, "Yes."

She nodded, averting her eyes to the floor, "And that's who took us?"

"Yes."

She nodded once more, "So, now we have to escape from their nest?"

"Yes." Amy looked at me now. She was still frightened, but in the dim light I could see something pass into her eyes—determination; a will to survive. "Okay, then I'm ready."

I smiled with a newfound respect for Amy. It took a lot of courage for her to accept our situation with the resolve she'd just shown.

I turned and led the way to the wall of tools. Amy quickly chose a pair of gardening shears before we stepped into the open doorway of the barn. The muggy, damp atmosphere indicated the storm was over, and the rain had ceased. The ground was drenched, and a light fog had set in due to the temperature drop.

I had no tingling sensation, so I assumed the area was vampire free for the moment, but who knew how long that would last? We needed to hurry. I stuck my head out into the night, inevitably exposing it, but I needed to get an idea of the area. As I looked out into the barn lot, despair and astonishment shot through me, and my knees abruptly became weak.

Through the fog-infested night, I recognized the area at once. The reason I thought the barn looked familiar wasn't because they all looked the same . . . it was because I was standing in the middle of the farm that was only five miles down the road from my grandparent's house.

CHAPTER 20

I'd traveled to that farm, formerly owned by Mr. and Mrs. Jones, countless times as a child with my grandparents. Whether it was social visits with laughter and card games, or my grandparents lending a hand to good friends on their farm, I had many fond memories of that place.

Mr. Jones passed away about seven years ago from a heart attack, and Mrs. Jones followed him into the afterlife within the following year. After the Jones' passing the ownership of the farm went to their two children, but they didn't want the responsibility and hard work that came with it, so they rented it out. The current tenant must have been Malus, and he was using the vacant stables for his followers to sleep in.

The only sounds saturating the night air were the chirping of crickets and the croaking of frogs. It was a tranquil sound that I missed and was often my lullaby as a child. I would open my window every night in the summer and fall asleep to their chorus.

I couldn't see signs of anyone through the haze, so I inhaled a deep breath and stepped out into the moonlight. As I looked at the familiar farm—the black picket fence which lined a pastured field and the dirt driveway that traveled through the woods and toward the house—all the facts we'd learned over the last month came together and made perfect sense.

Amy had mentioned mud on Jessica's car and an hour drive to the meeting place for the vampire cult. The driveway was gravel from the road to the house, but from the house to the barn it was only a dirt path large enough for vehicles and tractors to pass through. Lucian caught Malus' scent near my grandparents' house, not because he followed us, but because the entire time Malus and his followers were only minutes away. Unease swelled throughout my body as I thought about how near they'd been to danger the whole time.

If I was going to get us out of there, I needed to remain calm and focused. I hastily thrust all my uneasiness and feelings aside and concentrated on the situation Amy and I were in. "Watch for anyone and keep up, we're going to run."

I didn't wait for Amy to respond. Without delay I began to run down the side of the barn, along the fence row and straight for the woods. The sooner we could get out of there and get access to a phone, the better.

The ground squished underneath our feet, and I cringed at the noise—it would alert anyone listening for our escape. I kept telling myself that if we could just make it to the trees and out of the open sight of the pastures, we would be okay. I tried to run as fast I could without falling; I was terrified I would fall and land on the machete I carried.

Fifty more feet. Forty five. Forty. Thirty. An explosion of tingling consumed my entire body, nearly immobilizing me in mid-run, but somehow I continued. Twenty. I glanced back and saw an empty pasture. Amy was gone. Reluctantly, I stopped and turned toward where she should've been. Did she fall? How long had she not been following me? I knew she was behind me before the warning sensation, but once it began, it drowned everything else out, including her footsteps.

"Are you looking for this?" a voice called from behind me. I spun around to face the woods once again.

There was Amy, determination completely stricken from her face and replaced by fear and bewilderment. A hand came up from behind to cover her mouth, and an arm was wrapped around her shoulders holding her in place. I followed the path of the arm to see Jessica. But this wasn't the innocent, smiling version I'd seen in her picture, this Jessica was filled with disdain and wore a scowl.

I tightened my grip on the machete. "Hello, Jessica." Her scowl transformed into a malicious grin, revealing fangs. At least I knew who had knocked me out.

"Look, if you want me, fine, just let Amy go and leave her out of this."

"I don't want you," she snorted, "my master wants you." She regarded Amy, whose eyes had somehow managed to expand twice their size, longingly. "But I want her."

"You could really kill your best friend?"

"I'm not going to kill her. I'm going to turn her. Malus still needs more vampires before we can continue."

"Continue with what?"

She glared at me, "You'll find out soon."

A surge of fire erupted along my skin, sending me cringing to my knees. I'd never experienced that level of pain before with my warning ability. We must've been besieged by vampires for me to undergo the sensation to that magnitude. The tingling had morphed into a ruthless pain that radiated throughout my body, and drowned out everything else in its wake. I closed my eyes and concentrated, I had to force it to stop.

Over the last month, I'd noticed the sensation which warned me when a vampire was near usually died down, or disappeared altogether once I registered visually where the vampire was. But the fog was growing denser by the minute, so I knew I wouldn't be able to see all of them. I pleaded for the pain to stop and miraculously, it did.

The unexpected relief of pain was just as staggering as the abrupt eruption of it. I swayed on my knees, catching myself with my hands. I opened my eyes. Jessica's loathing glare hadn't faltered and neither had her restraint on Amy. Two men were now standing, one on each side of Jessica, and the one to her left had claw marks down the side of his face.

Lucian, I suddenly thought. He must be nearby with some of the werewolves. Amidst all the trepidation and uncertainty, it hadn't occurred to me that where I'd left Lucian a few hours ago was only a short distance from here. I couldn't believe I'd forgotten.

A newfound hope and optimism filled me as I slowly stood again. I scanned the areas to my left and right, trying to decipher the silvery shadows. I could distinguish five more human shapes, but I knew that couldn't be all of them. I'd been around a similar count of vampires when I'd been at *Silver Moon,* and I'd never experienced the sensation to that degree before. There had to be others beyond my vision in the concealing fog.

I wasn't sure what was preventing Lucian and his men from finding this place, but I hoped with this small gathering, they would now. All I had to do was buy enough time for them to stumble on it. "If I'm going to know soon enough, then why not just tell me now? It's not like I'm going anywhere."

The wounded man laughed. "No, you aren't. I know you're hoping your boyfriend will save you, but we took care of him and his pet dogs."

The blood drained from my face.

"How sweet, Ben," Jessica chimed in with the same shrill laughter I'd heard outside Amy's apartment before I lost consciousness. "She thought her boyfriend would save her."

"He's dead?" I whispered.

Jessica snorted again. "Not yet, but soon. Once our Master returns and takes care of you, then he'll finish him off."

Relief once again swept through me, and I released the breath I hadn't realized I'd been holding. "Where is he?"

"On a wild goose chase." Ben grinned. "Lucian and his pets attacked us, but we got away. Malus is leading them far away before he returns to make you one of us. Once that's done, he'll hunt Lucian down and kill him."

"Why not just kill him now?" If Lucian was alive, there was still hope of him finding me.

"Because turning you is more important than killing him. A fight could last a while, and he can't afford to waste time where you're concerned."

"Waste time for what?"

"For my plan, of course." I froze, recognizing the silken voice immediately.

Still clothed in the same attire as I'd last seen him, he appeared to be a ghostly dramatization emerging through the fog behind Ben. Malus stopped next to him, "An excellent job at catching her, Jessica."

Jessica looked at Malus in adoration, "Thank you, Master."

Malus began walking over to me, "I do apologize for the circumstances on how you arrived, but you didn't leave me any other option." He stopped just out of my weapon's reach. "If you didn't have constant surveillance, we could've handled this more civilly." He walked around me slowly, but remained far enough away where I couldn't easily catch him with a swipe of the machete. It took everything I had to keep my eyes straightforward on the three vampires in front of me and not follow Malus as he circled me.

"It's fortunate that you and Lucian came down here. I was listening, you know. I was careful to stay just out of distance from triggering your unique gift. Unfortunately, Lucian caught my scent. But that worked out to my advantage in the end." He faced me once again.

"How is that?" Just a little more time and Lucian would be here.

He sneered, "Once I heard you'd be on your drive, I sent Jessica to Amy's apartment and Ben and a few others to capture your live-in dog. I was going to capture you after we took out the wolves, and use Amy as bait later, if need be. I hadn't expected her to call you before Jessica arrived," he shrugged, "but all the same, you're here, and that's all that matters."

My heart skipped a beat, Aiden and Jimmy. That's why they hadn't answered the phone. "Where are they?"

"His friend was beaten and left for dead in the parking lot. But don't worry, your pet dog won't meet the same fate. I won't kill him. I need him for leverage, so you'll cooperate." Malus snapped his fingers. I heard movement to my right. I immediately turned, no longer worried about the vampires, my only thoughts on Aiden and Jimmy.

The visibility was limited in the misty fog, so I wasn't sure where they came from, but I could see five distinct figures coming closer. Two vampires were on either side of Aiden. He was in the middle of the group, bound by his wrists and ankles, gagged, and a naked bloody mess.

They threw him down at my feet. I fell to the ground and removed the gag. "Aiden, are you okay?" I desperately pleaded. I could see the extent of his injuries now. There were countless scratches, bite marks, and portions of flesh missing from his shoulders and chest.

He didn't answer. I checked his pulse—it was weak, but still there. Tears streamed down as I faced Malus, "You bastard."

"I admit, it's not the best way to gain your loyalty, but as long as you do what I say I'll keep him alive. I'll even do you one more favor and spare your Lucian, as well." Malus grinned. "You see, I've learned over the years, fear is the best means for achieving your goals."

I would do anything in my power to protect Lucian and Aiden, even if it meant this. "You obviously have me in a position where I have no choice but to do what you want." I stood. "So, what is this great goal you're attempting to accomplish?"

"Simple. I'm tired of hiding what I am. It's time the world knew about my kind."

That's what all this had been about? He wanted to out vampires? "So, why the dramatic following? Why not just go on national television and reveal what you are?"

"Oh, I plan to." He smiled, flaunting his fangs. "But revelation is not good enough; humans need to fear us again."

"You don't think there would be frightened people out there?" I asked incredulously.

His smile vanished as his eyes changed. "Your people have turned their fear of us into a romantic wanting. We're not seen as frightening creatures of the dark anymore, but hopeless romantics who will woo you and capture your heart." His anger was insatiable. "With my faithful followers," he gestured toward the two dozen or so vampires that now congregated around us, "in one week, we'll be ready to storm a public televised event and slaughter everyone in our path."

The vampires had surrounded us, encircling Malus, Jessica, Amy, Aiden, and me. Ben and the other vampire that had first appeared with him had melted into the ring of the enclosing vampires. They were all cheering and clinging to every word Malus spoke. It was clear he'd brainwashed them, and they truly believed they should go through with Malus' plan.

Malus continued, "That will be the beginning of our new reign over the humans. With fear in their hearts, they will succumb and obey us. Then they'll be our servants, while we rule the world, as it should be."

He came closer, raising his hand to trace down the side of my cheek, sending unnerving chills down my spine. "You cringe at my touch." His hurtful eyes lost the luminescent glow momentarily before returning with confidence. He smugly stated, "That won't last long. Once you're a vampire, you'll understand."

I averted my eyes. There was no way in hell I'd ever warm up to him. "Why turn me then? Why can't you just kill me or let me go?"

"I know you'll be powerful. Why wouldn't I want someone with your potential at my side? Your gift will be useful when dealing with the other vampires that would try to make us fail . . . human-loving filth like your Lucian. Plus, if you are who I think you are, it'll be easier to get certain vampires on board."

Did Malus just confirm my suspicions? That my father had been a vampire? Ellie said someone who was Born had until twenty-five to go through the Becoming, so had it just not happened yet? Or was I one of the children of a human and vampire that wouldn't go through that process at all? I still didn't see how my father could've been a vampire, and until I saw proof, I was going to assume it was all a coincidence.

The vampires tightened their circle around us as Malus continued, "With a large enough army, the humans will be our slaves. We'll rule the world, and the High council will have no choice but to adhere to my will." He glanced at Jessica, "It's time."

Jessica's canine's elongated, and her eyes changed. Without hesitation, she sank her teeth into Amy's unsuspecting neck. Amy flinched and tried to struggle.

"Do not resist," Malus warned. "It'll only cause unnecessary pain." Helpless to do anything, I refused to watch. I shifted my focus to the encompassing vampires. All of their eyes had changed as well, and they were staring at Jessica and Amy with envious hunger.

A thunderous howl erupted nearby, causing panic amongst the eager group. Jessica tore away from Amy, blood dripping from her mouth. She looked to Malus. "Hurry, finish it," he hissed.

Lucian was coming to save us.

Malus turned to me, "He will not stop me." More howls nearly drowned his words. "You will be mine." He hoisted me up swiftly, cradling me against his chest, and ran. The vampires scattered with confusion and mayhem, clearing a path for Malus to pass through. I tried to see over his shoulder, desperate to see Lucian, but the fog had become too dense to distinguish anything that far away; I could only hear the battering sounds of multiple struggles and threatening snarls.

I gave up trying to see behind us and looked ahead. We were passing through the tree line I was so desperate to reach only a few minutes ago. Instead of a safe haven, it now felt like I was crossing into my doom. I closed my eyes in defeat. Soon, I would be bound to Malus forever, and would never see Lucian.

I clenched my fists in frustration and realized I still had a firm grip on the machete. Hope surged through me. Malus had either forgotten I still had it, or he didn't think I would have the courage to use it. If it was the latter, he was so wrong.

It was gripped in my right hand, the one farther away from his body, and was in the perfect position to strike a blow to his chest. I inhaled a deep breath, focused on my target, and prepared to plunge it in.

Suddenly, something crashed into us, flinging me from his arms and slamming me into a nearby tree. The breath was knocked out of me, and my vision faltered. I shook my head, and once I could focus again, I saw Malus fighting an enormous wolf-like creature a short distance away.

It was poised on two hind legs, but there was an awkward bend in them, that suggested the creature could easily run on all fours. The hands were similar to a human's, but much larger, and they had long, curved claws. The werewolf was swathed in a coat of black hair, which wasn't as thick as a dog or a wolf, so you could catch glimpses of skin underneath the thin layer of fur. The face was more animalistic than human, but had a shorter snout than a canine and lengthened, pointy ears.

Malus was just out of reach of every swipe with its claws and its teeth glistened through each aggravated snarl. I don't know how long I laid there and watched them. I was scared to move, afraid I'd draw attention to myself. I didn't have any superhuman capabilities, and I was encased in a cluster of vampires and werewolves. Until I saw Lucian, my goal was to stay under everyone's radar and out of trouble. Plus, I wasn't sure I could move yet, even if I wanted to. I had collided with the tree hard.

Jessica came running up to aide Malus in the fight and leapt on the werewolf's back. She didn't have time to do any damage though, because no sooner had she landed on the creature, she was yanked off by another werewolf who'd joined the fight. I decided to use the turmoil to my advantage and silently make my escape. When I managed to get on all fours, I spied the machete only a few inches away from my hand. I grabbed it and stood on my first try. There was definitely going to be bruising, but I didn't think anything was broken.

Ben was next to make an appearance, but instead of immersing himself in the fight, he spotted me and dashed in my direction. I was only armed with a machete and lacked adequate combat skills against a vampire, so I made the split-second decision to run. I knew he was much faster than I was, so my only advantage was going to be the element of surprise.

After a few feet, I glanced back to see how close he was. Ben was much faster than I'd anticipated, and could easily grab me already. Before I could prepare myself, he lunged, knocking me down to the ground with unbearable force. Pain seared through my left arm and shoulder, which took the brunt of the fall. I saw him falling on top of me, in what seemed like slow motion, as he snarled, baring his fangs. I flinched in response and felt something in my right hand.

Without hesitation I tightened my fingers, and with a speed that shocked me, I brought the blade to my chest and positioned it straight up, just as Ben landed on the machete. A blood-curling scream tore from his throat as his momentum caused the blade to plunge in to the hilt and straight through his heart. Ben landed on top of me, trapping me underneath his dead weight.

Desperate to escape and find Lucian, I managed to push his lifeless body off and raised myself up. Jessica screamed as she saw what had happened. Anger filled her face, and she snarled, making it clear that Ben was more to her than just a fellow cult member. They must have been lovers.

She jumped from the back of the werewolf she'd repositioned herself onto and ran for me. I panicked, not bothering to remove my weapon from Ben's chest and ran. It was only when I heard her shriek with frustration that I dared look back. The werewolf she'd abandoned to go after me had caught up with her, forcing her to halt her pursuit of me and fight for survival.

I ran out of the woods and into the open pasture area between the barn and trees. I could hear the brawling sounds up ahead, and I ran faster; I needed to find Lucian. The look in Ben's eyes as he died and Jessica's face as she watched, replayed again in my mind, and I quickly tried to bury it. I'd never even wounded anyone before, let alone taken someone's life, but with the frenzied look that consumed Ben when he came after me, I knew I didn't have a choice. It was either going to be his life or mine.

I'd made it about twenty feet into the pasture when I tripped over something large. I cursed as I fell and braced myself for the impact. I'd been so busy frantically searching the fog for Lucian that I hadn't bothered to watch where I was going.

I got to my knees and easily found what had tripped me, it was a werewolf. It was breathing, but its eyes were closed, and the dusty brown fur was soaked with blood. I scrambled back, unsure if it would attack. I knew it had to be one of Lucian's men, but I didn't know if it would hurt me before realizing I was on its side.

"Now is not the time to lay down and rest," an agitated voice sounded from beside me. Startled, I looked over to find a glaring Brianna crouched beside me.

"I was running from Malus, and I tripped over the werewolf."

"Just like a clumsy human," she scoffed. "Where is Malus?"

"In the woods." I pointed in the direction I thought I'd come from. Without a second glance, she leapt up and ran toward the trees, disappearing into the fog. I stood and instantly locked eyes with Lucian. I almost screamed with relief and excitement. He was alive and, despite the distance between us, seemed uninjured.

The same emotions crossed Lucian's face at seeing me, but our moment of elation was short-lived—he was in the middle of a fight with two vampires. He had to take his eyes away from me and concentrate on his actions.

From my peripheral, I knew there were other fights taking place, but all else was forgotten in that moment—Lucian was alive. I watched while he evaded every attempt at attack the two vampires made. I would've thought the other two were quick and graceful, if they hadn't been fighting against Lucian. Compared to him, they appeared clumsy and uncoordinated. Lucian caught one of them by the arm, using it as a tool to propel the vampire around, until a cracking sound resonated. The vampire screamed in pain, and the other leapt onto Lucian's back, forcing Lucian to release the arm.

As Lucian threw the vampire off of his back, tossing him into the other one, an agonizing pain burst through my chest. I looked down to see the machete protruding through me. My knees became weak, and it took all the strength I possessed to remain standing.

"This is for Ben," Jessica whispered from behind. She'd escaped from her fight with the werewolf and had taken her revenge.

My eyes became heavy, but I forced them to stay open. Lucian had defeated both of his opponents and turned to look at me with a festive expression on his face. When he saw what had happened, it was immediately replaced with horror and disbelief.

The machete retracted, sending blood pouring down the front of my shirt. I struggled to grab her behind me, but I swiped at empty air. She'd already fled. My knees betrayed me, and I fell to the ground.

CHAPTER 21

L aying there, I'd never felt more helpless in my life. Despite the intense pain, I could feel pieces of me fading away into nothingness, and I was powerless to stop it. I struggled to look around, but anything beyond a narrow tunnel appeared hazy and unfocused.

Lucian's blurred face suddenly materialized through the outskirted fog. He was saying something, but I couldn't understand the words. I was plagued with the intense feeling that if I could just close my eyes, the pain would cease, and everything would be fine.

I felt my body jerk, and my eyes, which I hadn't realized had closed, flew open. Lucian was still there amidst a halo of darkness. He must've shaken me to get my eyes open again. He continued to speak, but I still couldn't make out the words. Lucian's face was a blur, but I wanted to see it clearly one more time, so I focused and strained my eyes to bring his exquisite features into focus. At the precise instant his face became clear, his words broke through the smog as well, crashing into me with force.

"Riley, hang on. Do not close your eyes."

I managed to whisper, "But I'm so tired."

His face was glistening, "Riley, I'm so sorry I couldn't get to you fast enough." Why was his face glistening? "If I hadn't sent you by yourself, none of this would have happened." I realized his face wasn't glistening, he was crying. It was tears I was seeing trailing down his cheeks.

I looked into those gorgeous eyes I'd come to adore, but they weren't the same. Sorrow had overcome them, dulling the majestic hue I longed to see. The pain was mercifully subsiding now, evolving into numbness. I knew I was on the verge of death, but all I could think about was consoling him. "It's not your fault, Lucian. You did everything you could. How could you have stopped it?" My words came out breathy and scarcely perceptible, but I knew he'd heard them. It was taking everything I had left just to remain awake and focused.

"I should've known he would do this," he paused, reluctant to continue. "Riley, listen to me, we can't stop the bleeding, and we won't be able to get you to a hospital in time." He lowered his head in defeat. "You're dying, and there's nothing we can do."

I somehow managed to raise my hand to the side of his face. His came up and engulfed mine, giving it a small squeeze. "Don't blame yourself. Neither one of us could have prevented this." I paused, on the verge of tears myself. His face started to blur again, and there was one more thing I wanted to say before I couldn't anymore, "Lucian, I love you."

"I love you, too," he confessed softly, his head still hung in despair. "I finally found you, and now I'm going to lose you, and there's nothing I can do—" he halted mid-sentence, Lucian's head shot up. A spark blazed into life once more in his eyes. "I can save you. Riley, listen to me. I can save you."

I always thought I wouldn't be afraid of death; that if my story had no chapters left to be told, I would welcome the ending. But now that I'd been thrown onto its doorstep, everything I thought I knew was wrong. I was scared shitless. I wasn't ready to be cast into the shadowy depths of an eternal uncertainty. I wanted to be saved.

"I can make you a vampire. It's the only way to save you."

Did I hear him right? Did he say become a vampire? My puzzlement must have shown on my face because he quickly added, "Yes. I can turn you into a vampire. It will save your life. But I won't condemn you to an eternal life of blood drinking unless you tell me to. Is that what you want?"

Sleep was pressing down on me, and I had to fight harder to remain awake. It made it difficult for me to consider what Lucian had just offered. Eternal life with Lucian, or ceaseless death in a matter of moments? The only hindrances with eternal life would be surviving on blood and remaining youthful while I watched everyone around me grow old and die. Could I handle that? Would it be worth it?

"Riley!" Lucian screamed, causing my eyes to burst open once again. "There's little time, you're fading fast. You have to decide now. Yes or no."

Staring at Lucian, I had one of those rare moments of clarity. I wanted nothing more than to be with him. I would gladly stroll through eternity alongside him, no matter what the consequences would be. Without hesitation I answered with a croak, "Yes."

Lucian's expression transformed from worry and fear to excitement and eagerness. Then something else passed over his face, a flicker of sorrow.

His eyes changed, and as he spoke his fangs slid down, "I'm going to drink your blood, then feed you mine. You have to hang on. Do you understand?"

I managed a small nod. I was too afraid to speak. It was starting to hurt to breathe, and I needed to save all the energy I still had for staying awake and alive.

He lifted my arm and sank his teeth into my flesh. I wasn't filled with euphoric pleasure as I had been on the other occasions he'd bitten me, but I didn't feel any pain, either. I don't know if my lack of pain was due to the fact I was willing, or to the effects of my dying body shielding me from it, as it was already doing for the wound in my chest.

I watched as he took more and more of my blood. I don't know how much I'd already lost, but I was definitely feeling the consequences of the amount he was taking now. The haze was growing and spreading with each second that passed, narrowing my vision to only Lucian's face. I tried to use Lucian as a focal point to keep my eyes open, but I wanted to close them so badly. I couldn't fight any longer, I slowly shut them.

Something was pressed against my mouth, but I couldn't move my lips in response. Someone must've opened them for me, though, because I could feel a warm and not-pleasant tasting liquid trickling in my mouth. My throat involuntarily flexed, allowing the thick liquid to travel down.

It was an odd sensation being able to feel it journeying downward into my body, warming everything in its wake. I vaguely wondered if I was hallucinating. The more I drank, the faster it flowed, swiftly spreading to my limbs. I flexed my fingers and toes in response to the balmy sensation and was astonished—just a moment ago I didn't have enough strength to do that.

The open wound on my chest, which had become numb, suddenly exploded with torturous pain. I winced and jerked in response. I turned my head and tried to curl my body into a ball amidst the pain, but Lucian's soothing voice calmly sounded, "It's okay, Riley. I know it hurts, but you have to keep drinking."

I opened my eyes. The haze had significantly receded, but my eyes were now filled with tears because of the agony I was feeling. I could barely see Lucian through them.

"The pain will get worse before it gets better, but I promise you it does get better," he reassured, as he placed his bleeding wrist to my mouth once again. This time I was able to part my own lips to let his blood flow freely into my mouth. I winced as I swallowed, preparing for the repugnant taste, but as it descended down my throat, I realized the taste had improved significantly. It was sweet and satisfying, which compelled me to indulge in my consumption and eagerly drink it down.

It continued traveling through my body, sending warm quivering sensations throughout. The pain in my chest was undoubtedly still there and becoming worse, but my solitary focus was on the feeling of the blood passing down my throat, coating my body with a thick warm layer just under my skin.

Lucian unexpectedly removed his wrist, ceasing the mesmerizing flow of the tantalizing liquid. I began to protest, but the pain in my chest that had momentarily subsided with my fixation on the blood, came roaring back with a menacing vengeance.

I screamed in agony. The pain had surpassed even the initial wound that Jessica had bestowed on me.

"Do you think she'll make it?" a distant, unfamiliar voice inquired.

A new pain began, projecting from the wound and encompassing all it touched in unbearable agony. I clenched my fists, striving not to cry out in pain again.

"I hope so," Lucian answered. "We were able to exchange plenty of blood, despite her injury." He paused, "It looks like the blood's stopped leaking out of her chest. I think she's already starting to heal." His voice held hope.

The fiery pain spread even farther, almost reaching my fingertips. My mind couldn't handle pain to this degree much longer. I was on the verge of passing out.

"It would be best to move her," another unknown voice resonated through the obstructing pain.

"That would be wise. If this worked, it'll take hours for her to turn," responded the first unfamiliar voice.

"Then let's hurry." Lucian's voice was the last thing I heard before relinquishing my fight and embracing the darkness. One last fleeting thought swept through my mind, would I wake up a newly turned vampire, or not wake up at all?

CHAPTER 22

I was afraid to open my eyes when I woke from my unconscious state. I wasn't sure if Lucian's plan had worked, or if I was awakening to a mysterious afterlife. I vaguely remembered coming-to and passing out several more times after Lucian gave me his blood. I thought I was in different places each time, but the memories were hazy— other than the pain. It was the worst feeling I had experienced in my entire life. It burned through my entire body, and I didn't think it would ever end.

I flexed my limbs experimentally. The pain that had encompassed my body had mercifully gone. In its place, however, was a new unfamiliar aching in the pit of my stomach and a burning dryness in my throat.

"Riley, are you awake?" Lucian calmly, yet eagerly asked as I felt a squeeze on my hand. Relief swept through me, and eager to see him, I immediately opened my eyes.

I was instantly spellbound. I recognized the familiar surroundings of his underground bedroom, but as I glanced around, captivated by the remarkable differences I was seeing, I knew I was a vampire.

Colors had become more vibrant and every detail, whether close by or on the opposite end of the room, had enhanced. I blinked, sat up in his bed, and took in everything in the room with a childlike fascination and wonder.

It was like I was truly seeing for the first time in my life. Every intricate detail of the room was no longer hidden from my sight. And it only took a matter of moments to scan every insignificant feature that it held.

"It's a lot to take in at first," Lucian began. "I can still remember when I opened my eyes for the first time after my Becoming. It's remarkable how much you don't even realize you're missing with human sight. You'll get used to it quickly, though, I promise." I looked at his bemused face, and my breath caught—Lucian was even more handsome than ever.

I lunged for him, wrapping my arms around him and holding him as tightly as I possibly could. With the emotional turmoil I'd endured, I was thankful it was finally over, and I wanted nothing more than to be near him. I buried my face against his neck and breathed him in.

I was surprised to discover he had a scent. I inhaled deeper, drawing in the delicate aroma that framed his body. Countless times I had done this before, but never had I noticed that exquisite fragrance. I remembered Lucian and the werewolves had tracked Malus by his scent and realized it wasn't only my eyesight that had improved, my sense of smell had as well. I wondered how many more differences I would have to adjust to in my new life as a vampire.

I pulled back and gazed into his emerald eyes, "Thank you Lucian, for saving me."

His face fell, "If I hadn't sent you home by yourself, this wouldn't have happened."

"I was the one who insisted I went by myself, remember? It doesn't matter, though, you can't change what happened. All that matters is that I'm still here. Besides, it was also me that decided to go to Amy's apartment without the boys," I paused, I'd forgotten about Aiden and Jimmy. "Are they okay?" I fearfully asked.

"They'll be fine," Lucian reassured. "They were beaten up pretty badly, but both are conscious and healing. They're in some of the other rooms down here."

I sighed with relief. I never would've been able to forgive myself if anything had happened to either one of them. "And Amy?"

"Well," Lucian began, "we showed up before Jessica could give Amy any of her blood."

"So, she's not a vampire?"

"No." Lucian answered slowly.

I raised an eyebrow, "Is she okay?"

Lucian looked away and cleared his throat.

"What aren't you telling me?"

"Well," he hesitated. "Jessica had managed to take quite a bit of blood before we showed up."

"Is she dead?" I interrupted. I hated to think everything I'd gone through to protect her had been for nothing.

"No." He answered quickly. "It's just," he stammered, "I think she was in quite a bit of shock about the whole situation. And with the blood loss as well, she was disoriented and attacked one of the werewolves from behind. He didn't know it was only a human and bit her on the arm. It was instinct more than anything. Once he saw it was only a human, he let go."

"Is she going to be a werewolf now?"

"It's still too early to tell. It usually takes a full day before the virus takes hold from a bite. But there's a good chance that she could be."

As long as she was alive and safe, I felt better. Actually, I felt completely renewed and like I had been asleep for days. But Lucian said it hadn't even been a full day yet. Curious as to how long I'd actually been unconscious I asked, "How long have I been out?"

"Only a few hours. It doesn't take as long for the body to make the transformation to a vampire as it does a werewolf."

The pain in my stomach, which had temporarily abated after my initial waking, began again. It emerged more severe than before, and the dryness in my throat was like I'd swallowed sand. I winced at the sudden unexpected pain and absently placed a hand over my stomach.

"Forgive me," Lucian said. "I was so relieved that you're still alive, I forgot to give you blood. I'll be right back."

Blood.

I had forgotten about that drawback. However undesirable the prospect of it was, though, I was going to have to grow accustomed to it and fast. Lucian had explained to me on several occasions that a vampire had to have blood to survive. He also said that only small amounts were required each day, which was something I thought I could cope with. Being alive and able to see Lucian and my family would be well worth it.

I found myself stunned, yet again, as I heard Lucian puttering in the kitchen. Every movement of his was clear and barley muffled. It sounded like he was in the room with me instead of down the hall and in the kitchen. I listened, transfixed until he entered the bedroom with three glasses filled with a dark substance.

He placed one on the nightstand before sitting on the bed next to me and handing me one of the glasses. I watched while he took a sip from his before I timidly glanced down at mine. The dryness in my throat had evolved to an impossible itch, begging for liquid nourishment to sooth it.

"It's alright, Riley." I shifted uncomfortably. "You'll be surprised at how much you'll enjoy it."

Tolerate, maybe. Enjoy, not so sure. I sighed, cleared my mind and thought of it as being an unfortunate side effect of being alive and able to be with Lucian. I brought the glass up to my lips, but before the blood touched them, I inhaled, inadvertently breathing in an intoxicatingly sweet aroma.

Two things happened simultaneously: my already superb vision became even better, allowing me to see even the most minuscule movement or flex of a muscle made by Lucian, and a dull ache erupted in my gums, followed by a release of pressure. I ran my tongue over my teeth; where my normal incisors had been, there were now two very sharp teeth which had grown longer than any of the rest. I looked to Lucian for guidance.

His eyes had become luminescent, and his own fangs had slid down. "Did you smell the blood?" he asked. Afraid of spilling the liquid, but also not wanting to move the glass, I slightly nodded my head once. "Don't be alarmed. You just had a natural reaction to the blood. Your teeth broke through for the first time, and your eyes look like mine."

It was hard to imagine my eyes with the same luminescent quality, but at that point it was hard to think about anything other than the enticing aroma I continued to inhale. All my reservations about drinking blood had been thrown out the window. Not only did I no longer care about drinking blood, I wanted to drink it.

"Drink, Riley." Lucian coaxed. "I'll explain all about your natural vampire reactions when you're done."

I closed my eyes and raised the glass. The blood passed through my lips and traveled down my throat, coating and soothing the aching dryness. It was just as sweet and satisfying as the aroma had promised and arguably the most delicious thing I'd ever tasted.

When I'd downed the entire glass, Lucian handed me the extra one he'd brought with him. It was only when I'd finished that glass as well that I felt my eyes bleed back to normal, and the pain in my stomach and the burning dryness of my throat had vanished. I knew my body didn't need any more blood, but I wanted more. "My throat doesn't hurt any more, but I think I could easily drink several more glasses. Is that normal?" I asked, my words sounding a little off thanks to my new teeth.

Lucian took the empty glass from me, placed it on the nightstand with the other two and crawled back onto the bed next to me. His eyes had returned to their normal shade as well, and his fangs were no longer visible. "The craving we have for human blood straddles a thin line between nourishment and addiction. So, yes, that's normal." He contemplated for moment, "Until you die, you'll have to live with the constant craving for blood. But once you get used to it, it's not as strong and doesn't feel like you *have* to have more, like you do now."

Now I understood what he'd meant by saying vampires only required small quantities each day to survive, but most chose to indulge with more. "Why did everything happen when I smelled the blood?"

He faced me, both of us sitting on the bed with one leg draping off and the other folded, our knees gently touching. It reminded me of that morning after Malus had invaded my dreams, and we were sitting on my bed discussing vampire myths.

"When you smelled the blood, your body reacted with its natural instincts. Theoretically, your fangs slid out, so you could bite into skin, and your eyes changed, so you could prepare for your prey's movements. You're a predator now, and they help you hunt your prey.

A predator—that's what I was now. I wasn't sure if I liked that, but like everything else, I didn't have a choice, and it was something I would have to adapt to. "How do I get my teeth to go back to normal?"

"Just think about it," he said it like it was simple. I frowned, but Lucian was right. As soon as I thought about them retracting, they did. I felt them slide back into my gums. I ran my tongue over my teeth as I had before, but I couldn't feel anything out of the ordinary.

"You'll need to practice, not only with your fangs, but your eyes as well. The more you practice, the sooner you'll be able to control them."

I thought about wanting to see better, and to have my eyes become luminescent, and I could immediately tell the difference.

"I'm impressed," Lucian proudly said. "You're a fast learner."

I suppressed a grin and let my eyes return to their normal gray. "What about work? Am I going to be okay around people, or is it like in the movies where I'm going to be a blood-thirsty monster?"

Lucian laughed heartily, "Again with the movies. Didn't I say you watch too many of them?"

I blushed, "I know, this is just all so new to me, and I don't know what to expect."

His laughter faded, "I'm sorry, Riley. You're the first vampire I've ever created, and I keep forgetting how new this all is to you."

I put my hand on his arm, "It's okay. This will definitely be a learning experience for both of us."

Lucian leaned in and cupped my face with his hand, "You will not be a monster, but you will have cravings for blood that you probably won't be able control in the beginning. Until you're used to your new abilities and know how to manage your cravings, I think it would be best if you remained here."

I opened my mouth to protest, but a knock on Lucian's apartment door interrupted what I would have said.

Lucian frowned, "I'll be right back."

While I waited, I took his advice and practiced with my new teeth and let them slide down and back up into my gums several times. With every release of the two new additions to my mouth, it felt less foreign and actually started to feel good when I released them—a little too good.

When Lucian came back to the bedroom, he was scowling.

"What's wrong?" I asked.

"That was one of the human workers from upstairs. She had Brianna on the phone to speak with me." He resumed his position on the bed. "She, along with several of the werewolves who weren't injured were tracking Malus, while the other vampires and I transported you and all of the wounded back here."

"I take it she didn't have good news?"

He gently placed his hand on my knee. "Not yet. They're still tracking, but she wanted to call and give me an update."

"What about the werewolf that was fighting him, did he die?"

"No. None of my men were killed. Some of them, like the one who fought against Malus, sustained severe injuries, but nothing was life threatening."

"What are we going to do if they can't catch him?"

"I honestly don't know." The worry and anxiety over this whole ordeal with Malus weighed heavily on Lucian's face. "That depends on his next move, but let's not worry about that until we have to." He looked me over, "Right now, we have to get you out of those clothes and into the shower."

I glanced down to see I still wore my white t-shirt and jeans from the night before. My shirt had a hole in the front where the machete had pierced through my body, and there was dried blood covering most of it. My jeans were a combination of blood and mud.

Lucian also still wore the same clothes he'd worn to my grandparents' house, and like mine, they were covered in blood, mud, and had a few tears in the fabric. "Why didn't you clean up after we got here?"

He placed both hands on either side of my face and pulled me to him for a chaste kiss. I closed my eyes, but I knew they'd

247

changed, and I could feel my new fangs sliding down. I wanted to part my lips and deepen the kiss, but he pulled away. "I couldn't leave your side until I knew you were safe."

I opened my eyes to behold Lucian's gorgeous face. His eyes had changed as well, and knowing we could now be together without fear for my safety brought a seductive smile to my lips. "Would you like to join me in the shower?"

Lucian flashed his fangs, "I thought you'd never ask." He hoisted me up in his arms and carried me to the bathroom.

EPILOGUE

Lucian thought it would be best if I cancelled all my appointments for the next two months. He said when I grew accustomed to my new abilities and my bloodlust was under control, I could return to work. For now, I would have to remain in seclusion in the basement of *Silver Moon*. I didn't know how long it would take me to get used to this new vampiric body, but Lucian assured me I would. I trusted his judgement, so we'll see.

I knew it was going to be hard to stay hidden away, but I didn't want to take the chance that I would be in a meeting with a client and suddenly couldn't control my eyes or teeth. Or worse, try to bite someone. Lucian also explained that I would never be able to fully prevent the transformation when I experienced strong emotions such as anger, bloodlust, or, apparently, in my case, anytime Lucian and I were intimate. With practice, though, I should be able to control those natural reactions to an extent and learn how to hide them if they made an appearance in the presence of humans.

After a few weeks, Lucian was going to have some of the club's donors come down to see how well I could refrain from lunging and trying to bite them. Hopefully, I could control myself. I don't feel comfortable with the idea of biting people, and I planned to only consume bagged blood, like Lucian.

The next few months were going to be trying and difficult, to say the least, but I also felt like it was a new beginning for me, and I was excited to see what the future brought. I never thought I would want or even like to be a vampire, but now that I was, I think I was actually going to enjoy being one. My goal was to take each day as a learning experience and to also enjoy every moment I had with Lucian. The thought of living forever was somewhat unsettling, but as long as I had Lucian with me, it didn't sound too bad.

I felt like I owed something to Mrs. Greenwell. I hated the way things had turned out, and I honestly didn't think Jessica was always so twisted. I truly believed that Malus had gotten in her head and made her that way. So, I called Mrs. Greenwell and told her the only thing I thought she would believe—that I couldn't find Jessica. I explained that as far as I could tell, she did leave with a guy at *Silver Moon* that night, but they'd both disappeared. Lucian was going to take her a full refund of the money she'd already paid as a down payment. She was obviously upset that I couldn't find Jessica, but it was better than telling her what had really happened to her granddaughter. Besides, she wouldn't have believed me even if I did tell her the truth.

Aiden and Jimmy were recovering at a wonderfully fast pace from their injuries. It should only be a few more days until they would be back to normal. As it turned out, Amy was infected with the werewolf virus, and she was taking the news wonderfully. She was actually excited about it and couldn't wait until her first shift on the night of the next full moon.

While Lucian was saving my life by turning me into a vampire, Malus and Jessica escaped. Lucian sent Brianna and some of the werewolves after them, while he transported me, Aiden, and a few others back to Louisville, but Malus and Jessica had too much of a head start. The werewolves relentlessly tracked their fading scent until it disappeared altogether.

The best we could tell, they had fled the state. Lucian sent out a warning to all the other Consuls in the surrounding states to be on the lookout for them. Now that we knew what his plans were, hopefully we could stop him before he could fulfill them.

I didn't think he would be foolish enough to come back to Louisville to try to finish his plan. Lucian and his team suffered no casualties during their brawl, while Malus and Jessica were the sole survivors of his cult. But if they did decide to chance their fate once again and come back, we'd be ready for them.

AUTHOR'S
NOTE

Thank you so much for reading *Silver Moon*! I hope you enjoyed the first installment of the Riley Hunter Series. If so and you would like to help support the series, I would appreciate it if you could leave an honest review on Amazon, Goodreads, and/or anywhere else. Reviews are a great way to support your favorite authors!

∞ ∞ ∞

The second full-length novel in the Riley Hunter Series, *Blood Moon*, will be releasing in 2019. Order your copy today.

Want to know more about Ellie? Find out where she came from and which member of the BloodGuard stole her heart. Order Ellie's short novella, *Dark Betrayal-A Riley Hunter Prequel* today.

CONNECT WITH AMANDA LYNN

∞ ∞ ∞

Follow to stay updated on new releases:

Facebook
Twitter
Instagram
Website

Keep up to date on everything Amanda Lynn. Sign up for the mailing list.

BOOKS BY AMANDA LYNN

THE RILEY HUNTER SERIES:

Silver Moon

Blood Moon-Release Early 2019

Hunter's Moon-Release Summer 2019

RILEY HUNTER WORLD:

Dark Betrayal

THE BLOODGUARD SERIES:

Book 1 (Continuation of Ellie & Kade's story)-Late 2019

∞ ∞ ∞

Made in the USA
Columbia, SC
29 March 2020